By the sa

The Hengest v.
A Brother's Oath
A Warlord's Bargain
A King's Legacy

The Arthur of the Cymry Trilogy
Sign of the White Foal
Banner of the Red Dragon
Field of the Black Raven

The Rebel and the Runaway
Lords of the Greenwood

https://christhorndycroft.wordpress.com/

As P. J. Thorndyke

The Lazarus Longman Chronicles
Through Mines of Deception (short story)
On Rails of Gold – A Prequel to Golden Heart (short story)
Golden Heart
Silver Tomb
Onyx City

Celluloid Terrors
Curse of the Blood Fiends

https://pjthorndyke.wordpress.com/

A CINC'S LEGACI

CHRIS THORNDYCROFT

A King's Legacy
By Chris Thorndycroft

2015 by Copyright © Chris Thorndycroft

All rights reserved. This book or any portion thereof may not be reproduced or used in any manner whatsoever without the express written permission of the publisher except for the use of brief quotations in a book review.

https://christhorndycroft.wordpress.com/

For Maia for her constant encouragement and my parents for their unwavering support

PICTS

HADRIAN'S WALL

BRITANNIA
SECUNDA

HIBERNIA

FLAVIA
CAESARIENSIS

BRITANNIA
PRIMA

MAXIMA
CAESARIENSIS

GAUL

BRITANNIA C.A. 444 A.D.

Place names

	Latin	British	Anglo Saxon	Modern English
	Britannia	Albion	Britta	Britain
	Hibernia	Eire		Ireland
	Cantium	Ccint	Cent	Kent
1	Londinium		Lundenwic	London
2	Tanatus		Thanet	Thanet
3	Rutupiae			Richborough
4	Durobrivae Cantiacorum		Hrofæscæstre	Rochester
5	Durovernum Cantiacorum	Cair Ceint	Cantwareburh	Canterbury
6	Corinium Dobunnorum			Cirencester
7	Viroconium Cornoviorum	Cair Guricon		Wroxeter
8	Eburacum	Cair Ebruac	Eoforwic	York
9		Din Eidyn		Edinburgh

"At length Vortimer, the son of Vortigern, valiantly fought against Hengist, Horsa, and his people; drove them to the isle of Thanet, and thrice enclosed them within it, and beset them on the Western side." – The History of the Britons, Nennius

PART I

*(Peorð) "Peorð biþ symble plega and hleahtor,
wlancum þar wigan sittaþ
on béorsele bliþe ætsamne."*

(Chessman) The chessman is a source of recreation and
amusement to the great, where warriors sit blithely
together in the banqueting-hall.

North East Britain, Late Summer, 447 A.D.

Horsa

The grey clouds were frozen over the calm sea. No wind scattered them nor drove the breakers to white foam. Summer was ending and the land seemed quietly afraid at the onset of winter when gales and thundering surf would break upon its shores once more.

Time was running out.

Along the beach rode a lone horseman, his fur-trimmed cloak billowing out behind him. His beard was tawny and his hair was long. He carried a spear but wore no sword at his belt, only the long-bladed saex of the Germanic peoples.

Three heads poked up from the seaweed-strewn rocks and startled the rider, causing him to rein in his mount and wheel around, gripping his spear in fear of an ambush.

The three men wore similar attire to him and all carried spears. "*Hwaet*, warrior!" called out one of them. "I can see that you are no Pict, but what are you? A deserter?"

"I seek the camp of Horsa," said the mounted man. "I carry a message to him from his brother."

"Are we to move inland? Is the final battle at hand?" asked one of the other men eagerly. "I am not the only one in Horsa's camp who is pig sick of this campaign. There isn't a Pictish settlement left that does not lie in smouldering ruins and there is little food to be found elsewhere."

"Hold your whining!" said the leader of the group. "You, messenger, does Hengest call for us? Why did not Aurelianus send one of his own men? Is it not he who leads the army?"

"Would you or anyone else in Horsa's camp trust one sent by that British dog?" asked the messenger. "I come directly from Hengest and my message is for his brother alone."

This seemed good enough for the three warriors and they beckoned the rider to follow them. He dismounted and led his horse by the bridle as they headed towards camp.

The smell of that morning's breakfast of roasted herring still hung in the blue smoke over the camp. The waves rolled gently in between the hulks of the beached vessels, nearly reaching the sealskin tents that had been pitched in small clusters around many hearths.

Horsa took the gold scabbard mounting from the messenger and studied it. He recognised it from his brother's scabbard which he had had made for his mighty sword *Hildeleoma*. There was no doubt that the messenger was genuine.

"And my brother says that they have Galana pinned?" Horsa asked him.

"They await only your coming from the east to crush her army once and for all."

Horsa leaned back into his throne of sealskins and wolf furs and closed his eyes. *Finally*. He had hated every bit of this campaign. All season he had led his ships up and down the eastern coast of Pictland, even up to the far north where it broke up into dozens of islands.

Their mission had been to harry the coastal settlements and prevent them from sending troops to the aid of the Pictish rebel, Galana, whose nephew, King Talorc, was allied to the Britons. Galana claimed that her infant son was the true ruler of the clans and the ensuing civil war had torn the north apart.

Horsa's men were born raiders and were as suited to the task as fish were to swimming. The stench of burning homesteads hadn't cleared from his nostrils for months. When he tried to sleep his ears rang with the sounds of slaughter, the death cries of warriors, the screaming of butchered families and the wailing of newly made widows and orphans. There had been no honour in this.

While his brother had engaged Galana in open battles, Horsa had been left with the pitiful homesteads and frightened families, most of whose menfolk had already left. Still, he had done his duty. But with every roundhouse burned he felt himself slipping further and further from who he was, further and further … *from Aureliana.*

He drank heavily most nights, but the more he drank the more he thought of her and the deeper his shame became. She was his hope for a future without bloodshed and the sound of weeping women. She was his white light in a world of black, acrid smoke. And the longer the campaign drew on, the dimmer that light seemed to him. He was terrified that her light might blink out altogether and he would be left in this cold, bleak north to die without ever feeling her soft, pale arms around him again.

But now, *now*, the end was in sight. This messenger brought with him the news that he had dared to hope for all season. The final battle was drawing close. If they could only smash Galana and her forces once and for all, they could all go home.

"Strike camp," he said, rising. "Beorn, pick out a guard party to hold the ships. You know whom to choose."

"Yes, captain," the massive, bald Angle replied, and he strode off to handpick his men.

"We take only weapons; no camp equipment or supplies."

"Is that wise, Captain," asked Aelfhere, the captain of the *Raven*. "No supplies? It may be a long march inland."

"Then we march on empty bellies," Horsa replied. "Hunger for slaughter is the only hunger we need. We march fast and hard and we do not stop until we have crushed our enemy and are free from this gods-cursed war!"

Hengest

"You have no authority over my men!" Hengest roared.

The tent was crowded and he felt outnumbered by the British officers who had assembled before Aurelianus to see justice done to two of Hengest's warriors. They had been accused of looting. Not really a crime during war, Hengest felt, but as usual it seemed that the British portion of the army was intent on making things as hard as possible for their Germanic auxiliary troops.

Hengest's two men stood by with their hands bound and their faces creased with incomprehension. *Poor, silly bastards*, Hengest thought. *They don't even know what's going on.*

"Looting may well be an integral part of your culture, Sais," said Aurelianus in a withering tone, "and I dread to think what your brother gets up to in the coastal settlements, but men under my standard do not act like common brigands. These men are to be punished, yours or not."

"That fortress belonged to Galana!" Hengest protested. "It held out against us for three days and took the lives of many of our men during the siege. We who shed blood for it have a right to its spoils, do we not?"

"All spoils are to be divided up by myself and my officers. Your men will get their share. We cannot set our soldiers loose upon civilians like scavenging wolves. Those days are over. We are a Christian army in a Christian land. We do not loot and pillage our brother man."

"And King Talorc's men? My men were not the only ones looting in the aftermath of that battle."

"King Talorc's warriors are allies, not auxiliary troops under my standard. We are here to help him win back his territory. If he wishes to pillage his own people, that is his business."

"You have your customs, Briton, we have ours," replied Hengest.

"But while you march with me, you and your men will adhere to my law."

"Well at least give these men over to me so that I may punish them."

"And have you treat them as leniently as you please, or worse, set them free? No. They must be made an example of. The army must know that insubordination will be punished severely."

Hengest ground his teeth but he knew he was beaten. The two prisoners were as good as dead and there was nothing he could do. He would like to storm the tent with Aesc, Ordlaf, Ebusa and all the others, kill Aurelianus and release his men, but that would be an unwinnable battle. Without saying another word, he turned and strode out of the tent, ignoring the pathetic gazes of his two doomed men.

"What happened, Father?" asked Aesc, who had been waiting outside.

"He refuses to listen to reason," Hengest replied. "I tried."

"And our two warriors?"

"They are to die, most likely."

"But that's not fair!"

"I know it isn't, Son. But Aurelianus leads this army. His word is law. For the time being."

The two men were hanged the following morning before the sun was fully up. Most of Hengest's men were still sleeping when it happened. It was clear that

8

Aurelianus had hoped to avoid any kind of disturbance by carrying out the executions before the comrades of the condemned knew what was happening.

There was uproar when Hengest's men awoke to find the two lifeless corpses dangling from the branch of an oak tree, their faces black and their tongues swollen.

The incident had put the auxiliary troops in a black mood. They didn't like the Britons and liked seeing two of their number executed by them less still. Hengest felt like he had lost their respect. They looked to him to protect them and to lead them onwards but how could they have confidence in him if he couldn't prevent the Britons from stringing them up over something as trivial as looting? The atmosphere was dangerous. If his troops decided to take justice into their own hands, he did not feel confident that he could control them.

"That our men have not already run riot and started stringing up Britons left, right and centre," said Ebusa, "is a testament to their faith in you as a leader. Let them seethe. They still follow only you."

"Thank Woden this war is nearly over," was all Hengest could say.

They nearly had Galana beat. All season they had engaged in small skirmishes with the Picts. Those blue-painted men of the north were the masters of ambush and their hit and run tactics had devastated Aurelianus's lines of supply. So far they had avoided open battle with the Britons. With Horsa and his raiders hammering the east coast, putting a stranglehold on supplies and reinforcements, Galana had become more and more reckless. Her warriors were hungry, outnumbered and desperate. They only had to force them into a pitched battle to smash them.

Now that chance had come. There was a valley two days march to the north where, Aurelianus's spies confirmed, Galana had set up camp. It was thickly forested on the northern side and would be hard for a large force to retreat through with any haste. Galana had got herself snared in a trap. A messenger had been sent to Horsa to call his raiders to the battle. With them approaching from the east and the Britons marching from the south, Galana would be caught between hammer and anvil. The valley would become a killing ground.

Perhaps that was the real reason his men had not mutinied, Hengest thought. They knew the end was in sight and looked forward to returning to their homes just as he did. One final battle by Aurelianus's side and then they were done as his mercenaries. He only hoped the treaty between Briton and Saxon could hold out just a little longer. It wasn't for his own benefit. In the lands to the south west, his daughter, Hronwena, was wife to the most powerful of all British rulers. If Briton turned on Saxon, things might get very difficult for her.

Hronwena

Hronwena watched the returning troops from a high window in Din Neidr. Cadeyrn was at their head. Their banners were torn and frayed; their armour dented and blood-spattered. Defeat was written all over their faces.

At table that night, her husband, Vitalinus, made much mockery of his son's efforts to oust the rebellious chieftain. Hronwena scowled. Despite having been stripped of his power by Cadeyrn, Vitalinus was still allowed to attend meals in the Great Hall.

"Even when I was a young man watching my father forge this island into some sort of unity, I never lost to a petty chieftain," he sneered. "And a Gael at that!"

Cadeyrn's teeth clenched on a mouthful of bread. "Benlli is more than a petty chieftain," he said. "His strength has increased bit by bit over the years. Had you quashed him when he first rose perhaps I would not be fighting him now. And as for the Gaels, you yourself have never fought them. You would rather employ others to fight your battles for you. Like Cunedag. Like Hengest." He glanced quickly at Hronwena.

"I have managed to keep the peace with Benlli since before you were born," said Vitalinus. "Now his raiders plunder our borders and steal our cattle. Perhaps your coup over me is not as popular as you had hoped."

"It is popular with all but Benlli," Cadeyrn replied coldly. "All the other lords have joined me in the fight against the Gael."

"And yet he defies you all. His territory has grown to include Cair Guricon, a town which he never would have dared attack whilst I ruled Britannia Prima."

"Perhaps Benlli is frightened of these rumours concerning Cadell for he knows, that should the old heir to Din Bengron resurface, I would support his claim."

"An imposter. A rural rabble-rouser."

"Many of the commoners believe in him and support him."

"The old family who ruled Din Bengron died by the sword when Benlli arrived here from Erin a generation ago. This Cadell thinks to insert himself into that lost bloodline and play on the hopes of the commoners who remember it. He is no more a prince than this bitch's husband! Once you have defeated Benlli – *if* you can defeat him – you must deal with this upstart also. And I must sit by whilst you lose every scrap of land I and my father fought so hard for."

"You have no choice!" Cadeyrn snapped. "You think you can worm your way back in to power but you will never rule Britannia Prima again! The people praise my name in the hills and herald the end of tyranny. Together with Vortimer, we shall re-forge Albion into a stronger, healthier land."

Vitalinus let out a short bark of laughter. "My two noble sons, what idealists! Every generation it is the same story; bring Albion back into the light, bring back the old days of peace. Why not even bring back the Romans? But what you do not understand is that the Romans were our enemies, boy. Oh, they ruled us for centuries and left their mark on this island in more ways than one, but now that they are gone we can truly start to be Britons again. And any utopian vision of the future you and your foolish brother have will forever be eclipsed by the days that saw me hold all of Albion in the palm of my hand. Whatever you two conspiring traitors do, people will look back to the days of Vertigernus and mourn his defeat by his wretched offspring!"

Cadeyrn drank the last of his wine as if to quench his anger and slammed his goblet down hard. "Guards! Escort my father to his chambers. I cannot stomach his miserable face over the dinner table. It spoils my appetite."

Hronwena was relieved to see the back of her husband. If she had her way, he would be locked up in the fortress cells, not taking his meals in the Great Hall or sleeping in the chamber one door down from her own. It repulsed her to think of him on the other side of that wall, knowing what he was, what he had done to his own family.

She regularly visited Enys and her son Britu. Deilwen's foster parents were keeping them well in their little hovel in the forest. She brought them food and cloth and ensured that they had all they needed. All she could do was wait until Cadeyrn and his brother, Vortimer, had decided what to do with their father. And that was taking far too long for her liking.

Cadeyrn ruled the province of Britannia Prima now and had the backing of the nobility. If it wasn't for the chieftain Benlli – who had sided with Vitalinus – things might move ahead quicker. There was also the matter of the war in the north which her father and brother were busy fighting with Ambrosius Aurelianus. She knew that Cadeyrn and his brother anxiously awaited the return of the army for they did not know if the mighty Aurelianus would side with them or their father. Civil war hung like a thundercloud over Britta and Hronwena had even heard Cadeyrn talk of sending to Gaul for Roman intervention.

She cared little for the fate of Britta. All she wanted was to sunder her marriage to Vitalinus and return to her family in the east. But it would do no good to simply flee. She wanted to get some sort of legal annulment of her marriage. She had heard that priests could do that and they might too once Vitalinus was stripped of all his powers. But until Cadeyrn had full control of his province, and he and Vortimer had decided what to do about Aurelianus and their contacts in Gaul, Vitalinus's fate could not be decided and she must remain his wife.

Horsa

The clearing had only recently been vacated. White ash lay undisturbed in the three campfires and a raven that had been picking a scrap of meat from a discarded bone went flapping away at their approach.

It was some sort of religious centre. Horsa had seen standing stones like these, with their carven Z-rods and snakes, many times in the previous months. An altar had been constructed of wood in the centre of the stones. It was such a chaotic thing that it took Horsa and his men several seconds to take it all in.

Rotten, twisted branches had been bound together to create an artificial tree. Skulls, some with skin stretched taught and even hair, dangled by bits of twine and creaked in the gentle breeze. The Picts liked heads. They thought that by possessing an enemy's head, they possessed his soul.

Then he saw the statue. It stood in a little enclave within the construction as if peeping out from its shelter. It was of wood, old, with moss growing in its cracks. Horsa had seen that face before. He felt cold all over as if something was beckoning to him through the mists of a lifetime. That face, with its gemstones for eyes, that haunting, aelfin expression was the very same face he had seen wrought in gold in Dane-land.

Years had passed since their expedition into the lands of the Wane-worshippers. He thought the demon-cult of Gefion had perished when he had cast that statue down into the watery depths and burned its worshippers alive inside their hall. And yet, here she was, in another land; the very same goddess who demanded human sacrifice and who had haunted his dreams ever since. This was the goddess who had placed a curse on him; he was sure of it.

Like the face of Gefion, Galana's screaming visage had haunted him for many nights, so much so that it had merged with the face of the goddess in his dreams. They were one and the same to him. Galana was the one woman who was a threat to him; the one woman who could fulfil the wyrd spoken to him by Ealhwaru, the Saxon seeress, who had taught him to fear woman's wrath.

"Ugly bitch, isn't she?" said Beorn at his side.

Horsa realised that none of the men who had been with him in that cave in Dane-land recognised the goddess. Gefion's curse was his alone.

"There's nothing here, Captain," Beorn went on. "Whoever camped here moved on days ago. Shall we continue? We have many miles march ahead of us before we meet your brother."

"Burn it," said Horsa in a hollow voice.

"Captain?"

"Burn this statue. Burn the whole grove. Leave nothing standing."

His men were confused by his demands but loyal enough to carry them out. Only when the altar and its statue were roaring merrily did he give the order to move out. They continued through the trees, listening to the crackling of the flames behind them as a goddess burned.

Hengest

Hengest gazed at the lines of Pictish warriors arrayed in the defile, the woods at their back. The smoke from their cooking fires could be seen through the trees beyond. Those fires would be deserted. Every man and woman in Galana's army had picked up a weapon and stood before them, defiant.

"They're mad," he remarked to Aurelianus.

"No, just desperate," the Briton replied. "And they have their damned Pictish pride."

"Quite so," put in King Talorc. "I am almost proud to call her my aunt. I would have done the same. When all other roads are closed off, the honourable Pict stands his ground no matter the odds."

Hengest could appreciate this kind of mindset for it was not so different from the Germanic sense of honour, but he doubted Aurelianus understood such views.

"What is our plan?" he asked the British commander.

"We hold here until your brother is nearby. No point attacking until every available exit is closed off."

"I doubt they could run from us."

"But we can wait. I mean this to be our final battle. I will not chance another of Galana's escapes."

"But will they wait?" Hengest nodded at the lines of shouting Picts.

"Probably not."

The sun reached its zenith and, as it began its slow descent, the Picts could not contain their restlessness, despite the odds against them, just as Aurelianus had predicted. They were born warriors and were not made for playing the waiting game. It was almost as if the descent of the sun heralded their last day in this world and they were determined to meet the darkness before the land did.

"Gods, they're marching!" said Aesc.

Marching was a generous way of putting it. Urged on by their leader and their priests, the Picts set forth in a howling charge, like dogs that could not be restrained any longer and had broken free from their master's leash.

"What do we do?"

"We hold," replied Aurelianus simply.

Before the Picts came within fifty feet of the British ranks, the Britons hurled their javelins. The enemy was obscured for a moment as the black shafts soared and then descended in a bloody hailstorm of slaughter. Warriors went down like spitted swine, stumbling, buckling and tumbling with shafts protruding from their breasts, necks and heads. Some fell with pierced limbs, dragged down by the weight of the javelins, to roll, screaming in agony.

Their comrades leaped over them and continued the charge, slamming into the British shields with all the more ferocity. All along the British line the Picts engaged, hacking, stabbing and kicking. They were stretched thin and the Britons, several ranks deep, pushed fresh men forward to reinforce gaps and replace bloodied, weary soldiers.

The enemy could not keep up the assault indefinitely and, shame and anger showing on their faces, they began to fall back, one by one at first, until it became a full retreat back to their leader. Blue-painted bodies littered the grassy valley.

"Why don't we push forward?" Hengest asked.

"The trees," replied Aurelianus. "Galana picked this spot for a reason. We may outnumber her but this defile is narrow. I can only send in as many troops as she can fight at any one time. To the un-trained mind it may look like she has backed into a corner but in reality she has protected her flanks from attack. She's smart."

Fresh javelins were distributed to the front ranks.

"Surely you don't expect them to attack again?" Hengest asked.

"They will keep attacking until every last warrior of theirs is used up," Aurelianus replied. "They are desperate and have nowhere to run. It is fight or die now. And given the choice, they will do both today."

Sure enough a second charge was soon set in motion. Galana sent all her warriors this time and, as the British javelins rose and fell a second time, Hengest almost felt sorry for them. The odds were so hopelessly set against them that they surely knew that death now hovered above them on black, feathered wings.

As the Picts began another retreat back to the treeline, King Talorc hawked and spat loudly with distaste. "There is no honour in this!" he exclaimed before spurring his mount and galloping off to where his own troops stood marshalled behind the British lines.

"I think our Pictish friend is up to his old tricks again," Hengest warned.

Aurelianus sighed. "I can't control the damned bastard. If he dies then the whole point of this war is lost. Hengest, lead your men after him and see that he doesn't fall. Besides, a strong cavalry charge may be the thing we need to shatter their resolve utterly."

"While you stay up here behind your shiny, polished troops?" Hengest asked him.

Aurelianus gave him a withering smile. "What are auxiliaries for if not to send into the enemy flanks? Besides, we need to hold the line at this rise to prevent the Picts from rushing forward to freedom."

"Don't bother to explain," Hengest said sourly. "I have learned all I care to know about Roman battle tactics during this campaign." He set off, calling for his ten *turmae* to follow him.

King Talorc and his warriors were already halfway across the plain by the time Hengest had got his men on the move. Dust swirled about their flanks as they charged and the ground rumbled as if caught in an earthquake. The fleeing Picts had not yet made it back to the treeline and Talorc's mounted warriors caught up with them, scything them down with their long swords.

Galana's lines jostled together to form some kind of defensive barrier, but it was too late. Talorc was the first into the melee, swinging his blade and yelling his defiance of his aunt. It was chaos. By the time Hengest's cavalry arrived at the battle it was very hard to tell which Picts were Talorc's and which were Galana's.

Arrows and slingshots sailed out from the forests and found marks in their ranks. Hengest saw two of his riders tumble from their horses, one pierced by an arrow and the other with a face smashed by a stone. There was a rallying war cry from the trees and more Picts surged forward to help their comrades.

"They've been hiding warriors from us!" cried Hengest, sensing the danger. "Talorc! Fall back! Fall back to the Britons!"

There was no telling how many warriors Galana had concealed in the forest and with the rest of the army standing on the rise with Aurelianus, there was no hope of reinforcement.

King Talorc was loath to flee as his aunt's warriors had done and was one of the last to disengage. As they retreated, Hengest kept looking over his shoulder to make sure that Talorc was with them.

"A trap," Aurelianus stated once they had limped back behind the British lines. "Surprising at this stage of the game."

"Galana's only been sending a fraction of her force against us," said Hengest. "Probably hoped to lure us closer to the trees where she could ambush us."

"Well, she lured Talorc and we very nearly lost him."

"At least now we know the real odds we face."

"Yes, it takes a Pict to know a Pict, apparently."

"What now?"

"We move down in wedge formations. Cavalry guarding our flanks."

"Oh? Finally? After Talorc and I were nearly butchered while you lot watched from up here, you want to bring the fight to them? Aren't you worried about getting blood on your armour?"

"I have received word from your brother. He and his raiders are advancing through the trees towards the rear ranks of Galana's forces. The trap is set. Now we pull the noose taut."

Horsa

A river ran between them and the Pictish camp. The thatched roofs of roundhouses could be seen through the trees.

Roundhouses? Thought Horsa. *They've been here for some time.*

This was not the hastily put together camp of an army on the move. This was nearly a village. Enclosures contained livestock and washing was hung up to dry on frames by the water's edge. The place was more or less deserted.

Through the blue woodsmoke Horsa could make out a woman wearing a Pictish hood going about her business and somewhere a baby was wailing. There was not a warrior to be seen about the place.

They began to cross the river, holding their spears and shields high as they waded across. Even in the final days of summer the water was bitterly cold. The woman on the other bank had seen them and cried out as she ran towards the roundhouses.

Horsa had not made it to the bank before the first of the retreating Picts came blundering through the trees. At first he thought they had wandered into a trap but then he saw the terror on their faces, their red blades and blood-spattered bodies smeared with blue paint.

"They're on the run!" called Horsa to his men. "Don't let any pass!"

Blades were drawn and spears were hefted as they climbed the bank and entered the village. Terror turned to abject surprise on the faces of the Picts and before they fully comprehended the situation, Horsa's raiders were upon them. Swords and axes slashed through bare

22

flesh and spears thudded home into heaving chests. A few of the Picts tried to rally into defensive groups but were too disorganised and confused to put up much resistance.

More and more Picts came hurrying through the trees; hundreds of them, fleeing the army that marched on their heels. Beorn wrenched his axe head free from a dead Pict's chest with a horrid sucking sound and looked up. "Gods, there's too many!" he yelled to Horsa over the din of battle.

He was right. The Picts were panicked, but the sheer number of them might overwhelm his raiders. His men had torched some of the roundhouses and fire and smoke roared and swirled about only adding to the confusion.

A warrior leaped from the smoke like a shade from a nightmare and Horsa ducked as a Pictish blade swung out at him. He drew his own up and to the side, spilling the guts of his attacker. He couldn't even see the trees now. All about him was smoke, leaping flames and red slaughter. He hoped that Hengest, Aurelianus and the rest of the army would be here soon to mop up the fleeing army.

But something else niggled in his mind.

Galana.

She was here somewhere. Her death would mean the end of the war. If he could only kill her himself, perhaps the curse of Gefion could be lifted and he would finally be free.

Bodies littered the ground – men, women, some even children – all dead and he had to step between their corpses. Still, the Picts were rushing from the forest. There seemed to be no end to them. Horsa scanned the faces of as many as he could. All were warriors. None were priests and he could not see Galana herself. Sweat poured down the sides of his face and his sword arm was heavy and weary from killing.

A herd of terrified pigs stampeded past, broken free from their pen and headed towards the water. He strode onwards, cutting down a fleeing Pict as he did so. He reached the trees where some of his men were already delving into the murk to engage the enemy. He caught flashes of red oval shields – hundreds of them approaching through the forest towards him. He heard the sound of carnage and screaming horses to his left. Through the drifting smoke he saw Hengest's cavalry striking down Picts like spectres glimpsed through fog.

"*Britannia Victrix!*" came a roar to his right, and Horsa saw Aurelianus and his mounted troops hacking their way through on the other flank. "*Britannia Victrix!*" bellowed the Briton again, exultant in the slaughter and his inevitable triumph.

King Talorc whirled his bloody sword around his head and screamed victory over his defeated aunt, his blue-smeared face running red with the blood of his own countrymen, and his eyes livid as if possessed by a demon.

The battle was over. The village blazed, its dead littered between the fires. Some Picts may have escaped through the chaos and into the forests beyond, but precious few.

"Where is Galana?" Horsa shouted to nobody in particular. "Galana! I have to find her!" He felt panicked. Aurelianus and King Talorc may exult in their triumph but the battle and the war was not over for him until he saw Galana's body.

Hengest rode over to him and dismounted. His steed's flanks were foamy with sweat. "On time for once, Horsa!" he exclaimed, embracing him.

Horsa seized him by the shoulders and shook him. "We must find Galana! If she escapes, all is lost!"

"Calm down, Brother! The battle is over. She is defeated."

"But where is she? I must see her corpse!"

"Some of the Britons are saying that she is lying a few yards in that direction," said Beorn, wiping the blood from his axe blade with a fistful of grass.

"Where?" Horsa demanded.

Beorn led him through the trees and asked directions from several Britons who were cleaning their swords and wiping the sweat and blood from their brows. Horsa could see the crested helmet of Aurelianus standing around with some of his officers. At his feet lay four or five dead Picts.

Horsa shouldered his way through so that he could see.

Galana was dead alright. Her face looked strangely peaceful beneath the swirling war paint. She was surrounded by several of her priests and lieutenants. They all had deep gouges in their bellies, right beneath the ribcage. Some still had the hilts of ceremonial knives protruding, gripped by stiff fingers.

"Took their own lives," said Aurelianus. "Defeat cannot be borne by such people. They fell on their own blades in the name of honour."

"They will be given the proper funerary rites by my people," said King Talorc. "She was my aunt. She was my bitter enemy, but she was my aunt. I will take her home with me to Din Eidyn."

"But what of her son?" Aurelianus said. "What has become of the infant pretender?"

Hengest

The roundhouses were searched and in the largest – the royal residence – they came upon a sad discovery. The young pretender's cot was a gilded thing with a horse motif. He was in it, swaddled in a white sheet. He was dead.

"Smothered by the looks of it," said Aurelianus. "Galana's defeat could not even be borne by the young and innocent. I wonder if she killed him herself before leading her army out to make its last stand against us."

The war was over. The north had been pacified and had a king to rule it in Britta's favour. They returned to Din Eidyn where the celebrations went on for days. Hengest wished it would all come to a swift conclusion so that they could return home. He got the impression that Aurelianus felt the same and Horsa seemed to be the most eager to return of all.

"I want to ride back with you to Londinium," he told Hengest, slurring his words. Homesick or no, he was enjoying the mead and celebrations as much as any Pict.

"But the ships must be safely captained back to Cantium," Hengest told him.

"Beorn can do that. There's no finer seaman in the fleet, myself included and I trust no man more."

"What's your interest in Londinium? I'm only going because it is expected of me. I have to represent our new kingdom at Lord Vertigernus's victory feast but it is sure to be a tiresome affair. I would much rather go straight home. Halfritha is waiting for me and I must see what Octa has been doing to my hall in our absence."

"Humour me, Brother. Would it not appear better for both of us to be present at the victory feast?"

"You'll have to get yourself a good horse. It's a long ride. And you'll get saddle sores the like of which you have never imagined!"

They set out the morning after the final drinking bout had come to its close; leaving King Talorc and his warriors snoring on the floor of the Great Hall. They made Eboracum in good time and, as he had done on their outward journey, Lord Elafius met them at the gates, only this time to welcome the conquering heroes.

Remembering the Britons' treatment of him and his people when they had passed through the town before, Hengest was under no illusions as to the hospitality they faced on this return journey and so ordered camp to be set up outside Eboracum's walls. This was preferable to bedding down in the fort's barracks with the Britons while Aurelianus and his officers feasted with Elafius up at the commanders' quarters.

Darkness had barely fallen when Cerdic the interpreter hurried into the camp looking for Hengest. He had been drinking in the town with the Britons and had some important news.

"I can't rightly say whether it's truth or no," the trusted interpreter told Hengest who sat in his tent drinking sour British mead. "But the soldiers of the town are convinced of it. They say that strange things have been happening while we have been away. They say that Lord Vertigernus has been usurped by his son."

"How can that be true?" Hengest asked incredulously. "We fought this whole damned war on Vertigernus's orders."

"Is Vertigernus alive?" Horsa asked from the furs on which he lounged.

"The word is that he is kept under lock and key at his fortress in the western mountains," the interpreter replied. "His son, Cadeyrn, is keeping him guarded and has taken his position on the council as ruler of Britannia Prima. It's all been ratified by Vortimer."

"Could be bad news for us," Horsa said. "Aurelianus wasn't the only one who wanted nothing to do with us. In fact the whole treaty between us and them was Vertigernus's idea. With him gone, what's to stop Aurelianus and the rest of the British leadership turning on us?"

"Aurelianus may hate us, but he is at least loyal to his lord," said Hengest. "He'll be as surprised as us to hear of Vertigernus's removal from power for there's been no correspondence between them this whole campaign."

"Surprised isn't the half of it," went on Cerdic. "I heard it from one of the palace guard that there was a great row during the feast. Elafius has been tight-lipped since we got here and Aurelianus knows that something is up. There's to be a meeting of the council in a few days in Londinium and Elafius won't tell Aurelianus what's been going on. He blew up over the wine and stuffed partridge earlier and stormed off to the barracks."

"I don't like this," said Hengest.'

"Nor I, but we've done our bit," said Horsa. "We won the war for them and now we're going home. Whatever problems the Britons have are their problems. I want nothing further to do with their politics."

Hengest felt panic rising. "It's not that simple, Horsa. If what we hear is true and Vertigernus is under lock and key then I want to know what that means for my daughter. Is she under lock and key too? Is she even alive?"

Horsa had no answer for him.

Aurelianus marshalled his troops at the crack of dawn and set off on the road south without saying farewell to Lord Elafius and without waiting for Hengest and Horsa to rouse themselves. Cursing the Briton, but at the same time pleased that they would be spared his sour company for the rest of the journey, they mustered their cavalry and set off on his dusty trail.

They marched at a breakneck pace, reaching Londinium in a fraction of the time it had taken to march north at the beginning of the season. The men were exhausted as the crumbling walls of the town appeared and looked forward to the bathhouses, wine shops and brothels with tired smiles.

But when they came within sight of the north gate, they saw that Aurelianus had encamped his army without the walls.

"Why isn't he billeting them at the fortress?" Horsa asked.

"I don't know," said Hengest. "But it doesn't look good."

By asking around the camp they learned that the gates had been barred to Aurelianus but anything by way of explanation had been denied them resulting in confusion and anger. Aurelianus had demanded an answer and it came later that afternoon.

A reception party met them at the gates. Lord Vortimer, ruler of Maxima Caesariensis, led the delegation. Bishop Calvinus was there along with other dignitaries and nobles. The absence of Lord Vertigernus was notable. Hengest had Cerdic translate the conversation between Aurelianus and Vortimer which was carried out in Latin.

"What the devil's been going on?" Aurelianus demanded. "I've spent all season in Pictland without a word from your father and now, having won the war, I pass through Eboracum hearing rumours that you have usurped him. Elafius does nothing to dispel these rumours and now I am forbidden entrance to Londinium and am made to wait at the gates like an invading host! Does all Britannia run mad?"

"All in good time, old friend," said Vortimer with a smile. "There have been changes, it is true, and all this is merely a precaution. Surely you can appreciate the sense in not allowing your army to camp within the town's walls until we can be sure of where your allegiances lie."

"My allegiances? I have just spent all summer up to my arse in mud, fighting those blue-painted devils on the council's orders! Where is your father?"

"My father is under house arrest in the west. I have called a meeting of the council and now that you have returned, we shall hold it tomorrow. All will be explained."

"So, it is true then. You have usurped your own father. Are you in command of Britannia Prima too, now?"

"I retain my rule of Maxima Caesariensis," Vortimer said. "My brother, Cadeyrn, rules Father's old territories in the west. I have merely taken Father's place as head of the council."

"Saints preserve us," said Aurelianus. "The rightful ruler of this island overthrown by the conspiring of his own wretched pups! It is a tragedy worthy of Seneca."

"I realise that this is not the homecoming you may have desired or imagined. And I dearly hope that I can count on your continuing loyalty to my family. But there have been changes of which you have been ignorant. I promise you it will all become clearer at the meeting. But for now, you and your valiant warriors are the toast of the city – nay, the island! Rest, wash away the dust of journey and I shall have meat and wine brought out for your troops. And you and your lieutenants, I hope, will join me in feast tonight. A new era is dawning on Britannia, of which you are to play a key part."

"Listen to me, Briton," Hengest said, striding forward and seizing Vortimer by the sleeve of his tunic. "What has become of my daughter? If she has been harmed then no treaty or British army will save you from my sword!"

Vortimer's guards lowered their spears and pointed them at Hengest. Vortimer seemed surprised at his sudden appearance as if he had forgotten all about the auxiliary troops that had accompanied the army. He shook himself free of his grip. "Rest assured, mighty Hengest. Your daughter is alive and well and still my father's wife. They live in comfort at Din Neidr under the protection of my brother."

"And our treaty? My agreement with your father? It still stands?"

An expression passed over Vortimer's face that Hengest could not read. Then he smiled and said; "It still stands. Briton and Sais are still friends, and you still have your lands."

Horsa

It came as a surprise to Hengest and Horsa when they received the invitation to attend the feast at the palace with Aurelianus and his lieutenants. The abundance of fine food and good wine was a welcome change to the strict rations they had endured all season and they tucked in ravenously, drawing mild looks of disgust from the assembled nobles.

After the feast, the guests moved and conversed by torchlight in the gardens. Vortimer and the other nobles talked excitedly, while Hengest and Aurelianus sat in sullen silence, each looking as displeased as the other.

Horsa sought out Aureliana. Gods, she was more beautiful than he remembered! It had been agony to sit at table and not give away his love for her by constantly gazing in her direction. She had played her own part admirably and had not once looked over to him.

She had seen him coming and moved away, her eyes insisting that he follow her. She led him into the gardens and vanished behind a hedge. They stared at each other for a moment and then, when it was clear that they were alone, flung themselves into each other's arms, their lips meeting, almost biting in their passion.

"I prayed to God every day that he would bring you safely home to me," she told him.

"You prayed to your god, and I prayed to mine," said Horsa. "All of them. Some bugger must have been listening."

"And Galana?"

"Dead."

"Did you …?"

"No, she died by her own hand."

"Then you are free of that dreadful curse?"

"I believe so. There is no woman alive now who can hurt me."

"Can your gods be so easily thwarted?"

"Easily? Let me tell you, my girl, there was nothing easy about that war. Every day was blood and screaming and death."

"I am sorry, Horsa, I did not mean to belittle your efforts."

"No matter, my British princess. I would go through it all again if your love depended on it. The fighting and killing was nothing compared to the pain at being so far from you."

They kissed again.

"But what now, Horsa? The war is over and you shall surely return to your home in Cantium. How will we see each other?"

"We will find a way."

"But things will be so much more difficult now. Lord Vertigernus has been usurped by his sons. Everybody in Londinium hates you and your brother. Oh, isn't it awful?"

"Hush now. Whatever happens, they cannot drive a wedge between us. I will not let them. I promise."

Vortimer

Two days later the council met in an upper chamber of the palace. Vortimer gazed at the faces of the other council members as he took his seat at the head of the table.

Father's seat.

"Are we not to be joined by your co-conspirator?" Aurelianus asked, indicating the empty seat at the table.

"Lord Cadeyrn is unable to make the journey to Londinium at this point," Vortimer said. "But, as he is my brother, I can speak for him."

"Council meetings under your father were never held until every member could attend."

"This is what you might call an emergency meeting," Vortimer replied. "There is not time to wait."

"Are we under invasion?" asked Aurelianus with mock alarm on his face. "I was not aware."

"You jest, but you do not realise how true your words may prove to be. Perhaps we are not under invasion right now, but in a year? Who knows? The Saxon threat grows ever stronger in the east. We must make arrangements with all haste."

"I can barely believe my ears," said Aurelianus. "I have only just washed the blood out of my tunic having fought side by side with the Saxons all season. Now I am told that they are our enemies?"

"Have you grown so cosy with them during your campaigning?" asked Lord Elafius. "I would never have had you down as their sympathiser."

"Have no illusions," Aurelianus replied. "My time with our Germanic neighbours has only increased my disgust of them. But the fact remains, they earned their land legally and we do not attack our allies. Your reshuffling of the council, legal or not, does not alter your father's treaty with them."

"On the contrary," Vortimer replied. "With my father gone from the council, the treaty is null and void. You never approved of it, Aurelianus. Why defend it now, when we are so close to ridding ourselves of the Saxons once and for all?"

"That is another point that concerns me," said Aurelianus. "Even if I offer my support to this war you are planning – and make no mistake, without my support there will be no war – we are not strong enough to oust the Saxons. You underestimate their numbers and their ferocity. Why do you think Lord Vertigernus enlisted their help in the first place?"

"As to that," said Vortimer, "we have already discussed sending to Aetius of Gaul for aid."

Aurelianus snorted. "Aetius? He can't lend any troops. He's got his hands full with Huns and Goths; not to mention that dribbling fool he serves at Ravenna."

"Maybe, maybe not," said Vortimer. "All we can do is put our case to him. And there is always Bishop Germanus. His interest in this island may sway Aetius, for is it not truly the clergy who rules the Western Empire?"

"My father had dealings with Germanus when I was a boy," said Aurelianus. "It got him killed."

"Yes," put in Lord Marcellinus. "I've often wondered why you so readily followed your father's murderer."

Aurelianus's face was stony. "My father was a traitor. His actions tore our family apart, not to mention Britannia. He went against the ruling of the council for his own gain. It all sounds remarkably familiar, come to think of it."

"Come now, Aurelianus," said Vortimer. "That unpleasant business was hardly the same as this. We are acting for the good of Britannia. Surely you can agree that my father's treaty with Hengest and his brother has the potential to bring ruin upon us."

"Your father, for all his failings, is a shrewd man, but above all, he is the legally appointed head of this council and as such, I will not defy his orders."

"And so?" said Elafius, his exasperated words causing spittle to gather in the corner of his mouth. "What will you do? March your army west to release him from Lord Cadeyrn's fortress?"

"If I must."

"Then surely you can see our trepidation at allowing your men the run of Londinium!" said Marcellinus. "If you cannot listen to reason, then your men must live in their tents outside the walls."

"Gentlemen," said Vortimer in a calming voice. "Anger will not get us anywhere. Perhaps we should adjourn and cool off for a few moments. Besides, I have a few words I would like to put to Aurelianus in private. Shall we?"

They rose and shuffled out to take the air in the gardens and drink some wine. Vortimer remained with Aurelianus. The general would notice how none of the other lords minded this brief moment of privacy and wonder at it, but it had to be done. The man wouldn't listen to reason. Vortimer had but one weapon up his sleeve that might convince the pig-headed bastard. If his mind could not be turned then perhaps his heart could.

Aurelianus

Aurelianus strode into the reception room of his villa; his hob-nailed sandals click-clacking on the mosaic floor. He turned left, heading towards the kitchens. The stable boy said that Seren would be there. He couldn't face his daughter just yet. He needed some confirmation, some proof that what he had heard in Londinium had been a lie.

It can't be true, it just can't!

Seren was mixing herbs she had picked in the gardens. Aleum, mint and thyme infused the kitchen air with their scents.

"Welcome back, Master," the little old woman said to him, putting down her bowl and bowing her head.

"Leave us," Aurelianus said to the head cook and the other servants in the kitchen.

They put down their knives and rolling pins and filed out silently. Seren looked up at him under worried brows, fear showing in her eyes.

"Has my daughter taken a lover, Seren?" he asked her.

The fear turned to terror in those small dark eyes. "M … master?"

"A lover, Seren," he repeated patiently. "Is there some young pup sniffing around that I should be aware of?"

This seemed to break the maid's resilience. "Master, I beg you! I wanted to tell you, but she forbade it! Have mercy!"

"Peace, good woman," he said, struggling to refrain from shaking the little nurse savagely. "I respect your loyalty to my daughter. My anger is not with you. Now tell me, who is it?"

"Oh, Master, it is too terrible! You will have me flogged and cast out, I know it! I have failed you! I tried to stop her, to tell her that it was wicked and wrong, but you know your daughter's stubbornness!"

"My God, woman will you name the bastard!" he bellowed.

But he knew the answer already, and even as Seren told him, he barely heard it. His brain knew the confirmation was only a formality for the truth had already been spoken to him by Vortimer hours previously.

She must have confessed her affair to Bishop Calvinus. That was the only way Vortimer could have got hold of the information that was now shattering his heart. He had seen Calvinus toadying around after Vortimer ever since they had returned and knew that the Bishop of Londinium was no longer loyal to Vertigernus, but to his son instead. Now Vortimer was using this information to bring Aurelianus into his plot against his father.

All these things were apparent to him and yet irrelevant as he stormed down the hallways towards Aureliana's room. Seren scampered along in his wake, her skirts hitched up and crying "Don't hurt her, Master! I beg you! Show mercy on your daughter!"

She thrust herself between him and the door to the chamber, her thin, frail body barring the wood against him. "With all respect, Master, I won't see it done! She's been a wicked girl but the Good Lord calls for compassion!"

He seized her by the arms and shoved her aside before flinging open the door.

For a moment he was struck dumb and could only stand in the doorway and stare. She was so like her mother. So beautiful and pure.

She had been waiting for him; no doubt having heard his thundering approach. A codex lay unravelled upon the bed next to her which she had been reading. Another one of those damned romantic works her mother had loved. He ought to have burned all those scrolls the day she died.

"Tell me it's not true," was all he could muster, as he gazed into those dark brown eyes, searching for a flicker of hope. "Tell me it's all a vicious lie or a game and that Seren is in on it."

"My lady, I am so sorry," said Seren behind him. "I had to tell him. I cannot tell a lie …"

The look on Aureliana's face vanquished any hope Aurelianus had. "Leave us Seren," he said.

The miserable nurse turned away, but remained in the corridor, anxious that no harm would befall her ward.

"At first I would not let myself believe that it could be true," he said. "I told myself that it was a trick of Vortimer's; a cheap lie to further his ambitions." He tried to continue but found himself choking up. She was so very much like her mother, the wife he had loved with all his heart and lost. Now he risked losing her too. His eyes teared up. She had not seen him cry since the day they had buried her mother.

Now she had begun to cry too. "I am so sorry, Father. I never meant to hurt you."

"It's not my pride that hurts, girl, it's the thought of losing you."

"You will never lose me!"

"Aureliana, you don't know what these men are like! I have spent all summer campaigning with them! They're animals! And that Horsa is one of the worst; a foul, bloodthirsty savage …"

"Stop! I won't hear these things about him! You don't know him as I do. He has done terrible things, he's told me, but he has a good, gentle side."

"Gentle side? We have used these men as hired butchers, God forgive us. Horsa was sent to burn and pillage the Pictish coast. Families have been slaughtered at his command."

"I won't! I won't!" she shrieked, covering her ears with her hands. "No more! Haven't you yourself killed innocents? Isn't every man in your army responsible for leaving women without their husbands, children without their fathers, families without their homes? Horsa is a good man. I love him."

"Love him?" Aurelianus exclaimed. "You cannot love one of these pagan wolves! It's simply not possible!"

"Father, I swear on the cross itself, that I love Horsa and he loves me and if it were not for the stupid wars and politics of this land, we would marry!"

He was knocked back. It was almost as if she was *trying* to hurt him now. How could she be so stupid? So blind? All he wanted to do was protect her, that's all he had ever wanted. Well, if she was going to get angry, so could he.

"I'm telling you now, girl that this stupid, dangerous affair has run its course. You will never see that man again!"

"You can't stop us!"

"Oh, but I can! If I have to keep you locked up with a whole century posted here in the villa grounds, then that is what I shall do. If he ever comes near you again, I'll have his head on my gates!"

"Father!" she sobbed, but the fight had gone out of her and she fell down on the bed weeping.

He could not stomach any more as he turned and made for the stables.

Vortimer

Vortimer was considering retiring for the evening when he received word that Aurelianus had returned to the palace.

"Twice in one day, Aurelianus," he called out, as the general entered the reception hall, removing his helmet. "I am honoured. Was there some item of the council meeting that you wished to discuss further?"

"Drop the games, Vortimer," Aurelianus snapped. "I know that you used the information about my daughter to win my support of your cause and I don't care. I want only to crush those heathen dogs."

Vortimer sighed. "I am sorry, old friend. I assure you it was no pleasant business and I only wish there had been some other way to convince you. But you can see how the facts speak for themselves."

"I do not condone what you and your brother have done for it goes against the laws of this land. But I don't condone many of your father's actions either. His treaty with the Saxons cannot continue."

"Quite. Else how many thousands of other British daughters will be defiled by Hengest's wolves?" He detected a wince of pain in Aurelianus's eyes as he said this.

"What is it that you propose?"

"I have had a letter drafted. All the other council members have signed it and it lacks only your signature. Come, let me show you." He led the way to his office where, upon his desk, anticipating Aurelianus's arrival, a letter lay open. Vortimer handed it to him and the general began to read.

From the Lords of Britannia to Flavius Aetius, Magister Militum and thrice Consul of Gaul, greetings.

PART II

(Ur) "Ur byþ anmod ond oferhyrned,
felafrecne deor feohteþ mid hornum,
mære morstapa þæt is módig wuht."

(Auroch) "The aurochs is proud and has great horns; it is a very savage beast and fights with its horns; a great ranger of the moors, it is a creature of mettle."

Hengest

The days grew shorter, but to Hengest, they seemed somehow longer. Ruling land took some getting used to. He began to feel like a prisoner in his own hall for the line of messengers, complaints and disputes that trickled in through his doors seemed to be never ending.

The reorganisation of Cent – as the Germanic population called Cantium – into something resembling a kingdom of their homelands was a tricky business. It had to be divided into hides with a thegn to rule each. Then the yearly tribute or *geld* had to be determined for each hide. Local levies called *fyrds* had to be marshalled and ealdormen appointed to lead them.

Hengest's own warband was stationed on the coast and it took at least a day for it to be mustered to reach the borders of Cent should an invasion occur. The fyrds were necessary to fend off attackers until the main military body could arrive. As it stood there was not enough communication, manpower or organisation for the fyrds to effectively fend off an attack as this new complaint now confirmed.

"We cannot win a war outside our own borders for fear of losing one within, it seems," said Hengest in a weary tone, as the thegn finished his report. "I heard nothing of these rebels before I marched north, and now it seems as if Cent is infested with them."

"They must be dealt with else more and more will join their cause and we will not have enough theows left come harvest," said Horsa.

"They don't even see themselves as rebels," said Aesc. "That's the trouble. They see themselves as free men who owe no allegiance to you, Father. They had their own British masters until we killed them or ran them off their lands."

"Theows come with the land just like cattle and crops," replied Hengest.

"Try telling them that. They see us as the invading horde and don't want anything to do with us."

"What of Ealdorman Osgar?" Hengest asked. "It is he who leads the fyrd in those parts. Why hasn't he sent to me for aid?"

"My ealdorman is a proud man, my lord," said the thegn who had brought the tidings of rebellion. "He doesn't want you to think that he can't handle the problem."

"Obviously he can't handle it if his theows are wandering off from their work and forming warbands. Does he know that you came to see me?"

The thegn looked at his feet. "No, my lord."

"Well, you did right. I've no idea what Osgar thinks he's playing at but I'm going to have to intervene before these rebels start knocking on our own doors. Who is this leader of theirs?"

"He goes by the name of Trefor," said the thegn. "Nobody knows much about him other than that he is a Briton who takes objection to our people owning British slaves and farming British land. More and more theows run away weekly; sometimes killing their masters when they hear of Trefor's band of outlaws. Soon he'll have an army and there'll be nothing to stop him burning every farm in Cent like he burned mine." The thegn's eyes grew wet at the memory of his scorched home.

"You will be compensated for your losses," Hengest assured him.

"There is no wergild that can restore my son to me," replied the thegn sourly. "I only want to wet my blade in the blood of these brigands myself."

"And you shall. I am sending my most savagely ruthless warrior to tackle this labour problem of ours. When he is done there won't be a theow left in Cent who will dare raise a hand to his master. Horsa, when can you leave?"

Horsa glanced at his brother in surprise. "You want me to go slave-hunting?"

"Can you suggest a man better suited?"

Horsa was silent.

"You have experience in this field if I remember correctly. Take your best raiders and set out as soon as possible. We don't know where this Trefor has his lair, but he seems reluctant to leave Cent. It shouldn't take you too long to root him out. Just follow the smoke of burning homesteads."

The thegn who had brought the news of the slave rebellion departed and Hengest turned to the next matter of business. The man who approached was dressed in the rich clothes of the British aristocracy.

"The agricultural concerns of your kingdom do not stop at escaped theows, I fear," said the man in British.

"What can I do for you, Briton?" said Hengest.

"I am Teguin, son of Vosenius, Master of Trade at Durobrivae."

"Ah, yes, your father is the man who does such a fine job of ensuring that all our goods coming in through Rutupiae reach our good friends in Londinium. How is dear Vosenius?"

"He is well, though your subjects in the east fare less so."

"Oh?"

49

"I am sure that you have had news of the scarcity of good aurochs, Lord Hengest."

Hengest sighed. "Day after day farmers come traipsing mud through my hall complaining of being sold thin, old aurochs by our British neighbours."

"When your people took over Cantium, my lord, many farmers simply fled, taking their cattle with them. The mighty horned aurochs, so vital for pulling the plough, have become something of a scarcity. Despite breeding all year round, there simply isn't enough of them to repopulate the missing stock, so farmers have no choice but to purchase them from the Britons. Farmers on the borders of Cantium are regularly swindled by the cattle-traders. Whether old, injured or malnourished, the aurochs that are being sold are far below the standard paid for. Something must be done."

"I had no idea that cattle-trading affected the interests of you and your father so severely, Teguin," said Hengest.

"As Master of Trade, the business of low-born farmers in the countryside is not usually something that concerns my father, it is true," said Teguin. "But it is our belief that this cattle-swindling is run by the various criminal gangs who operate in the shadow of my father."

"Criminal gangs?" Hengest asked.

"I am sorry to report that there are many such gangs who have an influence on trade and that they are most probably creaming the profit from this scam."

"I will investigate personally," Hengest told him. "I won't tolerate gangs in my kingdom."

The man smiled and seemed pleased at his sincerity. He bowed graciously and departed.

"Were you not so very different from these so-called 'criminal gangs' when you and Horsa took over Rutupiae, Husband?" said Halfritha, when court had adjourned and Hengest sat with his family and closest friends at their meat that evening.

"Perhaps not," he said, eyeing her closely. "But I rule this land now, not a collection of poorly organised gangs. If these Britons think they can pass off poor stock on us then they have a surprise coming."

"But what can you really do?" Halfritha asked him. "You can admonish the gangs who live in your territory all you want but the Britons who sell the aurochs come from beyond the borders of Cent. You can't start a war with them. Will you complain to Vortimer?"

"And have him think I can't handle the land his father gave me?" Hengest exclaimed. "I must deal with this without the help of our allies in Londinium. I will ride out and see to the business in person. Ebusa shall come with me. An impressive display of force on the border should be enough to dissuade the Britons and the gangs from any foul-trading in the future."

"Can I come too?" Aesc asked.

"No, my boy, I have been thinking about giving you something more exciting to do. You shall accompany your uncle Horsa and help him deal with these escaped theows."

Aesc and Horsa exchanged a look. "You distinguished yourself in war with the Picts and I think you are ready to ride out without your old man at your side. It is important for you to gain an understanding of our land and how it all works for you shall rule it when I am gone. My father used to send me out on political errands when I was your age back in Jute-land. In fact, it was on one of these errands that I met your mother."

He smiled at his wife and placed a hand on her arm but it felt lifeless to him. Her face was stony. He stifled a sigh and removed his hand.

"Look after him, Horsa."

"Like he was my own," his brother replied.

Aesc

"Who do you think this Trefor is?" Aesc asked, as they rode out, fifty mounted raiders at their back. It was his first time commanding such a large body of warriors and he was glad of his uncle's company. Officially, he was in charge of these men as his father had placed him in command, but there was no denying that they were Horsa's men through and through. He didn't know how far these raiders would follow his orders should their captain not be there to back him up.

Horsa shrugged. "He seems to have come out of nowhere. A slave that killed his master and roused a rabble in the countryside is all people seem to know about him."

"Why do so many follow him?"

"Perhaps they were just waiting for the right kind of situation to come along and it came in the form of Trefor. Not all leaders are great men. Some are just lucky."

"I bet you've met some great sea-captains in your time."

Horsa smiled. "The sea is different. It makes men hard and desperate. A leader has to fight to earn his place at the top and fight harder still to keep it. There is no room for incompetence for luck rarely smiles upon sailors. But yes, I have met some great ones."

They headed southwest towards the great forest of Anderida that straddled the border of Cent and the lands of the Britons. It was the farms on the outskirts of this forest that had been struck first and it was Horsa's thinking that the rebels had most likely made their lair under the cover of its trees.

The evidence of rebellion was more abundant the further west they went. Blackened timbers and razed buildings were all that remained of some homesteads, and the countryside seemed abandoned and desolate.

"They strike those who own the most theows," said the thegn who had brought the news of Trefor's rebellion to Hengest. His name was Ealdwine and he had accompanied them from Thanet on the road to Osgar's hall. "Thegns like myself are their biggest target. They don't bother with smallholdings that only own a couple of house-theows. My own land is a day in that direction. Do you wish to see it?"

"I don't think that's necessary," Horsa replied.

Aesc looked around at the emptied fields. "They must really resent us ruling over them," he said.

"It's not that simple," replied Ealdwine. "My own theows were Saxons mostly. And many who have joined Trefor's army are of Jutish heritage."

"Our own people abandon us?" Aesc was shocked.

"This was never about us against the Britons," said Horsa. "Any slave will bolt if he gets a whiff of freedom in his nostrils. And it may be more complicated still. When Trefor's men attack a farm they kill the owners and probably give the theows a simple choice; join Trefor or die a slave. I can't imagine many choose the latter regardless of any loyalty they may have to their dead masters."

They met a group of fleeing families carrying all their belongings on a cart drawn by two aurochs. The beasts showed their bones through their hides.

"Are you all from the same settlement?" Horsa asked them.

"From many," replied an old man, his back stooped from carrying a sick child whose head lolled about, barely conscious. "It is safer for us to band together on the road else we are prey to the raiders."

"They took everything from us!" said one woman who held a malnourished babe to her teat. "We have nowhere to go but we dare not stay. Why did we come to this accursed land? There is plague in the west and escaped theows lurking in the forest. And the Welsc cheat us with cattle like these wretched things!"

She had used a word that was rapidly gaining popularity amongst Cent's Germanic population. 'Welsc' meant 'outlander' and was indicative of how the settlers viewed the native population.

Horsa glanced at the wheezing aurochs that struggled to pull the cart through the mud. "My brother will clear up this business of cattle swindling and we are here to bring this revolt to heel."

The woman gazed at him. "You are Horsa, brother of the Folcwalda!"

Horsa nodded and the refugees began to gather about them. "This is Horsa the troll-slayer!" said one.

"What is this talk of plague?" Aesc asked them.

"Sickness," replied the old man. "It ravages the western lands of the Welsc and spreads without halt. It spares none, man or woman, old or young."

"Does this child have it?" Horsa asked, warily taking a step backwards from the old man who carried the infant.

"No. She is starving," the man said. "Her parents were killed by Trefor's men and she walked to the next farm. Two days alone with no food! The plague is an altogether different beast."

"It begins with coughing," said the woman. "And sweating. Then they start to vomit blood. Their bodies begin to decay while they are still alive."

55

"And none of you have it?"

The woman shook her head. "It has not yet reached Cent but we are heading east before it does."

They let the sad little train pass on their way to whatever wyrd was spun for them in the east. Aesc wished they could have done something for them, but his uncle's men had little enough food of their own and their business grew all the more urgent.

They reached Ealdorman Osgar's holding by nightfall. It was a medium-sized settlement, typical but for the staked palisade that had been recently constructed around it, penning in cattle, swine and dwellings. Men were digging ditches by torchlight overseen by a mounted nobleman with greying hair that reached to his middle and a short beard. He glared at them as they approached and the men threw down their tools and reached for their saexes.

"Peace, Osgar," called out Horsa. "We come to reinforce you against the rebels."

"Is that you, Lord Horsa?" Osgar called back. "I did not send for you."

"Am I your thegn to be sent for?"

"I meant no disrespect, Lord. I am merely surprised to see you."

"And my brother and I are surprised that you decided to tackle this rebellion alone and without our aid."

"Trefor and his bandits are a pest but we are safe enough here."

"With that flimsy palisade?"

"Come in and let us drink and eat and you shall see how safe we are."

As they entered the settlement and threaded their way through the dwellings and enclosures up to Osgar's hall, they passed the charred remains of a large homestead.

"What happened here?" Aesc asked. "Trefor's brigands or was somebody careless with some embers?"

"Oh, we suffered a minor assault," said Osgar. "But we repelled them once and we can do so again. And now that we have our palisade completed, we are even more secure."

Their meal was a good one and they were joined by the ealdorman's wife and daughter. The girl was pretty but seemed miserable. Neither she nor her mother spoke throughout the whole meal.

Aesc often found himself thinking of women these days. It was about time that he was married but his father had shown no indication that he was looking for a bride for his son. The only women Aesc knew were serving girls. The daughters of ceorls would never do for the future ruler of Cent. He had always assumed that his father would pair him up with a comely daughter of a thegn or ealdorman. He hoped that when he did, he chose one who was a bit more cheerful than Osgar's girl.

Conversation turned to the local fyrd. Horsa wanted to know where they were and why they weren't mustered at the settlement.

"I have them investigating the forests and trackways, looking for signs of Trefor's hideout," the ealdorman replied.

"The whole fyrd?" asked Horsa. "What if they should attack you here again? You don't have enough men to defend yourselves."

"They won't attack."

"How can you be so sure?"

"They can't get through to me without my men intercepting them and bringing me word of it."

After they had eaten, Aesc, Horsa and their men bedded down on the floor of the hall for the night. Fifty-odd sea raiders settled in by the glow of the embers began to snore.

"I must see to my family who live with my wife's sister," Ealdwine said to Aesc and Horsa, wrapping a cloak over his tunic. "Might I speak with you in the morning? Privately?"

"Of course," Aesc said. "Something on your mind?"

"I don't know if it's my place to speak, but I can't help thinking, you see. It was what you said about the aurochs earlier today."

"The Britons have been selling our people shoddy stock," said Horsa. "Know anything about it?"

"Tomorrow," promised the thegn. He turned to leave and then stopped, as if reconsidering. "You asked about that burned building on the way in."

"Yes?"

"I thought it odd at the time that Ealdorman Osgar did not tell you the full story. This settlement *was* attacked by Trefor's men."

"So he said."

"But he did not say that his daughter was raped during the attack."

Horsa frowned. "That quiet girl who sat with us tonight?"

"He only has one daughter and she's no maiden now. I just thought it odd that he didn't mention it."

"Very odd," agreed Horsa. "Sleep well, friend. And whatever more you have to tell us you can do so tomorrow."

The thegn nodded and slipped off into the night.

Aesc and Horsa looked at each other. "That explains the poor girl's misery," said Aesc.

"Hmm," said Horsa. "There is more at work here than meets the eye."

They awoke to find Osgar sitting at his table watching the flames of the hearth that had been rekindled by the theows. Aesc scrambled to his feet and rubbed the ache from his body. "You should have woken us, Ealdorman," he said. "We did not mean to oversleep."

"Sleep all you want," Osgar replied. "You are perfectly safe here."

"Tell me, Osgar," said Horsa, "where does Ealdwine's sister-in-law live?"

"In a dwelling on the eastern side of the settlement, I believe. Near the palisade. Why?"

"I have a mind to speak with him."

"You can't. I sent him out with a company this morning. I received word that some of Trefor's wolves were seen heading through the woods to the south. I ordered them to engage. I told you that my defences were more than adequate."

"We shall ride out and give them aid," Horsa replied, buckling on his sword and kicking Beorn awake.

"It'll all be over by the time you catch up with them," called Osgar, as they left the hall and made for the stables.

He had been right. It was over. Bodies littered the forest pathway and Ealdwine's was among them. As far as Aesc could tell, all the dead were members of Osgar's fyrd. There wasn't a single escaped theow among the corpses.

"They must have been overwhelmed," said Aesc.

"They were led to their slaughter," agreed Beorn. "Only ten of them. Poor bastards."

Horsa spat. "I don't know if Osgar is actively working against us or if he is just bloody incompetent! To send a paltry force of ten against Trefor's men? He just as near killed them himself!"

Aesc grimaced. Now they would never know what Ealdwine had wanted to tell them and it struck him that perhaps this brief episode of butchery had been designed to ensure just that. It was certainly odd that Ealdwine had been sent out when he had seemed so desperate to talk with them that morning.

They rode back to the settlement and gave Osgar the bad news. While the families of the slain mourned their dead, Horsa sent Beorn on an errand as they sat down to a midday meal of oatcakes and goat's milk. When they had finished, Beorn returned and told Horsa that all was ready. They took their leave again and rode out towards the forest.

"Why all this secrecy, Uncle?" Aesc asked him. "I appreciate that these are your men but I don't like being kept in the dark, especially as I am technically in charge."

"Apologies, Nephew, but I didn't want Osgar to know what we're about."

"You don't trust him?"

"Not nearly as far as I could throw him and he's a heavy bugger."

They came to a secluded homestead which consisted of a couple of roundhouses and a forge that was open on one side, so that the blacksmith could be seen hammering away at a glowing iron.

"Good work, Beorn," Horsa said, as they dismounted. "This place doesn't seem to have been touched by Trefor."

"Probably because it's a British steading," said Beorn.

"Or possibly because I own no theows," said the blacksmith, exiting his forge, sweat beaded on his sooty brow. "We did away with slavery before the Romans left so it's little wonder folks round here don't like you people starting up that practice again."

"Can we trust this fellow?" Horsa said to Beorn.

"I'm no friend of Trefor's," said the blacksmith, "and as you can see, I speak your tongue. I don't much care about who's in charge and Saxons pay me for my work which is more than I can say for Trefor's thugs. They've forced me to shoe their horses at sword point more than once."

"They have horses?" asked Aesc.

"Some. They have no cavalry to speak of, but they have a few stolen mares for Trefor and his captains to prance around on."

"Why are we here, Uncle?" Aesc asked.

"Because I intend to worm our way into Trefor's confidence and find out where his lair is and how strong his forces are."

Aesc gaped at him. "That sounds dangerous! And how can we hope to find him when Ealdorman Osgar cannot?"

"Escaped theows don't seem to have any trouble running into him," said Horsa. "We'll just pretend to be a pair of runaways seeking out the mighty Trefor."

"Just us?"

"Just us. My name will be Aelfstan – that's a name I have gone by before – and you shall be Deogol, my son. Now then, smith, do you have the collars?"

The blacksmith went over to his work bench and held up two large iron rings. "I just finished inscribing them before you got here." He handed them to Horsa.

Horsa smiled as he ran his fingers over the runes etched into the iron. They both read 'Ordlaf'.

"A little joke," Horsa said. "I'll give this to Ordlaf when we return. Tell him we were his theows for a while. Right, smith. Can you fix these on us now?"

"I'll just heat up the pins," said the blacksmith, stirring his coals. "Who's first? You or the boy?"

"Care to go first, Aesc?" Horsa asked. "Or Deogol, I should say."

Aesc felt sick and his legs were shaky.

"Come on, lad, it's not that bad. He'll be careful not to burn us, isn't that right, smith?"

"Uncle, I …" began Aesc, "I've worn one of these collars before. I swore I'd never wear one again."

"Gods, I'd forgotten, Aesc," said Horsa. "I'm sorry. I should have thought. But it's only for a short time. And we won't really be theows. We'll be joining a rebel army of escaped theows. And we can't very well pose as runaways without collars now, can we?"

Aesc nodded, unable to say anything further.

"I'll have the damned thing off you as soon as our business is done. I promise."

Hengest

The old Roman town of Durobrivae marked an important point on the trade route to Londinium. It was situated on the great river that separated Cent from the rest of Britta. A stone bridge had been constructed over the river centuries before, and the road wound its way south to disappear into the darkness of the Forest of Anderida.

The town was typical of its type: crumbling Roman architecture, filth and refuse in its unkempt streets and thieves and beggars rubbing shoulders with merchants and whores in its crowded marketplace. The only reason Durobrivae thrived when other towns like Durovernum lay abandoned, was its importance as a trading post and the compliance of its ruler with Hengest.

Vosenius – a merchant and a Briton by birth – was the ruling authority in the town. He had accepted Hengest's takeover of Cent readily, seeing no reason why political reshuffling should stand in the way of profit. Thus, Britons and Germanic settlers coexisted much in the same way as they did in the coastal towns.

It was late afternoon by the time Hengest and his retinue set up camp in the marshy outskirts. They headed into town on foot. There seemed to be a funeral taking place in the suburbs and the Latin prayers of the priest could be heard as they approached. Not wishing to intrude but keen to find out who was being buried, Hengest waited and watched the ceremony from a distance.

It was a large crowd and of them Hengest recognised only Vosenius. Once the rites had been said the crowd began to disperse and Hengest walked over to Vosenius. It took a while for the Briton to recognise him but when he did he all but got down on one knee.

"Lord Hengest! I received no word of your visit! We are unprepared! As you can see, we are in the midst of grief."

"Calm yourself, Vosenius," said Hengest. "I did not come here expecting a lot of fuss. Did your son not tell you that he visited me?"

"My son?" Vosenius asked.

"Teguin told me of his suspicions regarding the cattle swindle and wished for my intervention. This business of the aurochs is something that affects the whole of my land and I need it straightened out. I was on my way to visit Teguin now. Perhaps you wish to join me?"

Vosenius's face was stony. "I think it would be best if you followed me to my house instead. We have much to discuss."

Hengest frowned. "As you wish. Tell me, whose funeral was this?"

Vosenius turned to him, his eyes suddenly rimmed with red. "Teguin's."

Vosenius's house was one of the villas that peered over the ramshackle streets through its immaculate gardens, separated from the chaos it ruled. Vosenius called for wine and they sat down in a room columned on one side and open to the cypresses and hawthorns of the gardens.

"You'll have to forgive my wife," Vosenius said. "She has been inconsolable since Teguin's death and is not up to receiving visitors, even the ruler of Cantium."

"Pay it no mind," said Hengest. "I offer my condolences. I had only just spoken with your son and had no idea of his fate. How did it happen?"

"Murder, put simply," said Vosenius. "Teguin was riding back from some outing in the countryside. It was late and he had only one bodyguard with him. The man has been interrogated and I am confident that he knew nothing of it. Several unknown assailants attacked them and cut my son down from his horse. They stabbed him over a dozen times. The bodyguard was savagely beaten but managed to crawl to safety, damn him." Vosenius's hand shook as he placed his wine goblet down on the table.

"When was this?"

"Less than a week ago."

"He was returning from his audience with me. Do you think somebody bore him ill for calling on me for aid?"

Vosenius looked at him almost apologetically. "I've always admired you, Lord Hengest. When you overthrew that glutton Cassiodorus and took over his towns I rejoiced. Trade from the coast has not flourished so since Stilicho's time and I was only too happy to work for you to ensure the trade route across the river remained open. But you must understand that my position here is not easy.

"I have no troops like you do. Even Cassiodorus had his Saxon mercenaries to count on," at this he looked at Ebusa, but not unkindly. "Resources are short and I must rely on means that some may find disagreeable to ensure that trade is protected. Teguin did not hold with some of my methods and evidently thought to bring you in to clear things up."

"There has been no problem with regular trade," said Hengest. "I'm not here to dictate how you go about protecting it or what methods you use. I am here because of the business with the aurochs."

"Yes. Times are hard. My countrymen are probably selling off the worst of their stock and keeping the best for themselves. It's not unheard of."

"It's damned dishonest. And I don't believe that it's as simple as you say. I think that there is a conspiracy against us designed to weaken our grip on the land and potentially starve my people."

"Look, my lord," said Vosenius, "I protect the main trade route across the river. That's wagons of grain, amber, wool, pottery, wine and oil mostly. Agriculture is a bit beyond my powers. Cattle traders cross the river at numerous points south of here. They come and go as they please. Naturally if I were to come across one who was selling poor stock at high prices, I would punish him accordingly, but I cannot control every farmer who strolls over into Cantium looking to sell an aurochs or two."

"I am not holding you responsible, Vosenius," said Hengest. "I have no complaints about your doings. But your son seemed to think that the root of the aurochs swindle was here in Durobrivae. He blamed it on criminal gangs that operate here ..."

"I apologise," said Vosenius. "I did not mean to be so defensive. But this town has been hit hard by the political crumbling that has blighted Albion in recent years. There are gangs, it is true, but they are under control. Violence and corruption are kept to a minimum, I assure you. Tell me, will you do me the honour of staying here in my house for the duration of your visit?"

"Thank you but I have a camp set up on the town's outskirts. I should remain with my men."

"What will you do here?"

"Ask around. I may have to travel along the border in order to find out what has been going on. I will use Durobrivae as a base for the time being."

They finished up their wine as quickly as they could manage without causing offence. It was a little early in the day to be imbibing Hengest felt, but the man had just buried his son and it was understandable.

"Do you trust him?" Ebusa asked once they were walking the cobbled street away from Vosenius's house.

"He's a good sort but he seems to be under a huge amount of pressure," Hengest replied. "And I don't think he was telling us everything. For instance, one would have thought that he would have been tearing this town apart to find his son's killers, and yet he seems content to wallow in sorrow and wine. It is almost as if he knows who is responsible and is powerless to do anything about it."

When they got back to camp they found a bearded Angle and his wife looking for an audience. His name was Larcwide and he claimed to be a merchant and a figure of authority in Durobrivae. His wife was a pretty Briton. She wore a good deal of lead paint intended to cover up some bruising on the left side of her face. It didn't fool Hengest.

"When I heard that the great leader of our people had come to Durobrivae in person, I dropped everything to come and meet him," said Larcwide. "We must stick together in this new kingdom of ours else the Welsc will threaten to overrun us."

"Do they threaten you, Larcwide?" Hengest asked.

"They're not to be trusted. Vosenius is alright, but there are many Britons here who are not as loyal to you as your own countrymen are. They threaten my

67

businesses and bully my workers. We followers of Woden and his kin must band together to hold strong."

"And what is your business?"

"Horses mainly. I've the best. You must come and see them yourself. I'm sure I can sell you some at a very attractive price."

"You're a horse trader, then?"

"Among other things."

"Which are?"

Larcwide rubbed his beard as he thought for words. "I'm what you might call a pillar of the community. I take care of local businesses and protect them from Welsc troublemakers intent on mischief."

Hengest nodded. He had a good idea of what Larcwide was and how he operated. Hengest promised him that he would drop by and take a look at his horses. As the pair departed, Larcwide's wife cast Hengest an odd look, turning the bruised side of her face to him, almost as if she wanted him to see it.

That evening Hengest and Ebusa wandered back into town. Hengest dressed himself in simple clothing and left behind all of the gold trinkets that marked him out as the Folcwalda. He even left *Hildeleoma* behind, much as it pained him. If they ran into any trouble they would have to rely on their saexes as they did in the old days.

The town had a nightlife much as the coastal towns did. Wine shops were open and drunks staggered about, vomiting and urinating in the alleys. They spotted a brothel with curtained windows and painted women displaying their wares on the street outside. As they passed one tavern a man came hurtling out of it as if thrown by a meaty pair of arms.

"Damn you bastards!" shouted the ejected man before hurling a glob of phlegm on the cobbles. "I've put in twelve years of loyal service to that shit-eating rat! And now I'm not fit to drink in his tavern?"

By the look of him he had drunk a fair amount already that night. His face was purple with bruises; several days old. His lip had been split nastily and the dried blood was cracked. He staggered over to a gutter and vomited.

"This could be a fellow who might tell us what's what in this town," said Hengest to Ebusa in a low voice.

They walked over to the man who had just finished emptying his belly in a torrent of steaming wine and bile. "Are you so well received in all the wine shops in this town or are there a few you could take a pair of newcomers to?" Hengest asked him.

The man turned and peered at him in the darkness. "Newcomers? What's your business in Durobrivae?"

"Looking for work. I hear this is the town to come to for men with good sword-arms who have no desire to join Hengest's band in the east."

The man chuckled as he wiped the side of his mouth. "This used to be the very town you speak of until recently." He glared at the entrance to the wine shop he had just been hurled through. "But loyalty is undervalued these days. Find somebody else, strangers. I'm a nobody now. I can't help you into any crew."

"Perhaps not, but I'm sure you could tell us a good deal about this town so as we don't run into trouble. Come now, we're buying."

This seemed to encourage the man and he led the way to another tavern on the other side of the street.

They went in, sat down and ordered a full jug of local mead and some bread.

"Tell me," said Hengest, as their bruised companion slaked his considerable thirst, "who is it that owned that tavern you were just thrown out of?"

"Cian," said the man, setting down his cup and tucking into the bread. "My boss for twelve years and the toughest thug in Durobrivae."

"I thought Larcwide ran the illicit side of things here," Hengest said.

"There's three men who rule this town. Four if you count Vosenius. But he's only as big as the other three let him be. He pays them tribute, you see."

"Vosenius pays gang leaders tribute?" asked Hengest in astonishment.

"Has to. He can't run this town without them. There's Cian, Larcwide and Teilo. Cian runs protection for the bakeries and butcheries and is the biggest silver-lender in the town. Teilo controls the river fishing trade and the ferries. Larcwide sells horses mostly and won't permit anybody else to sell them within the town limits. They all have their businesses and are in a state of relative peace so long as nobody steps on anybody's toes."

"I can't believe it all runs as smoothly as that," put in Ebusa.

"We've had problems in the past to be sure, but nobody likes gang warfare in the streets and so the peace is kept at all costs."

"Any of these gangs involved in cattle trading?" Hengest asked.

The man shook his head. "Not much profit in it. Anybody can sell cattle."

"Anybody can sell horses."

"Not like Larcwide's horses. Those are the finest stock. Finer than Hengest's is what they say."

"Now let's be sensible …" began Ebusa, and Hengest smirked at his thegn's offended tone.

"Who in this town is afraid that Hengest might interfere with local businesses?" said Hengest.

The man shrugged. "Everybody and nobody, I suppose. He could certainly cause some bother for Cian and the others but he's busy enough sorting out the coastal towns, I heard. Got enough on his plate what with his treaty with Vertigernus to bother us."

"Somebody was worried," went on Hengest. "Worried enough to kill Teguin, Vosenius's son, because he went to Hengest for help. At least that's what I heard."

"Then you've been talking to the wrong people," said the man with a bitter grin. "Teguin went to Hengest alright, but it wasn't that what got him killed. I can tell you this now because he's dead and everybody will find out in time anyway. He was having his way with Arianrhod, Larcwide's wife."

Hengest blinked. "How do you know this?"

"Because I was his bodyguard. I knew Teguin and occasionally earned some extra coin protecting him. Cian arranged it. I was there the night Larcwide's thugs knifed him. I nearly didn't make it myself, as you can see by my face."

"Is this why you were thrown out of Cian's tavern?"

"More or less. Perhaps I let my drink get the better of me and mouthed off a bit, but that's more or less it, yes. Cian's livid that I let Teguin die. These bruises of mine don't impress him. He thinks I should have laid down my life for Teguin."

"Why? What does he care for Vosenius's son?"

"Teguin owed Cian money. Lots of money. And he would have paid but with him dead there's nothing to collect and so Cian blames me for crawling back to him with half the teeth broken in my head. Perhaps I should have died in the mud with Teguin." He reached for more mead and guzzled it down.

"You've been very helpful, friend," said Hengest, rising to leave. "Enjoy the rest of the mead."

They wandered out into the nighted streets. It was late and the streets were still busy. "This town's worse than Rutupiae with its gangs of thugs and thieves," exclaimed Hengest.

"There's a lot going on here that's amiss," said Ebusa, "but nothing to do with aurochs."

"We don't know that yet. We don't know what these gangs are mixed up in."

"What do you plan to do?"

Hengest smiled at him. "Stir things up a bit and see if I can't get a few of these characters to show their true colours."

Deogol

Their collars weighing heavy and cold around their necks, Aelfstan and Deogol followed the track through the forest with no real direction in mind. They had walked for over half a day and still the wooded expanse of Anderida continued before them.

"What if we don't find Trefor, Uncle — I mean, *Father*?" Deogol asked. "Will we turn back?"

"Tired already, Son?" joked Aelfstan. "Or are you frightened to join with the rebels?"

"Neither, but we can't walk on forever."

"You've a right to be worried. I hear that Trefor has trials for all who wish to join his army and any who don't measure up get strung up on frames for the sun to burn brown."

"Are you making that up?" Deogol asked.

"No! And those who are still alive after three days get staked out with an apple in their mouths for the wild pigs to find!"

Deogol was sure his uncle was teasing him and was not amused.

"You're right about the apples and the pigs," said a voice behind them in Jutish, the accent thick.

They both jumped and spun around, instinctively reaching for sword hilts. Each grasped empty air, feeling uncomfortably vulnerable.

Four armed men stood on the pathway. "Only we don't put the apples in your mouths," continued the one who had spoken. "We put them up your …"

"Don't frighten the lads unnecessarily," said another of the men in an equally strong British accent. "They might not even survive the three days tanning!"

The four men chuckled at this. Two of them were clearly Britons but the other two had flaxen hair and the tall-framed look of Germanians.

"Well?" Aelfstan asked. "Are you Trefor's men or are you a bunch of landless thugs with big mouths?"

That stopped them smiling and the leader of the group – a brutal-looking Briton with a nose that had been flattened – approached Aelfstan and snarled at him. "We're Trefor's men and you'd better believe it. Question is: who are you?"

"Aelfstan's my name, and this is my son, Deogol. We're runaways from back east."

"And you want to join Trefor's band, is that about the size of it?"

"We heard that he's hiring strong young men willing to fight."

"Hiring's not quite the word," said Broken-nose. "Trefor isn't some soft landowner willing to pay people to fight his war. If you'll get any pay then it'll be loot you fought tooth and nail for and Trefor demands loyalty in return. If he doesn't get it there'll be no messing about with stringing you up to sun for three days. He'll have something much worse planned for you."

"Well, are we going to talk all day," said Deogol, "or are you going to take us to him?"

"Eager lad, aren't you?"

"We've been walking for days with nothing but nuts and nettles to eat, but we've got fight in us, make no mistake about that. Take us to your master and we'll show him."

Broken-nose grinned as if at some private joke and said, "Come on then. Daylight's wasting."

They plodded on through the forest; taking overgrown tracks that neither Aelfstan or Deogol would have spotted. The men were jovial enough. Broken-nose led the way, jesting incessantly with the other Briton who was called Heilyn.

"We've got plenty of *Saeson* in our ranks," said Heilyn. "Like these two behind me. That's why we have an understanding of your language."

"We had heard that many of our people had joined with Trefor," said Aelfstan, shooting a glance at Deogol.

Deogol understood the look. If these Britons understood Jutish, then they would have to be careful not to say anything that might be overheard and get them into trouble once they reached Trefor's camp.

"What are your stories?" Aelfstan asked the two Germanic men behind them who had been silent until now. "How did you come to be Trefor's men?"

"We are Angles," said one of them. "Our master brought us to Britta from Angle-land. He was a cruel man. When we heard of theows that had freed themselves and lived in the forest, we slew our master and sought them out."

"Tell me, *Sais*," said Heilyn to Aelfstan. "Did *you* kill your master when you made your escape, or did you both sneak away in the night?"

"Killed a couple of his guards," Aelfstan replied. "Tried to get into my master's chambers and gut him like a herring, but I had my boy to think of."

The leader smiled.

That they were nearing Trefor's lair became apparent by the appearance of more warriors from the woods.

"New recruits?" asked one, brandishing a heavy British sword.

"They hope so," said Broken-nose.

In a clearing stood the encampment. Deogol was reminded of the Pictish villages they had seen tucked away in the northern forests beyond the wall. But this had more of a slapdash appearance as if its inhabitants were not as skilled or experienced in constructing their own shelters as their northern cousins.

Roundhouses were the favourite type of dwelling but their walls showed the wattle through their daub and the thatching was poor. There were tents too; scraggly, rat-eaten things from which dirty-faced children peered out impishly. The warriors and their women sat around fires drinking from clay jugs with weapons carelessly left to one side.

They were led inside the largest roundhouse where they found Trefor.

He was younger than Deogol had predicted – no more than twenty-five winters. He was shorter than Aelfstan, but stocky and had a thick head of curly black hair. Dark eyes lay sunken below a heavy brow.

"Names?" Trefor asked abruptly.

Aelfstan introduced himself and Deogol.

Trefor walked over to them and seized Aelfstan's iron collar in a meaty fist, drawing it close for inspection. "Ordlaf," he mused after one of his men had translated the runes for him. "There is an Ordlaf in Hengest's band. His standard bearer, I believe. Same man?"

"The same," replied Aelfstan.

"Is he dead or alive?"

"Alive. As I said to your lieutenant, I considered taking his life in our escape, but had to protect my son."

"Pity. Any wound against the hated Hengest is a boon to my people. Tell me, Aelfstan, you and your boy have shown no signs of the pestilence?"

"No, none."

"Do not lie to me. It will go the worse for you both if one of you shows sign of infection."

"We are healthy; both of us."

"Good. I cannot afford to have infection in my camp. Walk with me, both of you."

They left the roundhouse and headed out into the forest. Trefor's guards plodded along a few paces behind. Trefor put many questions to them concerning Ordlaf, Hengest and the power of the *Sais* horde. He wanted to know how strong their warband was and how many settlements there were and how many days march lay between them.

Aelfstan told him more or less what he wanted to know and largely stuck to the truth. Such information could be got hold of easily enough anyhow and their mission here was to ensure that Trefor would never get to use it anyway.

"Your people think they have the run of this place," Trefor said. "But their time will come. When my army is strong enough, I'll throw that bastard Hengest back into the sea myself."

"And what then?" Aelfstan asked him in a cool voice.

"What do you mean?"

"What will you do when Hengest is defeated and Cent is yours? Extend your rebellion to the rest of

Britta? There are slaves of all kinds on this island even though the Christian god forbids it."

"Fuck them. I'll be King of *Cantium* then. Vortimer himself will have to pay me tribute. Get some sleep now. I'll find something to busy you with tomorrow morning. You can bed down in my roundhouse. It's a bit cramped but you'll sort out your own dwelling in a few days."

They were left to return to the settlement alone while Trefor discussed some matter with his men. It gave Aelfstan and Deogol a chance to talk.

"Are we really going to stay with these people?" Deogol said.

"Not to your liking?"

"They're a bit rough but that's to be expected, I suppose. They've had rough lives and have only just escaped from them."

Aelfstan glanced at him in surprise. "Quite sympathetic, aren't you? These men are traitors and enemies to your father."

"Traitors? None of them swore a vow of fealty to my father. They were born into slavery most of them. Others were captured and sold just as I was. Just as Hronwena and mother were."

Aelfstan sighed. "You've had a rough introduction to the whole business. But slavery is a way of life. The gods made some of us strong and some of us weak and left us to fight it out amongst ourselves. It's only natural for some to rule others."

"When you were a raider, did you never have any empathy for the people you enslaved?"

"I tried to avoid the slave trade in general," Aelfstan replied. "Except when it was absolutely necessary. It's a dirty, bloodthirsty business and takes certain types to run it."

"But you have no problem in owning theows yourself."

"It's not really something I think about. Look, did your father ever take you on a hunt when you were younger, back in Jute-land?"

"Yes."

"Do you remember your first? What was it, a stag? A boar?"

"Stag."

"How did you feel when the hounds dragged it down and your father – or whoever it was – plunged his spear into it?"

Deogol grew embarrassed. "I was sick," he mumbled.

"But how did the venison taste that night?"

He thought for a moment. "Delicious."

"See? Just because we don't have the stomach for certain things doesn't make it wrong. Like I said, it's the natural order of things."

Deogol wasn't convinced. Venison might taste succulent but try telling the stag that. He supposed that he still had a lot of growing up to do; despite the men he had already killed. No doubt he would understand better when he truly became a man like his father and uncle.

The roundhouse was cramped as Trefor had said. A dozen warriors lay around the hearth in a circular form of snoring and farting shapes. The stench of unwashed bodies was accentuated by the heat of the fire and the close quarters. Aelfstan and Deogol slept as near to the door as they could manage and put up with the draught.

The following morning Trefor sent for them. They found him conversing with Broken-nose and Heilyn. "I've got your first task for you boys," he said, as they approached. "Put these on." He handed them cloths soaked in some foul-smelling ointment. "Fasten them around your noses and mouths."

Before they could ask what it was all about, Trefor left them to attend to some other business.

"Come on," said Broken-nose, his voice muffled behind his own cloth mask.

A few paces through the trees lay a man tied to a bier. His face was pale and terror showed in his eyes. His mouth was gagged with a dirty strip of cloth and he moaned at their approach.

"What's this?" Aelfstan asked, his own voice muffled.

"Just pick up your end of the bier," said Broken-nose, "and make damn sure you don't touch him."

The man's moaning became more frantic as they carried him through the woods. The two Britons did not seem to hear him at all; almost as if he did not exist. Deogol understood what was happening. This poor wretch had shown signs of the pestilence and they were taking him away from the camp to die alone in the forest.

They walked on and on, and when Broken-nose decided that they had walked far enough, they deposited their burden on the forest floor. They did not untie him or remove the gag from his mouth. He did not make a sound as they left him, only sobbing silently, tears of terror and dismay rolling down the sides of his face.

When he was out of view behind them, Broken-nose removed his mask and said, "Now's your chance to prove your loyalty to Trefor. We can't leave a comrade of ours to be eaten alive by wolves, plague or no. Better to put him out of his misery." He held out a dagger. Aelfstan went to take it but Broken-nose held it away from him. "The lad must do it."

"Why?"

"We need to know that the youngest of you has what it takes."

Deogol looked uncertainly to Aelfstan but took the knife, slowly.

"Make it quick," said Broken-nose. "And keep your mask on."

With a final glance to Aelfstan, Deogol turned and headed back the way they had come, the dagger gripped tightly in his fist. As he walked, he tried to remember how many people he had killed in battle and found that he couldn't. Killing used to bother him. Not anymore. But this was different. Killing someone tied to a bier? It didn't sit well with him and he worried that he would not be able to do it. He forced himself to think logically. The man had the plague. It was a mercy killing if anything. And besides, his mission depended on it. Moreover, their *lives* depended on it.

When it was over he returned to the group, cleaning the knife blade on a rag he had torn from the man's shirt. He tossed the bloody rag away.

"Well, that's done," said Aelfstan. "Let's head back. I haven't had my breakfast."

"Knife looks a bit clean," remarked Broken-nose, glaring at the dagger Deogol handed back to him.

"I wiped it clean for you," said Deogol. "Didn't you see me?"

Broken-nose eyed him suspiciously. "I think we'd best take a look at your handiwork, lad."

They put their masks back on and walked back to the bier.

It was apparent from a few feet away that Deogol had completed his task. The man's face and chest were masked with blood from the arterial spray. His throat was opened by a large, dark gash. Broken-nose grunted something and said; "Good enough."

As they headed back to camp, Aelfstan put his arm around Deogol's shoulders and said, "Well done. That can't have been easy but it was necessary. For many reasons."

Deogol shrugged. "It's wasn't too bad. I don't know why, but it just seemed … *natural.*"

The next few days were quiet ones spent lounging around the camp. It was a shoddy band with a distinct lack of order that clearly grated against Aelfstan's sea-hardened discipline. Rank seemed to have only the most ceremonial of existences. Trefor's word was law and he had a few chosen underlings such as Broken-nose and Heilyn who instilled order by violent means, but other than that everybody seemed to be on the same standing.

At least the food was good and in abundance. Deogol didn't know where they got it for the paltry attempt at pig runs and few scraggly chickens hopping about were not enough to feed the whole band; so he assumed that the juicy sides of beef they gorged themselves on had been robbed from nearby farms.

There were no training drills and the warriors were left to their own devices which involved drinking, fornicating and fighting, regardless of the time of day.

Deogol couldn't understand why they were hanging about. "We know where Trefor's lair is," he said to Aelfstan one day," and we've seen how strong

82

his band is, so what are we waiting for? Let's get back to Beorn and the others."

Aelfstan shook his head. "You've seen the weapons they carry," he told him. "British swords, Roman helms, good shields and mail shirts. These aren't just odds and ends picked up by runaway theows. Even our people seem to have British or Roman gear. How did they get it? Who did Trefor barter with to outfit his band with such stuff? There's something going on here and I intend to find out what."

"Do you think Ealdorman Osgar is in league with Trefor?"

"It would explain a few things. But not everything."

"I can't believe he would betray his own people."

"I could. If the price was right."

Two days later their boredom was ended by further orders from Trefor. Aelfstan had heard him discussing a shipment of something or other with Broken-nose, Heilyn and a couple of other underlings.

"Any chance of tagging along on this one?" Aelfstan asked them.

Broken-nose glowered at him. "You're far too nosey, *Sais*."

"Well, we've been sitting on our arses for days now. I was under the impression that this was an army in the making. So far I've seen nothing to suggest that you are any threat to Hengest's people in the east."

"Watch it," Broken-nose warned.

"My son and I don't even have weapons," Aelfstan went on. "We can't do much fighting for you unless we get some good iron in our hands like you all seem to have."

"I'm telling you ..." Broken-nose began, but Trefor interrupted him.

"You can both go along. It'll give you more of an idea of what we're about. Follow orders and don't get too inquisitive. It's a skill you seem to have a born talent for but I'm telling you to rein it in for now."

"As you say," Aelfstan replied.

Before they set off, Aelfstan and Deogol were given a saex each and a British spear. "You won't need them," remarked Broken-nose, "but the chief wants you armed anyway."

They set off at dusk and before they had emerged from the forest it was pitch black. The moon shone down on flat, poorly tended fields. It was cold. Puddles in the track ways began to develop uneven skins of ice.

"Must be somewhere near the border," said Deogol.

"Keep quiet," snapped Broken-nose in a low voice. He was looking about, searching for something.

A light winked in the distance and they made for it, hurrying along at a jog. Deogol welcomed the exercise for it warmed him. As they approached the light, several shrouded figures could be made out and a mixture of lowing noises met their ears. "Those are aurochs I can hear!" he said.

There were about a dozen of the beasts and the men who waited with them were warriors in Germanic war-gear. Deogol froze as he recognised them. They were men from Osgar's fyrd. He hung back behind Broken-nose and the others, motioning to Aelfstan to do the same but he had already seen them. They kept their faces in shadow.

"Planning on keeping us waiting all night, Briton?" asked one of Osgar's men in Jutish. "My balls are frozen."

"Think it's easy finding you lot in the dark?" Heilyn replied.

"And it's only going to get darker and colder," Osgar's man said. "I don't know if your masters are planning to keep this up through the winter but a curse on them if they are!"

"They're not our masters," replied Heilyn.

"Britons are Britons."

Heilyn snarled. "Hengest might take orders from them but Trefor follows no man."

"Oh no? From where we stand, he looks like Vortimer's lap dog more than anyone."

"Alright, enough!" barked Broken-nose. "We've wasted enough time. You men, get hold of these aurochs, two per man. We've still a long walk ahead of us."

Osgar's men sneered at them and departed, vanishing across the dark fields. Deogol and Aelfstan took hold of a rope in each fist and followed the Britons who were heading back towards the forest.

"Are these things paid for, then?" Aelfstan asked.

"What did Trefor say about asking too many questions?" Broken-nose reprimanded him.

"They're paid for," said Heilyn. "Not by us, but they're paid for."

"They're fine beasts," Aelfstan commented. "Finer than anything I've seen in Cent in recent months. Are they from across the border?"

"Shut it, *Sais*!" came Broken-nose's order.

Both Deogol and Aelfstan were frozen and worn out by the time they reached their destination; a small settlement in the forest apparently known to their companions. The aurochs had snorted and dragged their hooves every step of the way and Deogol was nearly dead on his feet with exhaustion.

Mercifully there was the light of hearth fires and the smell of cooking meat coming from the roundhouses but it seemed that the night's work was not over yet. Women emerged from their dwellings and came over to them with sharp knives. At first Deogol thought they had wandered into a female-led ambush and nearly reached for his saex but it quickly became apparent that the knives were for the cattle.

One by one, the aurochs were led forward to have their throats slit and cups of the steaming blood were passed around to briefly sate their hunger and to warm their bones. Then the work began.

Broken-nose explained that the cattle were to be skinned and the meat cut up, half of it salted and half wrapped in sacking. This was laborious work at the best of times, but in the middle of the cold night after such a journey, it was almost unbearable for Aelfstan and Deogol. But they offered no complaint and set to it with grim determination. Their only comfort came from the warm, slippery flesh that they worked with, soothing to their numb hands as they cut and sliced.

Deogol wondered how many times this had gone on; good cattle sold in secret and slaughtered. Whatever scam was going on, Osgar was in on it, and by the gods he would make sure that he was held to account for it.

Dawn was streaking the eastern sky by the time they had finished, and with great delight, they learned that they were to get some food and sleep before the final leg of their journey. Roasted beef, mead and bread baked that day were as nectar to Aelfstan and Deogol and only the effort of chewing and swallowing kept them awake. When they were full they bedded down on sheepskins by the hearth and slept the sleep of the dead.

Hengest

"I told you we couldn't trust those Welsc bastards!" Larcwide raved, as Hengest's men passed pails of water in a chain to douse the flames. "But I can't understand why Teilo would attack me now. Peace has held for a good while."

The attack had come in the night and the flames could be seen from Hengest's camp. He thought it best to come in person with twenty able-bodied men to lend the horse dealer a hand. Two of his stables had gone up in flames and, in the confusion, twenty horses had been stolen by Teilo's men.

"Thank Woden we managed to get them out of the stables before they were roasted alive," went on Larcwide. "I never bolt the doors in case of fire but the creatures were in such a panic that they nearly perished anyway."

"And you are sure it was Teilo's men?" Hengest asked him.

"Absolutely. It's a small town and I recognised a few of them. When I get my hands on them I'll have them torn in four directions by my horses! Bastards! They dare to steal my stock!"

It was dawn before the fires were completely doused. The men stood around, sweaty, sooty and burned raw in places.

"Thank you for your help, Folcwalda," said Larcwide. "At least we managed to stop the fire from spreading. Will you quench your thirst with me in my hall?"

"I had better get back to my camp," Hengest replied. "I have much to do tomorrow and dawn is already upon us."

"Any closer in finding out who's at the bottom of the aurochs business?"

"A little."

"Just like those Welsc to trick us. Not an honest man among the lot of them."

"I am forced to agree," Hengest replied. "I have been asking around Durobrivae and the more I learn the more shocked I am. Do you know that Teguin, Vosenius's son, was killed over some man's wife?"

Larcwide suddenly looked nervous. "Ah, yes, I did hear something like that. Ugly business."

"And the worst of it is that it wasn't even him who was fucking the woman."

Larcwide turned slowly to stare at him. "Oh?"

"No, he was merely running errands. It was his boss who was having the affair. Somebody he owed money to, Cian, I think the name was. Teguin was working off the debt by running all the risks for him. Poor bugger got more than he bargained for. Somebody got the wrong end of the stick and had him killed instead."

Larcwide's face was white in the pale light. They left him standing there and headed back through the marshland to camp.

"That was nonsense about Teguin, wasn't it?" Ebusa said to Hengest.

"As much nonsense as the story I told Teilo yesterday about Larcwide bad-mouthing him."

Ebusa snorted. "This town is going to go up like a kicked hornet's nest."

His words were true enough for the following day Cian's tavern was torched and three men were burned alive. It was gang war on the streets of Durobrivae. With Larcwide increasingly paranoid and waging war on both Teilo and Cian, there wasn't a safe place for anybody affiliated with the three gangs in the whole town.

It wasn't long before the chaos Hengest had unleashed began to bear some fruit. He knew that one of the gangs would be involved in some racket that extended beyond the limits of Durobrivae and that would most likely have something to do with the aurochs conspiracy. The gangs knew the ins and outs of each others' businesses even if Vosenius and everybody else didn't. Hengest just had to watch and wait.

He had spies in the town and scouts in the countryside and a report reached him that a gang of Larcwide's riders had set out by moonlight and were following the river south. They were armed and the clandestine nature of their activity smacked of a gang on the warpath.

Hengest led a company of thirty riders and set out on the trail of Larcwide's men. Whatever they were up to, it went against the usual gang violence that was generally restricted to the town and its suburbs.

They were not far from the edges of the Forest of Anderida when they came across Larcwide's men. They were easy to spot for they were shooting fire arrows, seemingly at random, across the river. Some stuck in the mud on the opposite side but some struck the bulwarks of a barge that drifted on the black waters.

Men onboard the boat struggled to dampen the flames. Arrows rained down on them and, with no man at the helm, the barge began to turn and drift closer to the bank.

Larcwide's men ran into the shallows and looped ropes around the vessel, dragging it up onto the mud.

Swords and axes hacked down the remainder of the boatmen. Enraged, Hengest spurred his troops on.

"Gang war is gang war," he shouted to Ebusa, as they galloped down the slope, "but this is pure banditry within my own borders!"

Larcwide's men were too engaged in their act of minor piracy to notice Hengest's men until they were upon them. The mud tugged at their fetlocks and made the battle seem twice as slow. It was dark and difficult to tell one man from another. Any who were dragged down from their mounts flailed hopelessly in the mud, unable to rise and were either stepped on by hooves or had their brains dashed out by swooping blows.

None of the boatmen were saved and the deck of the barge was awash with blood. Larcwide's men were beaten and thoroughly confused. Some of them may have recognised Hengest but if they did, they didn't know whether to carry on fighting or submit to the Folcwalda.

Hengest slithered through the mud to inspect the barge. Ebusa was already on deck and lifting the oiled cloth off its cargo.

The glint of polished iron twinkled in the moonlight. Swords, helms, spears and bucklers were bundled up in the hold. All were good quality British items reflecting the Roman style.

Hengest made his way over to Larcwide's men and seized one by the throat. "Whose barge is this?"

"Cian's" said the man. "We did this for you, Folcwalda!"

"Speak sense! Where was it going?"

"Down through the forest."

Hengest glared at the man. "To Trefor?"

The man nodded.

"Cian has been selling weapons to the rebels?"

"Not selling. Just supplying. The weapons are already paid for."

"By whom?"

"Vortimer."

Hengest ground his teeth. It all made sense. Vortimer had hated the treaty his father had made with them but he dared not break it. He was supporting the rebels because it was the only way he could weaken Hengest's foothold short of declaring actual war. Vortimer was probably involved in the aurochs swindle as well but there was no proof of that here.

"There's a hell of a lot of gear here," said Ebusa. "Trefor doesn't have that many men, does he?"

"He's planning something big," said Larcwide's man. "He's building an army and has found a new base. Somewhere fortified where he can recruit more and more members."

"Where is this base?" Hengest asked him.

"I don't know. If I did I would tell you. I'm a Saxon and don't like Trefor and what he stands for any more than you do. This robbery of Cian's barge was a welcome task to us. But you stopped it! How have we offended you, my lord?"

Hengest ignored him. "Somewhere fortified …" he mused. "Now where might that be?"

Deogol

When they returned to the camp in the forest they found it in an unusual state of activity. Blades were being sharpened, shields recovered with hide and mail scrubbed with sand to make it shine. Trefor was arguing with some of his lieutenants by his roundhouse.

"Who waylaid it then?" he demanded.

"We don't know," replied one in a nervous voice.

"So I don't have my weapons?" Trefor was nearly shouting now. "How am I supposed to outfit an army without proper gear?"

His lieutenants cowered from him and he stormed off.

"Are we to make our move at last, then?" Broken-nose said, as they walked up to them.

"Who knows?" said one of them. "Have you heard anything about this theft of the chief's barge?"

"We've been gutting and skinning cattle all night. How could we know about some bloody barge? What happened?"

"The chief was expecting another shipment from Durobrivae and it never arrived. We heard that there was some sort of fight on the river. People saw lights from fire arrows. Anyway, the boat's not arrived and the chief is mighty peeved that he hasn't got his weapons."

"We have weapons enough. Besides, there won't be any fighting for Durovernum. The place is a ghost town."

"Right, but the chief was hoping to recruit more folk and outfit them from his own supply. How's he supposed to do that now?"

"I don't care. Once we've taken Durovernum, not even Hengest himself and all his horses could oust us."

Deogol and Aelfstan shared a worried look. "So it's Durovernum Trefor is after," Aelfstan said under his breath. "With that town under his control, he could fortify himself indefinitely."

They set out within the hour; a ragtag column of armed slaves, singing and drinking from skins. Aelfstan rolled his eyes at the lack of discipline. "If Trefor isn't careful half his men will be too drunk once we get there," he said to Deogol.

They reached Durovernum a little after noon. Once past the earthen bank and sturdy walls it felt as if they had wandered into a forgotten age. This was a Roman town left more or less as it had stood in the days of Stilicho. The thirty-seven years that had passed since the legions had withdrawn had seen a gradual abandonment of the town by its residents. The Germanic settlers, who distrusted the old Roman ruins, left the town a crumbling testament to those who had ruled Cent before them.

They passed bakeries, potters and wine shops that looked like they had just been vacated were it not for the long grass that poked up through the cobbles. The town's residents had not been able to take everything with them so furniture, tools and drinking vessels lay about as if they had just been put to one side after a day's work.

Trefor established his pseudo-court in one of the fine houses adjacent to the old theatre; not far from the forum and basilica. He posted sentries and set men to work barricading streets with rubble, broken timbers and other junk, creating an impenetrable boundary around the nucleus of the town. Eventually, he explained, he would repair the walls and post guards on the ramparts, securing his grip over the whole town.

They feasted in the crumbling villa that night. Men and women lolled on moth-eaten cushions of the finest silk and drank the looted mead they had carried with them, while the beef Aelfstan and Deogol had spent the previous night slaughtering sputtered and drizzled in the kitchen fires. Trefor was sprawled on a throne fashioned from cushions and furs.

They were well and truly drunk when the messengers arrived. One of the guards Trefor had posted came in, his face raw from the cold and his eyes nearly watering at the sight of the warmth and food he was missing out on.

"A delegation from Hengest, chief," he said.

"That was bloody quick," said Trefor. "How did he know we were here? Send them in."

Deogol recognised the four men immediately as they entered the chamber, eyes wide at the debauched nature of their enemies. They were good men, trusted thegns of his father and he immediately felt nervous for them. Trefor was in an exulted mood.

"Finally we are worthy of the mighty Hengest's notice," he said. "What does the *Sais* overlord want?"

"To parley," said one of the messengers. "The Folcwalda recognises the strength and courage of the one known as Trefor and wishes no conflict."

There was a resounding cheer from the seated rebels but Deogol was not fooled. This grovelling offer of peace sounded nothing like his father. His father rarely sent envoys in his stead. That he was not here in person meant that he was up to something.

"Lord Hengest offers you terms," went on the messenger. "Leave Durovernum. You will not be assaulted by any man of his; he gives his word. You and your followers will be free men; free to own land."

Trefor hurled a goblet of wine at him. It struck him in the face and drenched his clothes. "Does Hengest think that I require his blessing to be a free man? I was born a free Briton and was taken into slavery by an underling of his. I bought my freedom back with blood! Every man and woman here is free by my law, not Hengest's! And now he offers these paltry gestures of peace? It is because we are too strong for him now! We take what we want and there is nothing he can do about it and this makes him afraid! Hengest is afraid!"

The messenger's face was set. "I shall carry your words to my lord," he said.

"You shall not," replied Trefor. "Hengest is a fool if he thinks he can send his men in to talk to me and get them back again. Secure these prisoners! Now that we have hostages we shall be the ones to make the demands!"

There was another resounding cheer and the four messengers were set upon, bound and dragged away to the jeers of the rebels. Aelfstan and Deogol looked at each other.

"What can we do?" Deogol asked.

"Nothing for now," Aelfstan murmured." We must wait."

Wait they did and it was a long wait. Trefor and his warriors were in the mood for celebrating. Barrel after barrel of mead was opened and they all got drunker and drunker. They began to drop off to sleep and Aelfstan decided that now was their chance. They slunk out of the hall unnoticed.

"Your father's up to something, I know it," Aelfstan said to Deogol, as they left the house and hurried through the gardens. "Otherwise he would have come in person to bargain with Trefor."

"I know. But what do you think his plan is?" Deogol asked.

"I don't know but I'm betting those messengers could tell us, if they haven't had all the sense beaten out of their skulls yet. Still feel sympathetic towards these theows?"

Deogol shook his head. "They don't care about slavery. They're opportunists on the warpath. Trefor himself said that he wants to set himself up as king. Give them half a chance and they'll be owning their own slaves before long."

The prisoners were being held in the old temple with a handful of rebels guarding them by torchlight. Deogol groaned when he saw that it was Broken-nose and his crew.

"What the hell do you two want?" he demanded, as they approached.

"Trefor sent us to interrogate the prisoners," said Aelfstan.

"Surely that can wait until morning. I'm surprised Trefor is in any state to be giving orders."

"He doesn't want them to get any sleep. Men are easier to break when they are tired."

Broken-nose eyed him suspiciously. "Very well," he said slowly, standing to one side. "But if this is some story you've cooked up to lend your countrymen aid, I'll see you both strung up from the highest building."

"They're not our countrymen," said Aelfstan, as they passed. "Not anymore."

The prisoners were bound hand and foot in the centre of the chamber, shivering on the cold mosaic floor. Deogol knelt down and drew his saex. The men peered at him in the gloom; astonishment written on their faces.

"Lord …" began one, but Deogol cut him short.

"Quiet. Tell me what my father is up to." He began to saw at the ropes as one of the men talked.

"We intercepted a barge laden with weapons headed for Trefor. We learned that he was marching on Durovernum and hurried to beat him to it, but he got here first. Your father has marshalled his troops on the northern side of the town. He hoped to find a way in while we were distracting Trefor with talk of bargaining."

Aelfstan shook his head. "Trefor has barricaded himself in here like a trapped badger. Hengest will lose too many men if he tries to storm the town."

The last rope snapped apart under Deogol's blade and the four men wriggled free, rubbing warmth back into their limbs.

"I knew there was something wrong about you!" came a voice behind them.

They spun and saw Broken-nose standing with his men, weapons drawn.

"I'm going to gut you myself, *Sais* scum!" he said and lunged.

One of the freed prisoners stuck his foot out and Broken-nose tumbled headlong into Aelfstan's arms. Aelfstan hoisted his enemy up and slammed his fist into his jaw, sending him reeling backwards to strike his head against the old temple font, stunning him. "You might as well know, my name is Horsa!" he said, and lunged at the man, striking him again.

Fighting broke out between the unarmed messengers and the rebels. Aesc drew his saex and sliced it across the belly of one, spilling his guts while two of his father's men hurled a tangle of rope into the face of another before barrelling into him and seizing his sword.

Horsa had Broken-nose in a wrestling grip from behind and was slowly bending his head forward into the stagnant water in the font. Broken-nose struggled but Horsa was too strong and, his forearms straining, he submerged his enemy's face and held it there.

Broken-nose thrashed about and water slopped everywhere but he couldn't get a breath. Eventually, the body hung slack and Horsa let go, allowing the corpse to slide onto the floor.

The rest of the guards were dead and the escaped prisoners had armed themselves. "What's the plan now, my lords?" one of them asked.

"We need to clear one of the barricades and get word to my father that the way is open," Aesc said. "But we need to move fast!"

They exited the temple and hurried down the streets that were black and devoid of torchlight. The moon was shrouded and it was bitterly cold. They turned left and headed up the street that led north-west towards the town walls. One of Trefor's barricades loomed ahead; a confusion of rubble and smashed furniture.

The men guarding it were half frozen and utterly susceptible to surprise as Horsa, Aesc and their comrades fell on them, spilling steaming blood onto the icy cobbles.

"Somebody needs to get out and head north to tell Hengest," said Horsa.

"I'll go," said Aesc.

"Too dangerous, lad. I'd go myself but I'm needed here to do the talking if any of Trefor's men accost us. One of the others must go."

"I'm the fastest runner," Aesc, insisted. "And I'm also in charge."

Horsa smiled in resignation. "Go on then. Don't stop running until you find him." He turned to the messengers. "Where are they camped?"

"About five miles north, on the east side of the river," said one.

"Hear that, Aesc? Think you can find them?"

"I know my way about my father's kingdom better than you, sea rat!" And he took off, dodging a playful cuff from his uncle. He scrambled over the blockade and pounded down the street towards the gate.

Horsa

Horsa said a quick prayer to Woden to keep his nephew safe. "Come on, lads. Let's get this blockade cleared."

They worked hard and fast, dragging, pulling and dismantling. It took the rest of the night and it was only as they were finishing that a group of Trefor's men came wandering over, drunk and looking for fun.

"What the hell's going on here?" one of them asked in British. "Who gave the order for this blockade to be cleared?"

"Trefor did," Horsa replied. "He wants the road clear for transport of shipments."

"At this time of morning?" He gazed, bleary-eyed at the others and suddenly started. "Wait a minute! You're not our boys! You're bloody Saeson!"

"And what does that make you?" said one of Hengest's envoys, plunging his blade into the speaker.

The rebels staggered backwards, fumbling for their weapons. Horsa and the others were upon them before they could retaliate and two were dead in seconds flat. A third hurried away, to call for help.

"We'll have all of Trefor's men upon us any minute!" said one of the messengers.

"Then we hold fast and keep this road open," Horsa replied.

They did not have long to wait before the fleeing Briton came hurrying back with ten men he had kicked awake.

"If only we had some shields," Horsa muttered. "This is going to be a short fight otherwise."

The Britons stumbled to a halt, slipping on the ice a few feet from Horsa, panic written in their eyes.

Horsa sensed that they were looking at something behind him and he risked a glance backwards.

Torches – hundreds of them – were sailing through the night, held by warriors on horseback. Their hooves rang out on the cobbles and the Britons fled as fast as they could in the opposite direction of the column that was thundering down the street.

"I wondered if I'd find you here!" said Hengest, reining his horse in. "By the gods, it makes a man proud to be awoken by his son who claims to have escaped from the enemy's camp!"

"That's a good lad you have there, Brother," Horsa replied. "He played the part of an escaped theow admirably."

"Who'd have thought he had it in him?" Hengest said, turning to flash a grin at Aesc who rode beside him.

"Thought you'd got lost, Captain," said another voice, deep and merry.

"Beorn!" Horsa cried, spotting more of his loyal raiders in the ranks. "How did you come by this path?"

"I picked them up on the way," Hengest explained. "They heard that I was marching on Trefor's heels and didn't want to miss out on the fun."

"Think we'd leave our captain to take all the glory himself?" Beorn added with a grin.

"Where's Trefor, then?" asked Hengest.

"Sleeping off a hangover in a house by the theatre. Come, I'll lead the way!"

They swept through the town with the joyful cheer of men on the hunt. A few groggy rebels stumbled into their path to assail them but were hacked down and trampled. The guards Trefor had posted in the gardens had fled inside and bolted the doors. Hengest set his men to work on them with axes. Soon they were down and they led the attack indoors on foot.

Trefor's men were still too drunk to do any fighting and the mosaic floor of the hall was soon red with blood and slippery with innards. No quarter was given to these runaway slaves, traitors and enemies of the Folcwalda. Trefor showed his true colours, weeping and cowering behind his toppled throne, his face masked with vomit and his breeches soiled. There would be no time wasted on a trial for him and he was cut down by several men and run through with spears.

"This town's a bloody nuisance," Horsa said to Hengest when it was all over. "Sitting here like a ready-made fortress for anybody who wants to inhabit it. Should we post a garrison here to hold it for us?"

Hengest looked around at the cracked walls and blood-stained floor with distaste. "No. Leave it with its ghosts. I have no use for it. If ever it stands in my way again I'll just burn the damned place to the ground."

"Well, I've got some news on the whole aurochs mystery," said Horsa, as they stepped outside to watch the dawn illuminate the ruined roofs of the town. "Ealdorman Osgar was buying up all the healthy aurochs from any Briton who wished to sell them and then passing them on to Trefor's rebels. Though I can't imagine what he thought to gain from his treachery."

"Vortimer," stated Hengest. "He's been undermining me from the start. He likely paid Osgar to buy up all the cattle just as he paid the gangs in Durobrivae to ship weapons to Trefor. It was his way of weakening us while strengthening our enemies."

"So is the treaty with the Britons over then?"

"No. We, at least, shall honour Vertigernus's treaty, even if his son does not. I have no wish to fight a war this late in the year. It is nearly Geola. We've won this round and showed Vortimer that he cannot outwit us so easily."

Horsa did not dare show his relief. A war with the Britons was the last thing he wanted for it would make it even more dangerous and difficult for him to see Aureliana. "That Osgar has some things to answer for, though," he said.

"Indeed. We ride for his holding as soon as we're ready."

Ealdorman Osgar had fled having heard of Trefor's defeat. They arrived at his homestead to find the walled settlement in a state of confusion. The thegns and villagers hung around looking like they did not know what to do next. Hengest did not hold any of them accountable for their leader's treachery. These lands of the west were far from Thanet and a thegn had to obey his ealdorman even if that ealdorman was a traitor.

In Osgar's bedchamber they found treasure which bore a distinct Celtic motif. This was British loot and not loot taken from raids either. It was quite clearly payment. One thing Horsa did not understand was the attack of Trefor's rebels on Osgar's holding and the rape of his daughter.

"He had to avert any suspicion," Hengest explained. "He no doubt co-conspired a controlled attack with Trefor. Who would suspect a man of colluding with the rebels if his own daughter had been raped by them?"

"That bastard is inhuman!" remarked Horsa.

Nobody disagreed.

Two days later Osgar was found cowering in a shepherd's hut. He was dragged back to his holding and summarily tried and convicted.

All the villagers turned out to see him hanged. They hoisted him up slowly from the gable of his hall and let him dance until the life was choked out of him. His body was left there to feed the ravens.

Another ealdorman was appointed and Hengest wished that Ealdwine was still alive to fill the position. With Vortimer waging secret war on him and corrupting his own subjects, he needed all the trustworthy followers he could get.

The weather was turning for the worse and soon they made arrangements to return to Thanet where the comfort of hall, hearth, mead and song promised to carry them through the winter. They rode off just as the snow was starting to settle on the dry, dead reeds of the frozen marshlands.

PART III

(Mann) "Mann biþ on myrgþe his mágan léof,
sceal þéah ánre gehwilc óðrum swícan,
for þám dryhten wille dóme síne,
þæt earme flæsc eorþan betæcan."

(Man) "The joyous man is dear to his kinsmen; yet
every man is doomed to fail his fellow, since the Lord
by his decree will commit the vile carrion to the
Earth."

Early Spring, 448 A.D.

Aurelianus

At a small port town on the southern coast of Britannia, several miles from the borders of Cantium, Aurelianus waited with Vortimer. The small merchant ship they had come to meet was a pretty affair with a carven swan's head at its prow and a large white square sail. It rode the green swell with pride; a clean vessel of purity approaching a dark and corrupted land. The sailors on board tossed lines to the men on the jetty and the little vessel was drawn in.

The man who stepped down the gangplank was in his late sixties. Wispy grey hair crowned a round face like a laurel wreath. The white of his bishop's robes and a glint of a heavy crucifix showed beneath his dark travelling cloak but Aurelianus was surprised to see that he was also wearing a leather cuirass.

A simple wooden shepherd's staff served as a prop for the old man as he stepped onto the jetty. Vortimer was too young to know this man but Aurelianus remembered him from his first visit, nearly twenty years ago.

"Ave, Bishop Germanus!" he said, kneeling down to kiss the man's ring. "I am Ambrosius Aurelianus, *Comes Brittanarium.*"

"Indeed?" the bishop said, bidding him rise. "I am pleasantly surprised to find that the old military titles are still in use here despite the isolation of Britannia from the empire."

"We do our best to hold to the old order of things in these times of chaos."

"Quite. I remember the *Comes Brittanarium* was a man called Aurelianus during my previous visit. But you are too young to be him."

"My father. I was little more than a boy then but I remember you, your grace. You and my father fought the Picts outside of Eboracum. The people still remember and praise your victory."

"God's victory, my boy. Tell me; is your father still with us? I would dearly like to meet him again."

"No, he ... he fell in battle some years ago."

"Welcome back to Britannia, your grace," said Vortimer, stepping forward. "I am Lord Vortimer of Maxima Caesariensis and head of the Council of Britannia. You may remember my father also, Vitalinus or Vertigernus, as he is sometimes known."

At this the bishop's eyes narrowed and his lips wrinkled as if at the sour taste of lemons. "Yes, I knew your father. Has he too passed away?"

"No, he remains with us, although his power is greatly reduced. My younger brother holds Britannia Prima in his stead."

"And you have taken his place at the head of the council? Is your father ill?"

"I think it is best if we discuss my father back at my palace."

The bishop looked at him with suspicion but agreed. "I must introduce you to my travelling companion, Bishop Severus of Treves," he said, indicating a man with a long brown beard who was directing the sailors in unloading several chests. He wore similar attire to Germanus, but no cuirass as far as Aurelianus could see. "Bishop Severus was a disciple of Bishop Lupus who accompanied me on my first visit."

"Greetings to you also, your grace," said Vortimer. "It is a long ride to Londinium but I have a carriage waiting for us and tonight we may feast and thank the

Lord that you have returned to us in our most desperate hour."

Aurelianus much preferred to ride with his troops rather than be driven in a carriage but he felt the situation warranted a concession in this regard and so he sat next to Vortimer with Germanus and Severus opposite him. As the carriage rumbled towards Londinium, the senior bishop spoke mostly of the situation in Gaul and the problems with the various barbarian tribes.

"General Aetius is currently engaged with the Franks who are laying siege to Arras on the Rhine Frontier. His friendship with the Huns is shaky at best. You have no doubt heard of their excessive transgressions on the territories of the Eastern Empire. Their new king, Attila, is a terror by all accounts and few doubt the sincerity of his ambitions. His peaceable relationship with Aetius will last only as long as it is useful to him, I fear. And every acre the Huns conquer force more and more peoples into Roman territory. As well as Goths living on the Peninsular of Haemus and Vandals in North Africa, Aetius has been forced to settle Burgundians in Sapaudia and Alans in Armorica. There is scarcely a region left in the Western Empire that does not ring with Germanic tongues."

"Including Britannia," Aurelianus said.

"Yes, the Saxons have been a plague on this island since before my time. I encountered their brigands upon my first visit."

"There have been developments," Vortimer said. "They too are a settled people now. That is why I arranged for you to land here and not in Rutupiae which is now within their lands."

"Hmm, I did wonder …"

"My father has, I am afraid, entered negotiations with them and has given them the whole of Cantium in exchange for their service as foederati."

"Fancies himself as a British Aetius does he?" the bishop said. "I am wholly against the settlement of barbarian mercenaries within the lands they are employed to protect. We have seen the cruelties inflicted upon the people of Armorica by the Alans and the injustice suffered there is a matter I intend to take up with the Emperor when I return to Ravenna."

"And so Aetius is unable to come in person?" asked Vortimer.

"Not in person, but I can assure you that his prayers go with me. He may have need of Britannia's support in the days to come and wishes communications to be kept open."

"With all due respect, your grace," said Vortimer, "we are in no position to give help to anyone. The situation in Britannia is far worse than Aetius understands, I fear."

"The Pelagian heresy? I am confident that the true word of God can once again bring the Britons around to the Nicene Creed. I was successful before and, with God's help, I shall be successful again."

Aurelianus looked sidelong at Vortimer. The letter they had all signed had mentioned the turning of many Britons to the heresy as well as the Saxon problem. It had been sent with the intent of convincing the authorities in Gaul that intervention was immediately necessary, but it seemed that the clergy thought that spiritual intervention rather than military was the order of the day. It was hard to conceal his disappointment.

Lord Elafius joined them at dinner that night. He had travelled all the way down from Eboracum to greet

Bishop Germanus. "Your grace, overwhelmed as I am that you came here to aid us in our fight against the evils on our island, I must confess that I have come to you with the intention of asking a personal favour."

"Then ask, Lord Elafius. And, if God wills it, perhaps I can help."

"I have a son. He is only thirteen. He is a good boy, a fine rider and has a kind and goodly heart. But I fear that he will never rule my province when I am gone for he has suffered a grave injury. He fell from his horse nearly two years ago and his leg was twisted. It has never fully healed and, despite the attendance of the finest surgeons in Britannia, it causes him near constant agony."

"My poor man, but what would you have me do?"

Elafius cleared his throat. "There are many tales told, your grace, of your healing of a blind girl on your first visit. They say it was a miracle. You merely held your reliquary to her eyes and prayed and suddenly she could see."

Germanus smiled but not unkindly. "Well, the vinegar lotion and viola odorata I also applied to her eyes may have helped but ..." He could see the desperation in the man's eyes. "Where is your son?"

Elafius's eyes lit up. "I have brought him here to Londinium."

"You brought him all the way from Eboracum just to see me?"

"I am desperate, your grace."

"Very well." He indicated a gold reliquary that hung around his neck. "I carry the very same bone fragment of Saint Lucian of Beauvais as I did on my first visit. After dinner, take me to your son and I shall see what I can do. Through prayer and my own medical training, perhaps your son shall walk again."

"I thank you from the bottom of my heart, your grace," said Elafius, his eyes nearly brimming with tears.

"Speaking of saints," Germanus went on, "I have a mind to visit the shrine of Saint Alban. I wonder; is Lentilus still Bishop of Londinium? Perhaps he wishes to join us."

There was a nervous silence.

"Bishop Lentilus unfortunately passed away last year," said Vortimer.

"I see. How sad. But then, he was even older than I and I do not expect that I have many more years left on this earth. Who has taken his place?"

"Bishop Calvinus."

"Calvinus? The name is not familiar. What was his previous bishopric?"

"He was a deacon, your grace. My father gave him the title as well as Lentilus's seat on the council."

Both Germanus and Severus raised their eyebrows at Vortimer. "He appoints his own bishops now?" said Germanus. "I think it is time that you told me exactly what your father has been doing these years I have been away."

"Bishop Calvinus was little more than a pawn in my father's hand," explained Vortimer. "At least he was in the beginning. I have since lured him under my control. He is a good man, but ultimately a weak one. Bishop Lentilus died after protesting my father's treaty with the Saxons. Many of us at this table found that a little suspicious."

"Surely you don't suspect your father of murdering an ordained bishop? I remember him as a ruthlessly ambitious man, but …"

"At first I refused to believe it too. But there have been other episodes that have resulted in his removal from power. His treaty with the Saxons was not merely political. My father is a lustful, degenerate man and desired the daughter of Hengest, the leader of the Saxons in Cantium. Their marriage sealed the treaty."

"So he married a pagan," said Germanus. "Was she not baptised before the ceremony?"

"She was not and as far as I am aware, she still worships the false idols of her people. But this is not the worst of it. It was recently brought to my attention that my father's previous wife was murdered to keep a secret safe. My sister, who I thought had died of a fever, is in fact alive and a son has been born of a union between her and my father."

The hall was silent as the two bishops digested this information.

"He married his own daughter?" said Germanus slowly.

"Not married. Raped. He kept her locked up at an old iron mine and told everybody she was dead. He planned to steal away her baby and raise it as the offspring of his new union with Hengest's daughter. This was his twisted idea for a pure bloodline."

"This is too monstrous," said Bishop Severus, still in shock.

"There are indications that my father performed the same foul deed with my older sister, Senovara, and that my brother, Cadeyrn, is the result of this blasphemy."

"God was wise in sending me here," said Germanus. "You may be pushed between barbarian hordes and the sea, but with such evil rotting away at the heart of your leadership, no victory or salvation can be won for Britannia. We must bring your father to account for his crimes."

"But will you help us in battle over the Saxons?" Aurelianus asked him. "Will you send for troops from Gaul?"

"I am not a fighting man, despite my connections with General Aetius. And I am old and reaching the winter of my time on God's earth. But I will aid you as much as I am able in ridding the Devil's touch from your lands and call upon God to bring you triumph over your enemies. As soon as I have returned from Saint Alban's shrine, we shall set out for Vitalinus's fortress in the west and put all to rights. Who did you say is in charge of Britannia Prima now?"

"My brother, Cadeyrn," said Vortimer. "He is young and is struggling to keep his territories together. The minor chieftains who held allegiance to my father are loyal to him but I don't know for how long."

"Then we shall bind them to him with the word of God," said Germanus.

While Germanus and Severus visited the shrine of Saint Alban, Aurelianus and Vortimer began making preparations for the coming war with the Saxons. They were outnumbered and faced a foe just as ferocious as the Picts but it mattered little to Aurelianus. All he wanted was to see their hold over Cantium shattered and, if at all possible, to gut that bastard Horsa on the point of his own spatha.

Vortimer was eager too, although he was no military man. He had lived in the shadow of his father for too long and now that shadow was sure to be dissipated by the light the coming of Bishop Germanus heralded. He was keen to exert his own influence on the island and what better way for a young politician to prove himself than by starting a new war? It was often the way and if this war was successful, Vortimer's influence and popularity would be immeasurable.

They set out for the west within days. Germanus wanted to put things to rights without any delay and Aurelianus knew that as soon as they faced Lord Vertigernus, the sooner they could return to the matter of the brewing war.

He felt some discomfort at the notion of facing his old master. It was not fear, rather shame. He had gone back on the oath he had sworn to him all those years ago and his betrayal was like a knot in his chest. But that oath had been sworn under threat of death. Vertigernus had slain his father and would have killed Aurelianus too had he refused to support him and forsake the memory of his father's brief rebellion. And when he thought of Aureliana and that vile heathen's hands all over her, *defiling* her, he felt the rage consume him and banish all trivial feelings of shame. All that mattered to him now was the war and Horsa's death.

Cadeyrn's struggle to keep his family's territory together was evident in the landscape they passed through. They could see smoke rising from a burned settlement and a group of mounted warriors galloping away from it.

Aurelianus called his men to follow and they set off after the warriors. He hailed the strangers and they wheeled about to face him. He prepared himself for conflict but the riders did not seem aggressive.

"You bear the Chi-Rho on your shields," said the leader of the riders, slowing to a canter.

"And you bear the serpent of Din Neidr on yours," replied Aurelianus. "Are you Cadeyrn's men?"

"We follow Cadeyrn; the true ruler of Britannia Prima, God keep him," said the rider. "You're Ambrosius Aurelianus, aren't you?"

Aurelianus nodded.

"It is an honour to meet you, sir."

Aurelianus indicated the column of smoke behind them. "What has happened here?"

"Just another settlement razed to the ground by Benlli."

"The Gaelic chieftain?"

"The same. We got wind of the attack too late and found nothing but corpses and burned homesteads."

"Are the Gael's warriors still in the area?"

"I doubt it. They know they are outnumbered and so resort to this kind of low hit and run tactic. We are returning to camp. Will you join us?"

"If your lord Cadeyrn is at camp, we follow you gladly."

Aurelianus's keen military mind spotted the weaknesses in Cadeyrn's camp as soon as it came into view. The gap between the trenches and the palisades was too great and they were camped too close to the river. The place would be crawling with fever should the campaign last into high summer.

Cadeyrn was supervising a training drill when they found him. Aurelianus had met him once when Cadeyrn had been a small boy. Before him stood a man, scarred and hardened by his first battles.

"I recognised you as soon as you came into sight, General," Cadeyrn said, beaming. "Your presence here is most appreciated. But is this all you have brought? Twenty men? Is your army camped nearby?"

"I am afraid that I have not brought the army with me," Aurelianus said. Seeing the boy's confusion he

118

thought it best to introduce Bishops Germanus and Severus.

"Will Aetius be here soon?" was Cadeyrn's eager response. "How many units will he be bringing?"

"Alas, General Aetius is too occupied on the continent to attend to Britannia directly," Germanus explained.

"He's not coming?"

Aurelianus felt the boy's disappointment. His downhearted face spoke for all of Britannia. "These good bishops have come in his place to unite us in the face of our enemies," he told him.

"Quite so," said Germanus. "Now tell me, what is the situation here?"

"Benlli has rebuffed my offer of allegiance and now he has used the opportunity presented by my father's incarceration to wage war on me. For years he was my father's man and now that I rule Britannia Prima, he is running amok, burning villages and stealing cattle."

"We saw some of his handiwork on the way here," Germanus said.

"Can he be defeated?" Aurelianus asked.

Cadeyrn sighed. "Now that you are here, perhaps. He has defeated me once in open battle and though I have since rallied many chieftains to my banner, his fortifications at Din Bengron and Cair Guricon are too strong for us to break. He will not risk marching his men out into the open. His only tactic is in cattle raids and banditry. He strikes and as soon as I can muster any response he is gone like mist on a summer's morning. It's a stalemate, I fear."

"Then he has complete control of Cair Guricon?" Aurelianus asked.

"Yes. He has imposed a curfew of all things. Anybody caught out of their houses after dark is put to death the following day. The gibbets dangle with unfortunate men, women and children."

Another rider entered the camp accompanied by cheers from Cadeyrn's men.

"My brother!" Cadeyrn said. "He is here at last!"

As he went off to meet him Germanus raised his eyebrows at Aurelianus. "Another brother? How many does he have?"

"This would be Pasgen, his younger brother," Aurelianus replied. "He must only be fourteen or so. I have never met him."

Pasgen was indeed young and full of the exuberance that always beats in a young lad's heart on his first campaign.

"Pasgen here has brought supplies from Din Neidr," Cadeyrn explained. "How is everything back home?"

"It goes well," Pasgen replied. "The Lady Hronwena is doing a fine job keeping Father in check and seeing that all domestic matters are taken care of."

"Any reply from Cunedag and his sons?"

Pasgen beamed and handed his brother a scroll sealed with red wax and imprinted with the image of a dragon: the Pendragon of Venedotia. Cunedag had been given the territory after he and his sons ousted the Gaels. They had since set themselves up as kings, with Cunedag as their overlord, leader of a mighty warband that had long been the envy of Aurelianus.

Cadeyrn broke the seal eagerly and unfurled the document. As he read it his face sank.

"You have sent to Venedotia for aid?" Aurelianus asked him.

"Yes. And they refuse."

"They refuse to fight?" Aurelianus asked in astonishment. "Is Venedotia not under the dominion of Britannia Prima? How can they refuse their lord?"

"You know how they are," Cadeyrn replied sourly. "Pictish blood still flows strong in that dynasty. Their forefathers were never truly Romans. Cunedag has made kings of all his sons and given them territories to rule. Kings, by God! Venedotia is as Albion was in the old days; tribal and primitive. They may have owed allegiance to my father who gave them that land, but they don't see me as worth spit and will never follow me. I had hoped that Benlli's being a Gael would have incited them to join in the fight against their old enemies."

"The closer one looks at this island," said Germanus, "the more fragmented it appears."

"These are dark times in which you come to us, your grace," said Cadeyrn. "What do you suggest I do?"

"I think it is time for the true lord of Din Bengron to emerge," Germanus replied. "I am told he still lurks about in the countryside."

"Cadell? He's a wild one. I've tried reaching out to him but he's not interested in any alliance. He paints me with the same brush he paints my father with and wants to fight his rebellion against Benlli on his own."

"Has his rebellion had any success?" Aurelianus asked him.

Cadeyrn shrugged. "Not much. He steals Benlli's cattle and Benlli steals his. That's all there is to it."

"Still, he may be useful to us as a figurehead to rally others around," said Germanus. "Does anybody know where to reach him?"

"I have scouts who can show you the way," replied Cadeyrn.

"Then we shall set out tomorrow, if you would be so kind as to give us shelter. We have ridden far."

"Of course."

"In the meantime," said Aurelianus, "perhaps you would permit me to give you some advice upon the layout of your fortifications?"

Cadeyrn nodded. "Gladly."

The mist of the following morning shrouded the valley as the guide led them to Cadell's village. It did not have much of a military appearance. It was a small cluster of roundhouses, all pig runs and smoky hearths.

If Aurelianus had not known that the young man who sat opposite him was the exiled son of a chieftain, he could have mistaken him for a common farmer. He had plenty of followers but these too seemed more intent on growing crops and raising livestock than marshalling troops.

Cadell leaned forward over the hearth and cut off another slice of meat. "I have many loyal followers in the hills. Swords hidden under thatch, warriors posing as cattle herds, remembering the good old days before Benlli came. They would flock to my standard should I raise it."

"And why haven't you?" Aurelianus asked him.

The man's face drew into a frown as if insulted. He was not even twenty and had the brash, headstrong pride of many young warriors. "I do not wish to visit such bloodshed on my own people," he said.

Aurelianus nearly rolled his eyes but restrained himself. It was a fair excuse, but an excuse nonetheless. The man was merely afraid.

"Your conscience is admirable," said Bishop Germanus. "We too wish to avoid bloodshed. General Aurelianus is in command of a considerable field army but we have decided to travel with the minimum of soldiers. Benlli may be a Gael but the people he rules are Britons who ought to be ruled by you. If there is a peaceable resolution to this conflict, we shall find it."

"Benlli is a tyrant and all fear him but my men and I," warned Cadell, once again showing his pride. "Even Cair Guricon is Benlli's town now. Cadeyrn can do nothing to reclaim it. The Gael's forces are too strong."

"They are locked in a stalemate as we speak," said Aurelianus. "I met with Cadeyrn yesterday. He expressed his desire to retake the town but told me he wishes for Din Bengron to once again be ruled by your family."

"Ha! The House of Vitalis are no friends of mine! Vitalinus did nothing when Benlli murdered my father and cast me out of Din Bengron. He even tolerated Benlli's rule for many years. I expect nothing from his sons."

"Cadeyrn is young, like you, and inexperienced. But I have faith in his good heart and his will to rule his father's lands with a just hand."

"What does he know of hard fighting? You compare him to me who has grown to manhood in these wild hills with my men, scratching a living from the hard earth, attacking Benlli's caravans on empty bellies and bare feet."

"If we help you retake your father's fortress, will you be a loyal servant to Cadeyrn?" Aurelianus asked him.

Cadell did not answer. "How are we to defeat Benlli with no army?"

"With God's aid," said Germanus.

"I am a good Christian, Bishop," said Cadell, "but I doubt mere prayer can turn the swords of the Gaels to lead."

"I shall win them over with preaching. And I shall begin with Benlli's court."

"You will have a hard time finding an audience there. Benlli is a pagan and the Britons he rules are a mixture of Pelagians and Arianists. Rome is as distant to them as the stars. They care not for your words." And with that he retired to his chamber.

Aurelianus and the two bishops bedded down by the embers of the fire. "Sleep well, Aurelianus," said Germanus. "We shall need our wits about us tomorrow."

"Is your plan really to march into Benlli's fortress and try and win him around with words?" Aurelianus asked him.

"The Gaels are superstitious but easily converted, or so I am led to believe," said the old bishop, as he squirmed about to get comfortable on the old sheepskin. "Years ago, I was acquainted with a British bishop by the name of Padraig. He had been captured by Hibernian raiders in his youth and spent six years as a slave on one of their farms. He escaped and returned to Britannia, then went to Gaul where he became my pupil. After he was ordained, the Pope sent him back to Hibernia to preach the word of God. The staff of Christ has been planted deep into its green hills by

124

Padraig and it will never be removed. Monasteries have popped up all over the island and year by year, more chieftains convert to the true faith. Words achieved this, not armies."

Aurelianus stared at the rafters; deep in thought. Something else was bothering him and he had been reluctant to bring it up with the bishop. "I beg your grace's pardon and what I am about to ask is not intended to cause offence."

"Speak, Ambrosius. You are a man of honest words and I never hold that against anyone. Your father was the same so tell me what is on your mind."

"In Eboracum and Londinium they praise your name for your healing of Elafius's son …"

"Now, let's not get carried away. The boy still needs a crutch to walk and may never do without one. I merely applied my knowledge of field surgery to begin the healing process anew."

"The people say that it was due to your prayers and the power you hold in your reliquary, just as you healed the blind girl on your first visit."

"Are you so certain that it wasn't?"

"But I saw you attend to the boy. You fixed his leg with medicine."

"By using plants created by Our Lord God and my own two hands which he fashioned. So however you look at it, God healed the boy."

"But it seems a little …"

"Dishonest?"

Aurelianus was relieved that the bishop used the word and not he.

"We are dealing with simple people here. They do not understand the higher powers that govern us and everything they know about God they learn from priests and bishops. They need simple answers. God loves us all but he loves us best when we help ourselves. So where is the harm in letting the people believe what they want to believe without troubling them or confusing them with details? The end result is the same."

Aurelianus pretended that he understood and they lay in silence for a while before the old man began to snore. He didn't know if he agreed with the bishop's words, but one thing he was sure of, Bishop Germanus was a very different man to the one he had grown up hearing of.

The following morning the grim gates of Din Bengron were heaved open to admit the visitors. They were led past dismal huts where families squatted in doorways watching dogs gnaw at bones. Stone steps cut from the rock wound up to Benlli's great hall that frowned from the crest of the hill. They were disarmed before entering.

It was a large roundhouse with pillars to support a thatched roof above a circular hearth in the centre of the room. Built centuries ago, its hanging banners and tapestries had since been swapped for Gaelic adornments and the tongues of the men who guarded it were Hibernian. It was dim and smoky and the man who sat in his throne on the other side of the hearth was barely visible. His enjoyment at intimidating visitors to his court by speaking to them from the shadows was evident in his voice.

"What do Christian bishops and soldiers who wear the armour of Rome want in my lands?" said Benlli.

"These lands are British, though you were not born to them," replied Germanus.

"And yet my word is law, not the word of Britons."

Germanus led the way around the hearth to stand before the throne. Its occupant was an elderly man though not a feeble one. His black hair was streaked with grey and his skin had a loose, leathery look, marred by thin scars hinting at a violent youth.

"We have come to Albion from Gaul to preach the true word of God to the wayward," said Germanus. "The Pope is concerned by the increase of interest in such heresies as those of Pelagius."

Benlli laughed, turning his head back and showing black gums and rotten teeth. "A long way to travel to meddle in the beliefs of others. Men call me a tyrant and yet I do not condemn others for their beliefs. But enough of such games. I know you, Bishop Germanus. Your coming to this island is news that reached my ears many days ago. And I know that your real intent is not to convert us simple pagans and heretics."

"Oh?" Germanus enquired. "Does my lord know the mind of a wandering bishop more than he himself does?"

"You and your armoured thugs are no true men of God. Your aims are political! Do you not think I know the mighty Ambrosius Aurelianus at your side? Do you think I do not know the friends of my enemies? Cadeyrn cannot defeat me in open battle so he wages war by sending his brother's allies and meddling bishops whose mouths are filled with lies."

Germanus seemed unperturbed. "It would be a strange kind of warfare that relies on unarmed bishops walking into the lairs of their enemies."

Benlli was silent at this; as if unsure.

"No, my lord, my crooked staff is my only weapon and my words are naught but the truth. As a high-ranking visitor to these shores I am afforded the luxury of General Aurelianus here as my personal bodyguard. I am sure you can appreciate that the Holy Father would hate to hear that some ill-fortune has befallen one of his bishops. Aurelianus's political views are his business and do not concern me."

Benlli's beady black eyes flitted from Germanus to Aurelianus to Severus and back to Germanus. "What do you want of me? I will not punish my people for having beliefs that are not yours."

"I do not ask for that," Germanus explained. "Punishment is for God to exact. I am merely here to instruct and to warn."

"Warn? You make it sound like a threat. What can two bishops and their *bodyguard* threaten me with?"

"I do not threaten you. But God watches from His seat in Heaven. He watches and He judges and those who do not follow His word face annihilation."

Benlli rose from his throne, his face red with anger. "You *do* threaten! You threaten me and my people with death should we not listen to your lies!"

Aurelianus looked about at the guards in the chamber who were tensing at the raised voice of their master. He felt utterly naked without his sword and began to doubt the bishop's wisdom in this venture.

"I am merely a messenger, my lord," stated Germanus calmly. "And I am come to warn you and your people that God has turned his eye of judgment upon you. I dreamt a dream last night; a vision sent to me from the Almighty above. A prophecy; this I swear."

Benlli sat down and eyed him suspiciously. The Gaels held visions in very high esteem.

"I dreamt of fire sent down from Heaven to punish the unbelievers. I dreamt of flames consuming this very fortress and of its blackened ruins smouldering in the morning sky."

"You lie …" said Benlli quietly.

"I do not. This dream frightened me and I knew then that it was my duty to warn you."

"I could have you hung for crow-food should I wish," said the Gael, his voice edged with ice.

"Kill an ordained bishop who came to your court in peace? A bishop who has powerful friends both in Albion and across the sea? You are a wise king, Benlli. I do not believe you would be so stupid."

"Get out."

The order was spoken by one who knew he was beaten. When Aurelianus saw the expressions on the faces of the guards as they left the great hall, he knew that Germanus had won a victory. They looked frightened. He was willing to bet that at least a couple of them were Christians and the words of the bishop had put terror in their hearts. Word would spread. Germanus had planted a seed of fear in the court of Benlli. And that seed would grow.

"What now?" he asked the bishop, as they retrieved their weapons and were escorted out of the fortress.

"We wait for the God-fearing to come to us. We must welcome them for every soul that leaves Benlli's side is a victory over him. But my work is not finished. I go to Cair Guricon to warn the people there of God's vengeance. Before Benlli's curfew falls tomorrow, we shall have won many dozens of further victories."

Germanus and Severus preached all the next day in the market places of Cair Guricon; warning of the fire from heaven that would consume Din Bengron that very night. Once the identity of the two bishops had become known throughout the town, many of its Christian denizens were won around to their preaching and joined them in condemning Pelagianism, Arianism and all other forms of heresy. When Germanus began to tell of his dream of fire from the skies consuming Din Bengron, they gaped at him wide eyed.

But as darkness began to fall, Benlli's soldiers descended upon the town with the intention of taking Germanus and Severus into custody. A mob of Christians, who were now convinced of their master's imminent destruction, accompanied the two bishops to the town gates and faced off the guards, hurling insults and stones. A riot nearly broke out and Germanus and Severus barely escaped with their lives.

When they returned to Cadell's village they found that it had nearly doubled in size. God-fearing men and women had been leaking out of Din Bengron all afternoon. Terrified of the prophecy they had headed into the hills. There, they had been picked up by Aurelianus's patrols and taken to the camp of their lost chief, and filled with hot mutton stew and promises of a return to the old days before the Gaels had come.

Even Aurelianus had been surprised by Cadell's emergence as a strong leader. His hospitality was admirable and he strutted about spouting words designed to boost morale and unite his people, filling their heads with dreams of retaking Din Bengron and starting anew. He wouldn't be out of place on any battlefield and Aurelianus was forced to admit that the young chief may have a chance at reclaiming his birthright after all.

They wore hooded cloaks of blue that night. There were eight of them: Cadell and three of his followers and Aurelianus with three of his soldiers. They stole across the hills like phantoms towards Din Bengron; unseen by the torch-lit guards on the spiked palisades.

It had been Germanus's plan and Aurelianus had mixed feelings about it. It seemed a sham. Germanus had preached all day long about fire consuming the fortress and now it fell to him to ensure that it did. But as a military man, the idea was not unsound. Din Bengron was made almost entirely of wood. It would burn a merry blaze for days.

Cadell did not show any reluctance to destroy his ancestral home. On the contrary, it fitted in nicely with his speeches of rebirth and renewal. Besides, the promise of roasting Benlli and his Gaels alive was too good for him to pass up.

The spark to ignite the woodpile was in the form of a wagon loaded with oil-soaked branches. The wheels were newly greased so as to ensure speed and ease of transport. Several shields had been tied to the top of the cart to protect those who pushed it.

They were within a hundred feet of the fortress before somebody spotted them. Torches waved about frantically on the palisade and more were lit as guards were called to their posts.

"Light all the torches you want, you bastards," Aurelianus heard Cadell say. "You'll have more than enough light in a moment."

An arrow thudded into the shield above Auralianus's head. "Increase speed!" he yelled. "Push!"

They pushed. The little cart went trundling across the bumpy grass. The stone foundations of the wall fast approached. It was dry stone laced with timbers that poked out at regular intervals. If they could only get those timbers to catch fire, that whole side of the fortress would go up in a blaze.

More arrows sang down on them. They kept pushing until the stone face of the wall halted them with a juddering crash.

"Back!" Aurelianus shouted. "Back, all of you!" He fumbled with his tinder box, cursing as arrows hailed down all around them. He managed to get an ember glowing and tossed it into the recesses of the cart.

The oil and wood caught immediately and went up in a great 'whoosh!' Aurelianus nearly didn't have time to get out of the way before the air was sucked away and the heat of the blaze engulfed him.

With the blazing cart bathing them in light, they were suddenly easy targets for Benlli's men on the palisade. One of Aurelianus's men stumbled as an arrow punched between his shoulder blades. He screamed and went down. Aurelianus slithered onto his knees to help the man up, aware that by halting, he was a sitting duck. "Somebody help me carry him!" he bellowed.

Somebody doubled back and dived down to grab the wounded man's other side and Aurelianus was surprised to see that it was Cadell. Together they dragged the man out of danger and made for the safety of the trees.

Out of arrowshot and screened by the woods they watched the fire spread. The timber beams that laced the dry stone wall had caught as planned and the wooden palisade that had been built on top of it had caught in a number of places. Screams could be heard from within as men and women rushed about trying to douse the flames. It was too little too late. The extent of the fire meant that the whole fortress would be destroyed before dawn.

"Well, we've done God's work tonight," said Aurelianus to nobody in particular. "According to Bishop Germanus, that is."

Hronwena

The coming of Bishop Germanus to Din Neidr was accompanied by much fanfare. As lady of the household, Hronwena had been told by Cadeyrn to see to the complete overhaul of the fortress. Stone floors were to be swept and scrubbed, hallways were to be decorated with spring flowers and the stores were to be fully stocked with fish, meat, vegetables and fruits for the inevitable feast that would welcome the bishop.

All this confused Hronwena. In her land holy men were certainly treated with respect, but they were, after all, only men. They were not treated like demi-gods as they were here in Britta. Vitalinus also surprised her just before the bishop's arrival. She knew that her husband had been virulently opposed to any interfering from the Roman clergy or military for years. She knew also that Germanus had been here before, years ago, and there was no love lost between the two old men. But, far from showing terror at the arrival of his old adversary, Vitalinus came down to the Great Hall the morning of his arrival.

"My sons may have stolen my territories from me," he exclaimed, "but I am still lord of Din Neidr, whether they like it or not. If Bishop Germanus wants to come into my hall, then he must stand before my seat as a visitor." And with that he sat down at the head table and there he stayed, calling for wine and slowly drinking himself into a stupor.

The rest of the nobles filed into the hall, Pasgen among them, quiet and timid. Cadeyrn arrived just after noon with the two bishops and Ambrosius Aurelianus, mud-spattered and weary from their days in the hills. Vitalinus forbade the household from turning out into the courtyard to greet the guests. He was determined to make them come to him.

The visitors strode into the Great Hall with an arrogance that equalled only their host's. Hronwena reluctantly took her place at her husband's side and watched. She recognised Aurelianus from her wedding a year ago.

"So, you cannot rule my island without sending to Gaul for help?" Vitalinus said to Cadeyrn, in a withering tone for all to hear. "Bishop Germanus, it has been too long."

"Far too long," agreed Germanus. "Had I known of your vile deeds I would have come much sooner."

"Vile deeds? I fear my sons have led you astray with their vindictive lies. Have I not done my duty to God and the church by ridding Britannia of the Pelagian heresy?"

Germanus sniffed as a servant handed him a cup of wine. "Londinium may be clean of that heretical branch, but here in the hills of the west, the teachings of Pelagius are all too existent. The court of Benlli was infested with heresy, as was Cair Guricon, the second largest town in your own territories."

"Well, God be praised for sending you to rid my lands of that Gael and his godless followers," said Vitalinus. "We can see the smoke of his burning fortress from here. Your handiwork, Aurelianus?"

The bishop's face was stony. "That was an act of God as punishment for his crimes. I myself tried to warn him but he would not listen. I can only be thankful that enough of his followers turned to the Nicene Creed in time."

"And what now for the mighty Germanus?" asked Vitalinus. "Are you here to deliver another of your prophecies? Is Din Neidr the next fortress to fall to, ahem, *God's wrath*?"

"Heaven forbid. I am here to bring you to task for your crimes against your family and your crimes against God."

Vitalinus was silent and took a sip from his goblet.

"I have heard many rumours that are shocking to my ears," Germanus went on. "Some say that you had Bishop Lentilus killed so that you could marry a pagan." His eyes flicked to Hronwena. She returned his gaze without flinching. "Some accuse you of murdering your wife. But I cannot address mere rumours. I am here to see if one particularly abominable crime laid at your door has any truth to it. The crime of incest."

"More vile rumours," said Vitalinus.

"You cannot deny this one!" Cadeyrn exploded. "We all saw Enys months after you said she had died of a fever! I myself have visited the child, the child she says you sired upon her and came to visit more than once!"

The hall rumbled with murmuring.

"Where is this child now?" said Germanus in a raised voice.

"There is no child!" shouted Vitalinus. "And my daughter *is* dead! These fools blather about nothing!"

"Only I and two others know where the child is kept," said Cadeyrn.

"Then send for it and its mother," the bishop replied. "That is the only way we can know one way or the other."

"Your grace!" cried Vitalinus, heaving himself to his feet. "All in this hall are against me. What proof is there in some common whore and her spawn these people say are my kin? You yourself would not know my daughter and all here who knew her in life are my enemies! You cannot believe their lies!"

"Send for the child and its mother!" the bishop reiterated.

"Lady Hronwena," said Cadeyrn, "Will you be so good as to ride out with your servant and fetch my sister and her babe?"

Hronwena rose. She would be happy to do the old bishop's bidding, though she had formed a quick dislike for the man. For over a year now she had been trying to bring her husband's reputation crashing down and sunder her marriage from him. It had been a fraught journey and many things had happened that she had not expected, but now, at last, with the clergy coming to bring him to task, that journey was nearing its end and perhaps freedom was in sight for her.

It didn't take long for her and Deilwen to ride to the little cottage in the forest. Enys and her babe, Britu, looked well. He was three years old and very inquisitive. It was hard to believe that so small a child could be the cause of so much interest and outrage.

On the return journey Deilwen rode with Enys and Hronwena carried Britu in front of her. She had to hold him tight to stop him from toppling off the horse every time he leaned out to peer at something. Hronwena's heart was warmed by him.

The feasting was well under way by the time they returned to Din Neidr. Enys trembled to be in the same room as her father once more and looked everywhere but at him. Little Britu was wide-eyed at the host gathered before them. Germanus rose from his seat.

"These are the two who are said to be kin to Vitalinus?"

"A lie," said Vitalinus, his voice slurred with drink. "I've never seen them before. Take this whore and her whelp back where you found them."

Ignoring him, Germanus walked around the table and bent low to look at Britu. His old face creased into a friendly smile. "Now then, my child," he said. "I expect you're wondering why you and your mother have been brought here."

Britu did nothing but stare at his creased face.

"Is your father in this room?"

Perhaps the boy's eyes flitted to Vitalinus. If they did, Hronwena did not see it.

"I have a gift for you to give to him," Germanus said, as he reached inside his robes and brought out a bone comb. He gave it to Britu. The boy took it with interest and stroked its spiny teeth. "Go on then, my lad. Give the comb to your father."

It was a demanding task for any child of three to wander across a hall crowded with silent, staring adults, but Britu performed it admirably. He tottered off, sucking on the comb as he went, straight to the head table, seemingly oblivious to the dire tension in the air.

Hronwena's heart broke to see him. *How dare we ask this of him? How dare we put such an innocent in this position? How dare we all?*

Vitalinus's eyes were livid as the boy walked up to him and plopped the comb, wet with saliva, into his lap.

The deed was done. And, like a messenger who had just delivered a death warrant, the little boy turned around and strolled back to his mother's side.

It was not until Vitalinus's chair, flung backwards by its rising occupant, struck the stone flags that the hall erupted into condemnation. Germanus flung out an accusatory finger and yelled something, but Hronwena did not catch it. She saw tears on Pasgen's face as he went forward to embrace his sister and meet his nephew for the first time. She saw the twisted expressions of disgust and outrage on the faces of the nobles. And she saw the billowing cloak of her husband as he stormed from the room, defeated, humiliated. *Finished.*

That evening, Germanus met with Cadeyrn in his chamber to discuss what was to happen next. Hronwena sat with Enys and Deilwen in the great hall and watched Britu eat bread and warm milk. When Cadeyrn emerged from his meeting with the bishop, his face was grave.

"The boy is to go to Gaul with him," he said.

"With who?" Hronwena asked.

"Bishop Germanus."

"Gaul?" asked Enys, wide eyed.

"He is to be raised as a member of the clergy. He will be safe and well provided for. Germanus thought it best that he be removed from all this and for him not to have such a British-sounding name. From now on he will be known as Faustus."

"But he belongs here, with his family!" said Hronwena.

"In the eyes of the church he is an abomination," Cadeyrn explained. "It is best that he is closely guarded and raised in the very best houses far from the sin that caused him to be."

Enys was choked with grief. "Please, Brother! I beg you! Don't take my baby from me!"

"It is not my decision to make, Enys. I am sorry."

"How can it *not* be your decision?" demanded Hronwena, rising angrily. "You are lord of this fortress and ruler of Britannia Prima! Your brother is the highest man in all Albion! How can this foreign bishop come here and make demands?"

"You do not understand! We may be sundered from the empire, but the clergy still have authority over all that occurs on this island, authority bestowed upon them by God."

"Not my god," mumbled Hronwena as she sat down. She gazed at Britu who was sopping up the last of his milk with his bread, watching them with wide eyes. *How can they call such an innocent, precious thing an abomination?* she thought. *What right do they have?*

"Germanus and I leave for Londinium in the morning," said Cadeyrn. "Faustus will go by a different route to Isca, accompanied by some of Aurelianus's soldiers, where a boat will take him to Gaul."

He left them alone and Hronwena spat in his wake. "That craven bastard!"

Enys began to weep uncontrollably and Britu, concerned by his mother's distress, clambered into her lap. This only made her weep more and clutch at him as if he were about to vanish from her arms that very instant.

"Listen to me, Enys," Hronwena told her. "They shall not take Britu. We'll find a way. I haven't fought this hard and put so many lives in danger for you to lose your boy now. Berwen didn't die so that Britu would grow up not knowing his mother. We'll find a way. I promise."

Aurelianus

They found Londinium in a state of preparation. The army was still going through the drills Aurelianus had instructed his officers to carry out in his absence and already he could see that they had improved. The fort was full to bursting with new men levied from countryside militias and plucked from the household guard of various nobles Vortimer had pressured into contributing. Aurelianus had hoped to billet Cadell's warriors with them but instead sought out accommodation at the palace.

Vortimer met them in the reception hall. He was wearing a Roman muscle cuirass emblazoned with the serpent of Din Neidr on the left and the fish of Londinium on the right with the Roman eagle hovering above. His father would have disapproved of such an arrangement of heraldry but perhaps such symbolism was called for during these times. In the adjacent room officers were looking over maps of south-east Britta.

"Ave, Brother," said Cadeyrn, embracing him. "Ready to march off to war already? We were looking forward to resting our bones in your palace a day or two. You know how draughty Din Neidr is."

"Time is of the essence," Vortimer replied. "While you lot have been having fun in the western hills I have been chomping at the bit here. And the sight of those hill warriors in your company excites me no end."

"Cadell is here to join the fight," said Cadeyrn, indicating the reinstated chieftain of Din Bengron who looked around the chamber in awe.

"Then I take it that the Gael is dead?" Vortimer asked.

"It is like he never existed," said Cadell, coming forward. "And the same can be said of Din Bengron, I am afraid."

"Oh dear. That is distressing."

"Nothing that can't be rebuilt," the chieftain replied.

"Was the war really so destructive?"

"It was an act of God," said Cadell, dutifully, casting a look at Bishop Germanus.

"And your grace," said Vortimer. "You survived the wilds of my homeland once again, I see."

"There is nothing this island can throw at me that the power of our Lord cannot help me repel," replied the bishop.

"And our island is the better for it, I am sure."

"Am I to take it that you intend to march east immediately?" Aurelianus asked Vortimer.

"What better moment than the present? Hengest will no doubt receive word of our coming well in advance and I wish to give him as little time as possible to organise a response. Are you ready for our first war against the Saxons, Brother?"

"As ready as we'll ever be," answered Cadeyrn.

"And your grace?" Vortimer asked Germanus. "Will you inspire our troops as you inspired the soldiers of the previous generation to victory over God's enemies?"

"I will do what I must, as always," replied the bishop. "I am a good deal older than I was when we repelled the Picts, but I still feel the breath of Our Lord in my bones and while I do there is nothing that can dull my words."

"Then let us march!" exclaimed Vortimer with all the gusto of a seasoned general. "Let us drive our enemies into the sea from whence they came!"

Hronwena

The mountains sank down to rolling hills and wooded dales as they journeyed south. A mist descended, turning all to grey ghosts. Hronwena squinted at the trees ahead. The mist made it difficult to see the small group of horsemen as they entered the forest. Spots of rain touched her face. At least the trees would provide some shelter.

For three days they had followed the trail of the soldiers who were escorting Britu to the coast. The three-year-old boy Deilwen carried on her saddle had given up wailing after the second day. They had tried to explain to him that he was heading off on a fantastic adventure across the sea where a new life full of wonder and mystery was waiting for him in Gaul. Hronwena felt terribly guilty telling him this and wondered if the soldiers they followed were telling similar tales to keep Britu quiet.

"I still think we should have made the swap before they left Din Neidr," said Deilwen.

"He was too closely guarded," said Hronwena. "It has to happen on the road."

They had picked up the child at Deilwen's home. His name was Guern and he had been a poor orphaned babe the kind old couple had taken in just as they had taken Deilwen in years before. Whatever future the clergy in Gaul offered the lad, he would surely find it preferable to a life of poverty in the British hills. If only they could get him into the possession of the guards and get Britu home to his mother.

Hronwena did know how she was to convince the guards to go along with the plan. She had plenty of gold in her pouch to tempt them into handing over Britu and delivering the little imposter to Gaul in his stead. None knew his face there and it would be many months before Germanus would see him again. He would never notice that the boy delivered into his care was not the boy he had seen at Din Neidr.

They entered the forest and followed the stream in the wake of the soldiers. Damp twigs snapped dully under their horses' hooves.

"I don't know how we'll get a fire going tonight with everything wet through," said Deilwen.

"No fire," Hronwena replied.

"But surely now that we are in the forest they won't see our smoke," said Deilwen. "I'm nearly wet through and we haven't eaten a hot meal since we left. This poor mite is catching his death. Hark how silent he is now!"

Hronwena reached over and felt Guern's forehead. It didn't feel feverish but the lad was cold and miserable. "It won't be long now until we can return with Britu. I intend to make the switch before we leave this forest."

"I still don't understand how you're planning to manage it, my lady."

"I'm not too sure of that myself, Deilwen." She absently weighed her pouch in her hand and hoped she had brought enough.

It wasn't long before the light of a fire could be seen through the trees as the soldiers made camp for the night.

"That's our signal to stop," Hronwena said, dismounting and digging out a blanket from her saddlebags. She threw it down on the ground. "We huddle together for a bit but we mustn't sleep."

"Aren't we going to go and talk to the soldiers?" Deilwen asked.

"Not just yet. I need more time to think. We wait until they are settled in and then I'm going over to have a look at their camp. Maybe talk to them a bit, see if I can't work out how loyal they are before I offer them a bribe."

Snuggled up on the blanket with the boy between them, Hronwena and Deilwen stared fixedly on the flickering light through the trees, imagining roasted mutton, stewed hare, mead and warmth. They could hear the men laughing and talking until they grew quiet and then lapsed into silence.

It was hard to stay awake. Somewhere an owl hooted but the night was young. The sky was a deep blue through the treetops, not yet the black of night. Hronwena heard the soft breathing of the boy and felt her own eyelids drooping.

There was a shout from up ahead. Her eyes snapped open. The sound of clashing iron drifted through the trees followed by more shouts.

"What's going on?" hissed Deilwen. "Are those silly bastards fighting?"

"I don't know," replied Hronwena.

They waited and the shouts died away leaving only eerie silence. The light of the fire was still visible.

"I'm going to have a look," said Hronwena.

"Let me go, my lady!"

Hronwena wrapped the end of the blanket tight around Deilwen and Guern whose eyes were wide with fright and hurried off towards the fire.

"The bastards must dwell in these forests," one of the soldiers was saying. "Outlaws most likely. The trees must be infested with them."

"How many of them do you think there were?" asked one of the others.

"Dunno. I saw at least five."

"I reckon that too."

Hronwena crept closer. She saw the two speakers silhouetted against the flames. A third figure lay on his back and by the orange light she could make out blood on his face. There was no sign of Britu.

"Well, they did for Marcus, the whore-sons. Got him while he was sleeping."

"Could have got us too. And they took the blasted boy! I told you we should have left a watch."

"Well I didn't think … hey! Who's that?" He had spotted Hronwena and pointed his sword at her. "Come here! Show yourself!"

She rose from the bush she had been hiding behind and walked towards them.

"What's a woman doing skulking around a forest at this time of night?" demanded the other soldier. "Did those scum leave a whore behind?"

"No. I am a travelling healer. I am camped not far from here and heard trouble. Are either of you wounded? Your friend perhaps?"

"He's beyond the help of any healer. You're travelling alone?"

Hronwena nodded.

"Brave for a woman. Your accent is hard to place. Where are you from?"

"Here and there. What happened?"

"We were set upon by bandits. They killed our companion."

She tutted. "Three soldiers in such fine armour set upon by godless rogues? Did they take anything?"

"A boy we were escorting—*ow!*" the soldier yelped, as his companion kicked him.

"A boy?"

"Um, well, you see, it's sort of official secret business," said the soldier who had dealt the kick. "We are escorting a nobleman's son to his villa in the south."

"Why steal a boy?"

"Ransom. It's not uncommon. A boy being escorted by soldiers clearly comes from a wealthy family."

"But where would they have taken him?"

"These bandits make many hideouts in the hills and forests. But they would need to find out who the boy is and who his family are in order to demand a ransom. Corinium Dobunnorum is the nearest town. They probably plan on asking around there."

"Then you'd best get a move on!" Hronwena said.

"Not before daybreak. We'd lose our way in this darkness. We'll have to wait until first light, and then set off double quick."

"When I get within a sword's length of the bastards …" began the second soldier.

"Save it," his companion snapped. "No point wasting energy now. Let's get a bit a rest before we give chase. We've got to get that boy back before …" he glanced at Hronwena and fell silent.

"Do you mind if I share your fire for the night, boys?" Hronwena asked them. It was true what they said: there was no point in tearing off after shadows in the night.

The two soldiers looked at each other and grunted their agreement. They were too riled by their recent ordeal and too angry to much care who shared their fire.

Hronwena sat down and watched them bury their comrade in a shallow grave dug with their helmets. They hammered a wooden cross fashioned from rotten branches into the mound. She couldn't see why they bothered. The grave was too shallow and the cross too flimsy for there to be anything marking the spot within a week.

When the two soldiers drifted off to sleep once more, Hronwena slipped back to where she had left Deilwen and Guern, cursing the blundering stupidity of Aurelianus's men.

Hengest

The first news of the war that was to consume Britta came upon a blood-streaked dawn. A ceorl, who had been hunting in the forest of Anderida, had seen the approaching columns of British soldiers and had nearly killed his horse in his mad gallop to his master's hall.

His master, a loyal thegn of Hengest, rode to the coast and crossed to Thanet before the British army had made it out of the forest. Within the day, Hengest had his warriors gathered from every coastal town and marshalled them by the ruins of Durovernum.

"Where the hell is Horsa?" he demanded. His brother had been patrolling the waters with his fleet for the past few days.

"I sent word to his ships," replied Octa. "They were just off Dubris this morning but I'm sure my man got to them."

"Then why aren't they here?"

"It takes time for the ships to be brought in and Horsa to ready his men."

"Time we don't have."

Ebusa galloped over to them. "Vortimer has crossed the river," he said. "The residents of Durobrivae are fleeing the town."

Hengest cursed. "And what of our fyrd in the south west?"

"No news from them. It is my mind that they stood their ground and were overwhelmed."

Hengest couldn't believe he had lost a fyrd already. "I should have been there to join them in the fight," he said bitterly. "What good is a Folcwalda who cannot protect his people?"

"We must strengthen ourselves with Horsa's raiders before we engage," said Ebusa.

"No," Hengest replied. "I want to knock them back before they know we are here, and I've waited for my brother long enough. Ride out!"

"My lord!" Ebusa protested.

Hengest wheeled on him savagely. "Do you think I will have it said of me that I cowered in the east while my fyrds died for me? Aurelianus and Vortimer have advanced far enough. We ride!"

The cavalry and infantry units set forth with a blowing of horns and a flutter of banners. They cut across country with Hengest and Ordlaf at their head, through vale and thicket to meet the Britons who marched ever eastwards.

The battle was a disaster. The Britons, having drawn support from every village, tribal chieftain and town in the vast expanse of the west outnumbered Hengest's men. Hengest, his heart wrenched from his breast at the thought of losing all he had fought so hard for, forced himself to call a retreat and his warband limped back to the coast.

Licking their wounds in the coastal towns and worrying what the dawn might bring, Hengest sailed back to Thanet to comfort Halfritha.

He found Horsa drinking sullenly in the Great Hall.

"Gods, Horsa, we sorely missed your blades today. Where were you?"

"I didn't get the message until the warband had already marched. By the time I made landfall, I did not know in which direction you had gone. What happened?"

"We were damn near slaughtered. Aurelianus is coming for us with a keen blade. That gods-cursed whore-son has no sense of honour turning on us after we fought tooth and nail to win his war in the north for him. What was it all for?"

"He has always hated us," replied Horsa. "He only needed an excuse to turn on us."

"Well, he's got his damned excuse, worms take him, now that Vertigernus is all but a prisoner of his own sons. They were there today too; cowering behind Aurelianus. I could see their banners through the mist of battle; too far away for me to drive *Hildeleoma* up their stinking arses, more's the pity."

"What now?" Horsa asked. "Parley, surely."

"Parley? With those mucus-filled pups? Not only do I spit on the idea, but they wouldn't hear of it either. They won't stop until we are all driven into the sea. No, hard fighting is the only way out of this one. On the morrow we attack at first light. Come at them while they're still sleeping off their victory celebrations." He did not wait for Horsa's response but retired to his private chambers where Halfritha awaited him.

Halfritha knew of their defeat already. She did not run forward to hold him or to help him out of his armour. She merely sat in bed, watching him as a theow unbuckled his greaves and cuirass. "Were there many losses?" she asked.

"Yes," he replied. "But I called the retreat before it got too bad." He stretched his arms out so that the theow could remove his mail shirt. It was a heavy thing and the boy staggered out of the chamber with it. "We attack at first light. I can't give Vortimer the chance to pen us in on Thanet. That would be a death trap."

"I remember you once said that this island would be the safest place for us. Now it looks like the grass will grow on our barrows before the year is out."

"Don't say that!" he snapped. "We have boats enough. If it comes to that we can sail away."

"Back to Jute-land?"

"It won't come to that. I fought so damned hard for my kingdom, I'm going to fight doubly hard to keep it."

"And your children? What of them?"

"If it comes to it, I'll send you and Aesc away. He won't share his father's fate."

"Then you are willing to die here? Fighting for your kingdom?"

"That's what a leader does."

"And Hronwena? Will you leave your daughter in the hands of your enemies?"

"As far as I can tell, she has no part in this. She's still Vertigernus's wife in the west. This war of his sons is a mere rebellion."

"Vertigernus has lost all his power, so it is said," replied Halfritha. "And our daughter is no doubt Vortimer's hostage. Why not sue for peace with the Welsc and demand her as a condition? Her marriage to Vertigernus is useless now."

"Not necessarily. If I can only defeat his bastard sons I might have a chance of repairing the treaty with the Britons. I wouldn't worry as to her safety. They'll not harm her while they know they can use her against me. I expect they'll make their own demands soon."

"While you plan on attacking them?" Her face was incredulous.

"I cannot show weakness. That would be our downfall. I must not betray my people."

"A father should fight for his family," was her response, and she rolled over so that he could not see her face.

"That's what I am doing," he said, but he knew that it was useless. He called for the theow to bring him a horn of mead. He wanted to sleep deep while there was still darkness left.

Horsa

Horsa finished off his own horn and left the hall. Beorn was sitting opposite him, polishing his axe-head as he always did upon the eve of battle. All warriors had their own peculiar ways of staving off the sweating feeling of doom.

"Beorn?"

"Captain?"

"Return to the *Bloodkeel*. Have all our men onboard their vessels and out of the harbour. Make for Dubris and set up camp on the shore. Nobody is to know of this."

"But the battle …"

"I want no man of mine playing a part in it until I say so."

Beorn lowered his voice and looked about. "We're not going to join your brother against the Welsc?"

"You must trust me on this, old friend."

"Where will you be?"

"I am running an errand tonight. I will not be back until tomorrow."

"Hengest won't like this."

"You serve me, not my brother."

"Yes, Captain."

Horsa took a mare from the stables and rode off, following the old Roman road to Londinium, skirting to the south to avoid Vortimer's camp on the river. None barred his way and, some hours before dawn, he cantered off on a beaten track through the trees. He knew the way well. Few were abroad at this hour on the best of nights but with the scent of battle and death still drifting on the wind from the east, he was alone on the roads.

The lights of the villa were a beacon to him as he tied up his horse at the tree line and made his way through the wavering grass towards it. He scaled the wall at a point he knew was something of a blind spot to the guards that patrolled it and dropped down onto the gravel with barely a crunch. An oil lamp burned in the window above and he hooted his usual cry of a moor owl.

Aureliana poked her head out and he scrambled up onto the sill and swung himself into the room.

"Oh, Horsa!" she said, as she flung her arms around him. "Thank God you are still alive! I nearly clawed Father's eyes out when I learned of his plans and did my best to stop him leaving, but he had me locked in my room! It's all too terrible! I blame that Gaulish bishop, Germanus. Everything was fine until he came here stirring up trouble!"

"Now, Aureliana, you know that's not true," he said, inhaling the soft scent of her hair. "Your father has hated my people from the beginning and he is not the only Briton to do so. This war was only a matter of time."

"I have not slept for fear of what might have become of you. Is the situation so terrible in Cantium? Has your brother fended off my father's men?"

"The situation is dire. My brother was forced to retreat, something my people try to avoid at all cost. Your father's men were too many. They have pushed Hengest back to the coast."

She looked at him askance. "You were not at the battle?"

"No. I cannot fight your father."

"But how can you refuse? It is your people who are being killed! You might all be killed if you do not fight!"

"Then I shall die with a British spear in my chest before I strike a blow against your father. I cannot raise a hand to him for to hurt you would be more than I could bear."

"Oh, Horsa, my Horsa! You are a fool but I love you for it! But damn this whole thing! Who was ever so wretched as to fear that their father might live for it meant the death of their lover?"

She kissed him and they lay down on the bed together. They wept and made love, wept and loved again for there was nothing left for them to do but to love each other and howl at the futility of the world and its hateful ways.

Hengest

"What do you mean they're gone!" roared Hengest when Octa brought him the news over an early breakfast. It was nearly dawn. The chill left by the departing night saw a fury of activity on Thanet. It was no different across the straight in the coastal towns.

"The harbour master said that they sailed out in the night," Octa replied.

"And he didn't come to tell me? Have that harbour man put in irons. I'll deal with him when I get the chance."

"Horsa probably paid him to wait," Octa said. "This whole business reeks. Your brother is up to something if you'll forgive me for saying so, but I can't believe he would desert out of cowardice."

"He's never shown cowardice in his life," Hengest replied. "He doesn't know the meaning of the word. But there is something going on which he is not telling me. But, by all the gods, his games could cost me this battle and my kingdom!"

"Will we ride out without him?"

"We have to. Another day and Vortimer's men will have dug themselves in on the coast like limpets and we won't have a chance of retaking Cent. We may die trying, but our sword arms are all we have left. Time is not our friend now."

"Let us hope that surprise can give us the edge we need."

"Is my ferry ready?"

"Yes. Shall we leave?"

"Not before I offer up a sacrifice to Woden and Thunor. Care to join me?"

The Saxon nodded. Time was indeed short but they needed all the help they could get.

With the stench of charred meat hanging in the air and the wooden faces of the gods dripping with fresh blood in the sacred groves on Thanet, Hengest crossed to the mainland and led his warband out once more, the rising sun making flames of their spear tips.

Hengest sent out scouts to assess the layout of the enemy camp. They returned with the news that it was clearly divided into various factions. Aurelianus commanded the largest portion of the army and, true to Hengest's prediction, his corner of the camp was the most disciplined with sober, watchful guards and orderly rows of tents.

Vortimer and Cadeyrn had their own areas marked out by their banners of the serpent and the fish. They were small contingents and had a few guards, but the majority of their armies seemed to be sleeping off the previous night's drinking.

Then there was a shambling mess of tents belonging to various western hill chieftains Vortimer had either paid or otherwise convinced to join in his war. These were hopeless tangles of campfires, dwellings and slumbering groups of warriors that lay clustered like barnacles.

It was obvious which side of the camp to attack. It was the weak link in Vortimer's hastily built defences.

They attacked before the sun had fully turned its gaze on the land. Hengest's cavalry thundered across the patch that hosted the camps of the chieftains. They hurled torches and slashed tents. Half the camp was ablaze before a proper alarm was sounded. Warriors staggered out of their tents, strapping on helms and cuirasses, desperately trying to comprehend the situation as hundreds of Germanic warriors tore through their camp.

Hengest could make out the wavering banners of Aurelianus, Vortimer and Cadeyrn in the distance and wished that they were closer. By the time they had mopped up these petty chieftains, his real enemies would have been alerted and either have fled or put together a considerable defence.

It turned out to be the former. Even Aurelianus must have been caught unawares by Hengest's attack. Before they had made it through the camp Hengest could see the banners disappearing into the mist of the dawn and the columns of men marching away from the battle as he cursed them.

Leaving their allies to be butchered, the Welsc crossed the river and set up camp on its western bank. Hengest knew his men did not have the strength to pursue and called a halt just as the outskirts of Durobrivae came into sight. His dawn raid had achieved what it had been intended to do. It had pushed the Welsc back out of Cent and it had sent a clear message to Vortimer that they would fight and fight hard for their land. To the death if need be.

Aurelianus

"Are you so sure of this, your grace?" Vortimer asked Bishop Germanus. They stood on the same quay as they had done several months ago and Bishop Severus was overseeing the loading of that same swan-prowed vessel. "It's not too late to change your mind. We could use your help further in routing the Saxons. They have won a minor victory but they cannot win the war. God is on our side."

"And that is the reason why you no longer need me, my boy," said Germanus. "I have done all that I can for you in your fight against the pagans. But as I have told you before, I am old and am no warrior. You may outnumber Hengest's forces, but a river bars you from his lands and with neither side daring to cross it for the time being, it looks to be a long war. Besides, I have pressing business in Ravenna. I intend to present the case of the Amoricans to the Emperor. Britannia is not the only land that cries out for justice. I wish you luck in your plight and my prayers will be with you. You will win; of that I have no doubt."

They watched them depart on the morning tide. Aurelianus was sad to see him go. The old bishop had been very different to the man he had expected to meet and their work together had done something to his outlook on God and life. But he was a true Roman and had been a good friend to Britannia. Now they had to carry on the fight without him.

He rode back to the camp while Vortimer took the carpentium. When they arrived one of his soldiers hurried over to him.

"General, there is someone here to see you. A woman. Says she's from your villa."

"Seren?" Aurelianus guessed, and swung off his horse. "Take me to her."

"Master!" cried Seren, as she hurried forward, short of breath. "I came as quickly as I could!"

"What's the matter? Why have you left Aureliana? Is she well?"

"Well enough, Master! Well enough to receive barbarians into her chamber in the small hours!"

"*Him?* Has he visited her?"

"Had I known it at the time I would have had the guards butcher him! And I called them to seize him as soon as I knew, but it was too late and he was away!"

"What happened, woman?"

"I heard noises. Talking. The wall between our two chambers is very thin as you know, Master, and so I rose and tried to come in upon them by surprise, but they must have heard me for he was off out the window like a rabbit. I tried to shout to the guards on the wall from the window, but your daughter clamped her hand over my mouth. Oh, she's a wicked girl, Master, begging your pardon. The very devil has got into her this past year. It's not the first time they've met since you returned from the war in the north, I'll wager."

Aurelianus swallowed and found it hard. To think that she would betray him in such a manner was too much for him to bear. It was bad enough before, when that man was just some barbarian oaf she had taken a fancy to, but now, mere days after they had fought a bloody battle … it wrenched his guts around. He was sorely tempted to ride back to his villa that instant.

But perhaps Seren was right. Perhaps the devil had got into her. Confronting her would do no good. She was clearly under the spell of that yellow-haired Satanspit. He could not stop her loving him. But he could stop him from loving her.

Permanently.

Vortimer and Cadeyrn were in council. The tent was crowded with officers and maps were spread over a table, their corners held down with goblets of wine.

"I wonder if I might have a word, my lord," said Aurelianus to Vortimer, as he entered.

"Certainly," Vortimer replied. "Let's step outside."

The afternoon was turning into a hot one. Men sunned themselves as the blood dried on wounds and flies crawled ravenously.

"What is on your mind, Aurelianus?" asked Vortimer as they walked.

"I am given to understand, without intending any offence, that you have certain contacts who can perform work the nature of which may not be spoken of openly."

"This is a rather round-about way of talking for you, Aurelianus," Vortimer replied. "Do you mean assassins and spies and the like?"

"That is my meaning, my lord."

"Then I do wish you would say so. You make it all sound very sordid."

"I apologise, my lord."

"What is it I can do for you? My servants are yours, as it were."

Aurelianus looked about, more nervous than he had ever known himself to be. If his daughter were ever to learn what he was about to say, he would lose her forever. "I need a man killed."

"Don't we all? But who on earth could have displeased our Aurelianus so much that he dares not use his own sword to dispatch him?"

"Horsa."

Vortimer stopped, momentarily surprised. They continued walking. "Is this about your daughter?"

"Yes. They have continued to meet despite my having forbidden it."

"I understand your anger, but this request has come a little late. Had you asked me when we were still on peaceable terms and he and his brother were in their hall on Thanet drinking themselves stupid, there may have been a chance. But now that we are at war with them, they are constantly on their guard and surrounded by their men.

"They met two nights ago. He came to my villa and defiled my daughter beneath the noses of my useless guards."

"Two nights ago? Are you telling me that after we had smashed the Saxons, Horsa still had the strength and audacity to sneak past my lines and pay a visit to your daughter?"

"He was not at the battle."

"What?"

"He has refused to enter hostilities against me on account of his love for my daughter. I have this from my daughter's nurse who got it from her."

It took a while for Vortimer to respond to this and when he did he let out a short bark of laughter. "He is the most audacious barbarian I have ever known and also the most wonderfully foolish! I thought something was missing from Hengest's mad charge the other day. So Horsa and his brave raiders are at odds with Hengest! This is fantastic!"

"He is not currently with the army. My scouts report that he and his raiders are gathered off shore at Dubris."

"Then we can smash them in one fell swoop!"

"It would not be advisable to abandon our lines, my lord. If we march on Dubris, then Hengest will undoubtedly push for Londinium."

"Quite right, we cannot abandon our current position. But this changes everything. If Horsa is not at his brother's side, then it may very well be possible to fulfil your request."

"Do you have somebody who can be used at short notice?"

"Oh yes. I have the perfect candidate in mind. I have used them several times in the past and their skills are, shall we say, unorthodox, which I think is what is required for this particular task."

"Just one thing, my lord. This business must remain between us."

"Of course, Aurelianus. Have no fear. This is as much my battle as it is yours. None shall know of what has passed between us."

Hronwena

The weather had brightened by the time they left the shelter of the forest and green hills swept away from them for as far as the eye could see. There was no sign of activity on the road to Corinium. Everywhere lay the signs of poverty and plague. Many rural communities lay abandoned, robbed and neglected and the people, thin and emaciated, scratched out a living as best they could.

"My lady, how do we know we're even on the right track?" Deilwen asked in desperation. "We must turn back soon. Those bandits could have gone anywhere and we are exhausted and starving."

"We're not returning without Britu," said Hronwena firmly. "I made a promise to Enys. We will get her son back."

"Guern won't last much longer. And how are we to get Britu back even if we do find him? Two soldiers are as good as useless against an armed band of thugs."

Hronwena had left the soldiers at daybreak. She had returned to Deilwen and Guern and led them across country, parallel to the road. She didn't want the soldiers to learn that she was travelling in the company of a small boy.

A derelict mansio lay between them and the road up ahead. During Roman rule it had been a waypoint for travellers to sleep, eat and acquire fresh horses. Now its plaster walls were crumbling and its tiled roof was sagging and yet, a wisp of smoke could be seen coming from some outlet, hinting at habitation.

"Could be anyone," said Deilwen. "Not necessarily the bandits we seek."

"Look!" said Hronwena, pointing to the trees that encroached upon the mansio. "Our old friends seem to think this could be the place!"

Below them, partially screened by the trees, Aurelianus's two soldiers were lurking, their backs to them, as they surveyed the mansio.

"They must be desperate if they are planning on attacking," said Deilwen. "Two against untold numbers of bandits?"

"They may stand a chance," Hronwena said, forcing some optimism into her voice.

Deilwen looked at her. "You're planning something," she said.

"If we can somehow exchange Guern for Britu *before* Aurelianus's men make their rescue attempt, then they will be forced to take him to Gaul with them. They are obviously desperate to recover their charge. They'll have no choice after going to the trouble of rescuing him and we'll be on our way back to Din Neidr with Britu."

"But how is it to be done, my lady?"

"Those soldiers don't look like their making their move just yet so I'm going down to see what I can find out."

"No!" said Deilwen sharply. "I'm putting my foot down if that's alright, my lady. I've let you go and put yourself in danger far too much already. This time, I'm going. Now, take Guern."

Hronwena did as her handmaid said and lifted the poor, hungry boy up into her saddle. "Be careful, Deilwen," she said.

Deilwen dismounted and sneaked off down the hill towards the ruined mansio, taking a side route that concealed her from the soldiers' view. Hronwena rocked Guern to sleep, hugging him tight.

After a while, Deilwen came hurrying back, her face showing great excitement. "It's those bandits alright! They've got Britu locked up in a grain hut behind the main building. I heard two of the bastards placed on guard talking about him. Then one headed back indoors."

"Did anyone see you?"

She gave her a mischievous look. "You're not the only one who can sneak about, my lady!"

"Only one man is guarding him?"

"Looks like it. The others are in the courtyard round the front, sitting on their arses."

"Let's get down there."

"You want to make your move now?"

"Time is of the essence. If we can put Guern in Britu's place before those two fools down there manage to rescue him, they'll have to take Guern to Gaul."

"What if they fail to rescue him?"

Hronwena did not answer. This had been the real worry in her plan. If the soldiers failed, poor Guern would be left in the hands of bandits. She told herself that it was no worse than doing nothing and leaving Britu to his fate.

"This is very dangerous, my lady!" Deilwen said, as they descended the rise through the trees.

"That's why you're going to put your charm and clever tongue to good use. Go to the front entrance on foot and tell them something, anything, to get their attention."

Deilwen looked worried at this prospect but did as she was told. "I'll tell them I'm part of a wagon train that got stuck in the mud and need the help of several strong lads. The prospect of plundering a helpless wagon train will surely lure them away. It may even make it easier for Aurelianus's men to make their move."

"See, Deilwen? I told you I needed your wit on this journey. Good luck."

"And to you, my lady."

Hronwena led the horses around the mansio until the crumbling facade of its rear could be seen through the wavering branches. She hitched the two mounts to the trunk of an elm and lifted Guern down from the saddle. He could tell that something was up for his eyes were big and bright.

There was the grain hut. A bandit was wandering about, chewing on a chicken bone. "Now then, Guern," she said to him. "Be a good lad and do exactly as I say. We're going into that building over there but we mustn't make any sound. There are bad men about and they mustn't hear us. Can you be quiet like a mouse?"

The boy nodded.

"Then we shall be as two sneaky mice." She felt terrible for what she was planning. How would the boy feel when she left him all alone in the grain hut with bad men all about? But Britu was so close! And she was sure that the soldiers would be here soon to rescue him.

There came shouts from the mansio and she saw the guard hurry through a gate to heed somebody's call. Deilwen's ploy was already in place. She hurried across the grass towards the grain hut; her progress slowed by Guern's weight.

Once she reached the hut she put him down and fumbled at the door. It was tied with a length of dirty rope. She drew her knife and sliced through it. She opened the door and saw Britu's pale little face peering out of the gloom. Hronwena swept him up in a hug.

"It's alright, Britu. I'm here to take you back to your mother."

There were more shouts from the other side of the building and the sound of many horses. Hronwena took Britu out of the hut, pulled Guern close and kissed him on the forehead. "This will only be for a short time, I promise," she said, and pushed him inside. She tried not to see his pained look as she closed the door, sealing him in with the darkness.

"My lady!" came a cry from behind her. She whirled around and saw Deilwen waving at her from the trees. "Quick!"

She wanted to fasten the lock with something to avoid suspicion but there was so little time. "Listen to me now, Britu. You remember Deilwen, don't you? She's over there, look! Run to her! Run as fast as you can!"

The little boy took off; his short legs carrying his tottering form in a staggering pattern towards Deilwen's open arms. Hronwena fumbled with the old rope, desperately trying to refashion the semblance of a knot with the two sliced halves.

There were shouts and the clang of swords nearby and that gave Hronwena some hope. Aurelianus's men were making their move at last. Horses galloped around the corner and lowered spears at her. She saw British armour and shields painted with the serpent of Din Neidr. Blood was smeared on their blades. She gaped at them in incomprehension.

"And what do we have here?" asked the lead rider. "A thief? A Whore?"

"I'm trying to rescue this boy," said Hronwena, undoing her handiwork and flinging open the door to the grain hut. "These bandits kidnapped him."

The rider dismounted and peered in. Guern was sitting on his haunches looking bewildered. "And who is this boy to you?"

Hronwena tried to think of a lie but a soldier she recognised came jogging around the corner and flung out his arm at her.

"That's the woman I told you about!" he said. "She came to us last night and said she was a travelling healer and had heard us being set upon by the bandits. Then, this morning, she was gone! What's she doing here?"

"Wait a minute," said one of the riders. "I know her! She's the Lady Hronwena! That Saxon woman Vitalinus married. I've seen her at Din Neidr."

"Well well," said the first rider. "I think I know what's going on here. You were trying to get the boy back, weren't you? Trying to reunite him with his mother, is that it?"

Hronwena saw Deilwen, hovering about in the woods with Britu in her arms, unseen by the soldiers. "Yes," she said, looking the Briton in the eye. "That's more or less it."

"I knew there was something funny about her …" began Aurelianus's man.

"You're a brave woman to defy the bishop's orders and come down here on your own," said the rider. "But all you Saxons have horseshit for brains. Lucky for the boy that we came along in time to stop those bandits from killing you both. There's not much left of them now.

"We are under the standard of Lord Cadeyrn, your stepson. We're on our way to the war in the east and

171

happened upon these two fools that were sent with the boy." He turned to the soldier. "Well, the boy is back in your hands. I suggest you and your companion make for the coast with all haste. That boat won't wait. And try not to lose him a second time, eh? I don't know how Aurelianus trains you fellows, but those soft Roman ways are no match for the hard life we mountain men know. You have to keep your eyes peeled and your ears sharp."

The soldier grunted and took Guern by the hand. If he noticed that it was not the same boy – and Hronwena did not see how he couldn't – then he was too afraid or embarrassed to mention it. After all, here was a boy to send to Gaul and that was their mission. *Off you go, little man*, she thought as the soldier led Guern away. *And good luck to you.*

"Now what are we going to do with you, missy?" Cadeyrn's man asked her. "I can't spare the men to escort you back to your husband. We ride to Vortimer. I suppose he will have to decide what is to be done with you." And with that, he mounted his horse and trotted off, leaving her in the care of his men.

Hronwena looked over to the trees helplessly and saw that Deilwen and Britu had vanished. *Well done, Deilwen*, she thought. *Get that boy back to his mother.*

Hengest

We might actually win this war, thought Hengest as he gazed across the river at the British encampments. They were digging ditches. It was a clear sign that they felt threatened and planned to hold fast and defend rather than push another attack.

If only my bastard brother would get his head together and join us.

Horsa had camped on the shore by the ruins of Dubris; a tactical manoeuvre that would protect their flank should the Britons try to cross the river further south. But his reluctance to actually engage the enemy was still worryingly apparent.

Hengest could not understand it. He had had trouble with Horsa's men before but that had been years ago when he had barely known them. And now, after they had been through so much together, it felt like their army had split in two with each half following a different brother.

He had sent envoys to Horsa's camp. He had been too busy organizing his defences to go himself. They returned with word that Horsa had refused to see them. They had spoken to Beorn instead and had been told that, although Horsa's loyalty to his brother was absolute, there was something personal that stayed his hand from fighting the Welsc.

Well, thank the gods that the second battle had gone in their favour. Surprise had beaten the Welsc once but it would not do so again. Hengest was under no illusions. If he was to beat Vortimer and Aurelianus once and for all, he would need his brother and his raiders.

Horsa

The camp on the sandy shores by the suburbs of Dubris was smaller than Hengest's inland camp. Only about half of the raiders had pitched their tents and lit their fires; the other half remained onboard the vessels that hung out on a blue haze beneath leaden skies. Horsa wanted to keep his fleet mobile and within hailing distance.

It was sometimes hard for him to remember that he was not actually part of this war. The campaigning in Pictland a year ago had turned his mind to that of a military tactician and it was a hard thing to switch off. Then he remembered Aureliana's sweet face and, although he would never let her father have the run of Cent, he would hold fast, never attacking. If he had to die defending Cent, then so be it, but he would not attack Aurelianus.

A young scout approached bearing news. "The Welsc were spotted scouting their side of the river, Captain," he said. "They took one look at us and scarpered."

"That's good," Horsa replied. "We can't have them crossing the river."

"They won't get through us, Captain!"

Horsa liked this young man. He reminded him of Asse who had briefly captained the *Fafnir* before Ceolwulf's men had slaughtered everybody on board. "What's your name, lad?"

"Ceadda, Captain."

"You're with the *Raven*, aren't you?"

He nodded.

"How long have you been with us?"

"Two months. I joined after my dad died of the plague. I was the only breadwinner left for the family and I couldn't make ends meet. My mother and sisters were going hungry so I had to leave them and get employment elsewhere."

"What was your father's trade?"

"He was a hooper."

"Can't you pick up his tools and earn a peaceful living?"

Confusion was written on the lad's face.

"Whether we join this war or not, there will be peace one way or the other. We all need to think of the future."

Ceadda looked down as if embarrassed. "My father owed his neighbour a lot of money. I have to work the debt off and I can't do that hooping barrels. There's much better pay to be had under you. When the debt's paid off, I'll go back, if you'll give me leave."

"Any man of mine is free to come and go as he chooses," said Horsa. "I demand no oaths of fealty. Unlike my brother."

"Thank you, Captain. Maybe when this war is over we can all live peaceful lives. Family and home is what everybody's fighting for anyway, isn't it?"

Horsa looked out at the waves rolling in. "Ceadda, would you do me a favour?"

"Anything, Captain."

"Run along and see that my horse is saddled. It's about time I explained myself to my brother."

The lad nodded and hurried off. Horsa continued to stare at the waves. Then, he let out a great sigh as if the world was intent on tearing him in two directions. He rubbed the bridge of his nose thoughtfully.

"Hard work being the boss," said a voice near him.

He had noticed the girl around the camp before. She was hard not to notice, with her short tunica and exquisite thighs, but this was the first time she had ever spoken to him.

"What?"

"Stressful. Especially when you're not appreciated by your superiors, family or no."

"Hengest is not my superior," Horsa snapped. He didn't know why he was talking to this wench. He had known girls like her all his life. Camp followers. Whores looking for a bit of silver fucking lonely warriors who were far from home. Had he seen her around a couple of years ago, he would have carried her off to his own tent and not thought twice about it afterwards. But that had been a different Horsa, younger, yes, but *different* somehow. Women did not excite him as they had done before. Well one woman did, but Aureliana excited him in ways he had not known were possible.

"I can't see any man being your superior," said the girl. "You are a bear among men."

Horsa grimaced. "I'm not interested. Go and ply your trade on somebody else."

"I'm not a whore," she said, firm but not offended.

"What are you doing hanging around my camp then?"

"My name is Callista," she said. "I earn silver by sewing up wounds, applying poultices, that sort of thing."

"You're wasting your time here. We've not seen any battle and I intend to ensure that we don't. You'd be better off over in my brother's camp. I hear he has many wounded."

"I'm not interested in your brother." She rose and walked away.

A nearby raider from the *Raven* whistled through his teeth at her. "You can give me a fuck if the captain isn't interested."

"I'm not a whore," she said once again, and meandered off through the camp.

Ceadda returned and his head swivelled to catch a glimpse of Callista's backside moving very pleasantly beneath the cloth of her tunic. Horsa smiled.

"Have you ever had a woman, lad?" he asked him.

Ceadda flushed, noticing the sniggers of the men. "Not as such, Captain. There weren't many girls my age where we lived."

Horsa scrambled to his feet and dusted the sand off his breeches. "We'll have to sort something out for you when I get back then, won't we?" he said, patting Ceadda on the shoulder as he made his way over to his horse.

He rode to his brother's camp alone and as he entered it he felt the eyes of everybody upon him. He felt like a traitor. Well, perhaps he was, but there was nothing he could do about it.

Hengest was standing outside his tent. Ordlaf and Ebusa were nearby and the three of them gave Horsa the same expression the rest of the army had given him. Nobody greeted him.

"I am sorry, Brother," he began. "My absence at the battle was not out of any disloyalty to you."

"I wish to believe it, but I see no other cause," Hengest said.

"Can we talk in private?"

Hengest nodded and ducked into his tent. He poured out mead for them and they sat down, the sturdy camp table between them. There was nobody else in the tent and Horsa was suddenly aware of how long it had been since the two of them had had the chance to sit and talk in private, as brothers.

"I needed your raiders against the Welsc," said Hengest coldly. "Not to mention your own sword arm."

"I apologise and I intend to explain myself fully though I know that my explanation will not be received with any understanding."

"Try anyway."

"I am in love."

Hengest blinked. "A jest? I am not in the mood."

"No jest. I have never been more serious. I have fallen in love with a British girl."

Hengest slammed his horn down on the table, spilling mead. "And for that you refuse to fight our enemies? Love? What do you know of it? You have whored your way around the northern world without a care for anybody! Now you talk of love when I need you to talk of war?"

"I knew you wouldn't understand," said Horsa through gritted teeth.

"What's so special about this one?"

Anger bubbled within Horsa but he tried to control it. "Do you remember how you felt about Halfritha when we were boys? Or are you so hardened by your ambitions that those memories no longer have any place in your heart?"

"We are not the same, you and I, Horsa."

"But is it so inconceivable that I could fall in love as you did? Despite my past?"

"Alright, so you love the girl. But what is that in the grand scheme of things? The Welsc have betrayed us and are trying to push us off this land that we have fought so hard for! We have to fight! And doing so will surely not put this girl you love in any danger. I have many Britons in my army and many live in Cent with their families. It's their fight too. Aurelianus and his masters in Londinium are our enemies; not every Briton on the island."

"The girl I love is Aurelianus's daughter."

Hengest's expression froze. He leaned forward and cupped his face in his hands and remained so for some time. "Am I such a blind fool that I could not have seen this? How on earth did it come about?"

"What matter now? I love her more than I have loved anything. She shines a light on me that I cannot live without. And it is for that reason that I cannot fight her father and bring sadness to her heart."

"What am I to do? I cannot win this war without you, Horsa."

"It is my wish that you do not."

Hengest exploded. "Then what do you want? Do you want our people to be driven off their lands and forced back to Jute-land? What possible outcome would suit you, Horsa?"

"I don't know!" he shouted. "I didn't get in to this voluntarily. I didn't have a battle plan. All I know is that I cannot fight!"

"Then get out! Leave this camp and return to your ships! If you will not side with me against our enemies, then I don't want you here!"

Horsa stood up and left his brother, wrenching the tent flap shut behind him. He ignored the stares as he made his way to his horse.

Back at his camp he did his best to drown his sorrows. His raiders knew his mood and knew enough to leave him to it. But Callista was new and did not know him as they did. She sat down next to him presenting him with a fresh horn of ale. "Is Hengest still not seeing eye to eye with you?"

"He just doesn't understand," said Horsa. "It's like he has forgotten what love is like. All he thinks of is war."

"Aye, perhaps he has forgotten that there is more to life." She placed her hand on his thigh feeling the muscle that bulged beneath the rough spun wool. "I'm no whore but you can have me if you want."

Horsa laughed. "Not a whore? You have a funny way of showing it."

"It wouldn't be for payment. Or love. Just two lonely people who like each other sharing a moment. You do like me don't you? I can tell that you do. I like you …"

Her hand wandered across his thigh to cup his balls. He seized her by the wrist and thought about striking her but then another thought took him. "Come to my tent tonight," he told her.

She smiled with the satisfaction of a victor.

Antoninus

Antoninus waited in the clearing with the moon on his face so that he would be visible to Maelona when she came through the trees towards him. He had picked her up from her errands before; loyally awaiting her return from whatever task Vortimer had sent her on.

He often let his imagination wander on nights such as these, thinking about her fine, shapely thighs clasped around some unfortunate victim, choking off any defence as she slid the dagger in.

He liked to picture himself as the victim, and as he thought of her wild, black hair clinging to her naked breasts as she squeezed tighter and tighter, his eyes would close and his member would stiffen until it hurt.

But that was hopeless dreaming. Maelona had made it more than clear on a number of occasions that their relationship was strictly professional and if any part of his body came into contact with hers, he would quickly lose it.

Still, a man was allowed to dream.

Tonight it was to be Horsa and Antoninus wondered if she would actually fuck him first before she finished him. She had come to him that afternoon to tell him that tonight was the night. The Saxon raider had finally succumbed to her charms and had invited her to his tent. Antoninus smiled. Horsa was known for being particularly lecherous and debauched; even for a Saxon. He would get more than he bargained for tonight.

Something came rushing through the trees towards him and he peered into the gloom. It was Maelona. Why was she running? Fear showed on her face; an expression he had never seen before on her beautiful features. Sweat shined on her brow. The trees rustled as other figures on horseback pursued her, fighting through the forest.

Saxon voices sounded out and a spear whistled through the leaves, missing Maelona but thudding a few paces from Antoninus.

Damn! She must have been found out. But had she accomplished her task? *Only a few more paces, girl, you can do it!*

Another spear whickered through the night and caught Maelona in the back. It ripped through her chest, its ugly, red point emerging just above those heavenly breasts. She gasped, stumbled, her eyes fixed on Antoninus with a pleading expression.

She went down, earth and leaves churning up as her body hit the ground, sliding towards him. She lay still a few paces from him, dead. He could see that her hands were red and wet with blood.

So she *had* succeeded. *Well, it was lovely knowing you, Maelona …* Antoninus let the reins of her horse slip through his fingers. He needed to put as much distance between himself and the approaching Saxons and could not afford to bring the mare with him. His heart lamenting the dreadful waste of beauty, he galloped off through the trees.

Beorn

Beorn's eyes were wet with tears as he rode back into camp. He had led the party in pursuit of the assassin whose corpse was slung over the pommel of his saddle. She was dead and that was unfortunate. He had been looking forward to winkling the names of her employers out of her with a hot blade.

The figure he saw waiting for them at the edge of the camp made him suddenly afraid that he was looking upon a ghost. But the flesh was too solid and the eyes too alive. "Gods, Captain!" He bellowed with joy. "We thought you were murdered in your bed!"

"And so you rode out without even checking that it was me?" said Horsa.

"I heard noises from your tent and looked in and saw … you … on your side with a dagger in your back. Blood was everywhere … Somebody saw the assassin running for the trees."

"And now my assassin is dead, I see."

"We tried to take her alive but there was somebody waiting for her with horses. We couldn't risk losing her and so tried to pin her down. The aim was too good. You know her?"

"As do many men in this camp. She's been mincing around showing her thighs and trying to seduce me for days."

"Then who was it she …?"

"Ceadda. A young boy who did me a service. I sent him to my tent to enjoy himself in my place as a reward. *Eala!* What a reward! I shall never forgive myself."

"Who do you think sent her?"

"Could be any one of many men," Horsa replied. "I have no shortage of enemies."

"Do you think that your brother …"

"Stow that horseshit, Beorn!" Horsa snapped. "Hengest would never betray me like that, despite my betrayal of him. No, this has the stink of a Briton all over it."

Vortimer

"What am I going to do with you, Stepmother?" Vortimer asked. "You seem intent on complicating matters. My brother treats you with the utmost courtesy by leaving you as lady of his house when he could have cast you out as kin to our enemy, and you repay him by trying to disrupt his plans. Tell me, what is the life of Britu, our nephew, to you?"

"You would never understand," came the reply in that barbaric accent of hers.

Vortimer and Cadeyrn had been going over battle plans in his tent when news came that Hronwena had been apprehended outside of Corinium trying to stop their little nephew from reaching Gaul.

"You are a liability, my dear," said Vortimer. "Just across that river is your father. I question the judgment of my brother's men in bringing you here. Yet what is to be done with you?"

"We could send her back to Din Neidr," said Cadeyrn. "This stalemate looks set to continue. I can spare the men."

"Stalemates can be deceptive, Brother," Vortimer replied. "We have no idea when her father may renew hostilities and then I shall need every one of our men ready to repel the Saxons. No, she will have to remain here. I could send her to Londinium. There are many cells in the palace that would be more than suitable for a Saxon whore. Do you know that they sleep on straw like pigs?"

Cadeyrn shifted uncomfortably. "Hengest may be our enemy," he said, "but his daughter has never proven herself to be."

Vortimer nearly rolled his eyes. His younger brother had clearly developed a soft spot for their stepmother. "She may not seem our enemy, but we cannot trust her. She must not be allowed to communicate with her father. I have a mind to interrogate her further. Send her to my tent. I am too busy to deal with this now."

Cadeyrn eyed him with suspicion.

"Don't look at me like that," he said. "I have nothing sordid in mind."

"For a moment then, you sounded like Father."

"Another jest like that, and I'll have you digging latrines with the rest of the men."

"My lord," said a soldier at the entrance to the tent. "A man called Antoninus to see you."

"Leave us!" Vortimer commanded of all in the tent. Hronwena was taken away and as the last of the soldiers and officers filed out he placed a hand on Cadeyrn's arm. "Not you, dear brother. I should let you in on this little development. If I'm not mistaken, here comes some very good news indeed. Ave, Antoninus!"

"Ave, my lord!" said the soldier.

"You come to me alone? Surely my Maelona has not fallen to your charms and lies naked and exhausted in your tent?"

"Maelona … she's dead, I am afraid,"

All trace of jest vanished from Vortimer's face. "Dead? She failed?"

"No, I believe she succeeded, but they got her with a spear as she ran from the camp."

"And you are sure that she completed her mission?" Vortimer demanded.

"She had blood all over her hands," Antoninus remarked. "And riders came after her with a hot vengeance."

Vortimer sat back and stroked his short beard. He had never known Maelona to fail or botch a mission. Bad luck, that's all it was. Caught in the act. It was a terrible shame. He would miss her services, not to mention her exquisite scent.

"Who exactly was this woman?" Cadeyrn enquired. "And what was her mission?"

"The assassination of Horsa," Vortimer replied simply.

Cadeyrn raised his eyebrows in surprise. "I did hear a report from my scouts that the Saxons on the coast are preparing one of their pagan funeral pyres as we speak, yet there has been no battle in that area."

"Then he really is dead," said Vortimer, almost dreamily. He rose and called in one of his officers. "Go out and spread the word that Horsa the Saxon is dead," he told the man. "That should boost morale. Oh, and make sure that Aurelianus is the first to hear of it. It will please him greatly."

Hronwena

Hronwena looked around the lavish tent with interest. The Britons certainly knew how to live in luxury – even in the field. Vortimer's bed was a mass of furs, wide enough to lie on and stretch one's arms out without touching the sides. There was a writing table, a comfortable chair, a stand with a basin and jug of water and over in the corner stood a rack with his armour and helmet, polished to a high sheen.

She wondered how this compared with her father's living quarters across the river. *Gods!* To think that he, Uncle Horsa, Aesc and all the other familiar faces that she had not seen in over a year were just across the river … It was all she could do not to flee from the tent and make a mad dash for the water.

But no. Her mission was not yet finished. She hoped to all the gods that Deilwen was well on her way back to Din Neidr with Britu. She would never forgive herself if anything befell the pair on their return to Din Neidr. She had to find out what had happened to them and help them in any way she could.

But she could not ignore the danger her family was in. She was surrounded by men set on her father's destruction. She still felt the burn of anger at him for forcing her to marry Vitalinus but he was her father. And Aesc was over there too and beyond their lines lay Thanet and her mother. Her own people faced annihilation at the hands of the family she had been married into. There had to be something she could do!

Vortimer's armour winked at her from the other side of the tent. Its polished sheen irritated her. It seemed arrogant, as if dazzling her with its owner's intentions. She walked over to the armour and touched it. It was cold and yet felt so very fragile, as if a mere hand could destroy it.

But of course, a hand could destroy it.

She knew the rune spells. She could undo Vortimer.

There was no sign that she was to be disturbed any time soon. She looked about for a sharp implement. Her knife had been taken from her when they had brought her into the camp. On Vortimer's desk lay a short-bladed knife for sharpening quills. She seized it and reached inside Vortimer's breastplate for a smooth surface.

The rim around the neck provided a suitable candidate and she began to inscribe the runes, scratching deep, digging her hatred of him into the metal as far as she could manage so that no oiled cloth or handful of sand could rub it off.

Seren

The wine merchant had a body as broad as one of his barrels and yet he still managed to get his arms around the casks and carry them down from the cart and in through the trader's entrance to the kitchens.

"Mind you don't chip the plaster like you did last time," Seren heard the housekeeper warn him.

The wine merchant grunted as he staggered along the hallway and deposited his load at the top of the stairs where a servant would carry it down to the cellars. "Hot work," he said, accepting a cup of water from the housekeeper. "Or it might just be you that's making me sweat, my pretty," and he pinched the housekeeper's rear playfully. She squealed and flicked the hem of her apron at him.

"You keep your hands to yourself; I've told you so before!"

"You put up a good fight, sweetheart, but anyone can see you're madly in love with me!"

The housekeeper whooped with laughter and Seren rolled her eyes as she continued chopping carrots for Aureliana's supper, trying to ignore the two flirts.

"Well, that's the last of them," said the wine merchant, red in the face as he set down the final cask. "How about a kiss for a service charge?"

"Get away with you!"

"Come on, lovely! I don't know when I'll be able to come by with another delivery. It's not easy with the war in the east, and things are set to become a lot bleaker."

Seren set down her knife and hurried over to him.

"You've come through Cantium?" she said.

"It's the fastest route to Gaul."

"What news?"

"Your master has the Saxons penned in but not the strength to oust them fully. Least not until now. The war looked set to continue on into the winter but the Saxons have just been struck a blow that'll see Aurelianus finish them."

"What's that?"

"Horsa's been killed. Hengest's own brother and joint commander of their army. Their morale has hit rock bottom and a third of Hengest's warriors will follow no leader but Horsa. Their days are numbered."

The two women gaped at the man who, suddenly feeling that the room had become a little colder, decided that it was time for him to leave.

"Lord save us," said Seren to the housekeeper once the man had gone. "We can't let the Lady Aureliana learn of this! It would break her heart!"

"Agreed," said the housekeeper. "But she'll find out sooner or later and then what? Her father will be trumpeting it about that he killed Horsa the Saxon to get his men up and on their feet. She'll find out somehow."

"We'll handle that when the time comes," Seren said. "Until then, she must be kept in the dark as to ..." she let out a startled cry and the knife dropped from her hand.

Aureliana stood at the entrance to the kitchen. She had heard every word. Her eyes brimmed with tears and her face looked as if it had been drained of blood.

"Oh my poor girl, listen to me ..." Seren began, but Aureliana was off, running down the hall.

Aureliana

Aureliana's sobs choked her. It couldn't be true! It just couldn't! But deep down she knew that it was. Oh, the merchant might have been wrong, but somehow, deep within her bosom, she had always known that this war would take her Horsa from her.

How could God be so cruel? Was this her punishment for loving a heathen? It had to be. The bishops and priests had been right all along. She was a wretched sinner and the agony she felt now was her just reward.

What could she do now? Carry on, pray for forgiveness and hope that God, in his mercy, would send her another man to fill the yawning gap within her soul that Horsa had so recently vacated? Wait ten years, twenty? Would she be a spinster before a little of the happiness she had known returned to her?

She fell on her bed and wept at the thought of the long years of loneliness ahead of her. And it wasn't just Horsa she had lost. She had lost her father too; for she could never bear to be in the same room as the man responsible for the slaying of her beloved. She found that she didn't hate him. She had no energy left for hate. She could only despair in the face of the awful world that caused such things to happen.

Seren tried the handle on her door. Aureliana did not remember locking it but supposed that she must have. "My lady? Are you all right, my lady?"

"Go away, Seren."

"My lady, I am so dreadfully sorry. Won't you let me in so that we might talk?"

"Nothing you can do could ever help me!" Aureliana found that she still had a little hate left after all. Seren had told her father of her affair. And through that, she had been indirectly responsible for Horsa's death.

"I'll go then, my child," said Seren, sounding miserable. "But I'll bring some broth up later. You must eat, no matter how you feel."

Aureliana lay on her bed for a long time. The sheets below her face were damp but she did not care to move. Her mind fixed on the years of misery that stretched before her. How could she carry on? How could she go through the motions of everyday life, eating breakfast and Seren's blasted broth, going to church, socialising with silly girls her own age who had never known anything of love.

No.

She couldn't bear it and no god could expect her to. Perhaps Horsa's gods would have understood. If the god she had been raised to revere could not see that she had but one way out of her pain, then to Hell with him. Perhaps there were other gods. Or perhaps there were none. All she knew was that her time in this world was used up. It was time for her to go.

She rose and drew her tear-stained sheets up to her. She began to twist them, twirling them tighter and tighter until she grasped a hard cord between her fists. Then, she softly unlocked her door and stepped out into the corridor.

Horsa

Horsa frowned at the group of riders he could see crossing the bridge. It was only a small stone thing built by the Romans at the narrowest part of the river. With Hengest guarding the bridge north at Durobrivae this was the only other bridge into Cent.

He had ridden out with some of his men that morning to check his defences. Hengest had apparently had the same idea for Horsa could see Ebusa's plumed helmet on the other bank amidst a company of his riders.

"What's he doing on the other side of the river?" Beorn asked.

Several of Ebusa's riders were struggling with somebody on the mud.

"They've got someone," said Horsa. "A prisoner." He galloped on ahead, crossing the bridge and heading down the bank, kicking up spray from the river's edge.

"*Hwaet*, Ebusa!"

The tall rider's plumed helm turned. "*Hwaet*, Horsa! Good to see you alive! There have been rumours you were murdered in your bed."

"Hengest knew that it was not me who fell to the assassin's blade. I sent a rider. Did he not tell you?"

"Yes, but it is good to see you in the flesh all the same. Do you hold the bridge?"

"I may wish to have no part in this war but I will not let Welsc march into Cent unchallenged. Who is it you have there?"

"She says she was out collecting firewood but is clearly not dressed for it. And she has the manners and soft skin of a serving wench grown old in some lord's villa."

Horsa peered at the face of the old woman who struggled in the grip of two of Ebusa's Saxons and his heart suddenly skipped a beat. "Seren!" He dismounted and hurried towards her. "Release her! She's harmless!"

Seren gazed fearfully at him as if she were not at all sure that she was not seeing a ghost. Then her expression turned from fear to outright misery. "Oh, Lord Horsa!" she wailed. "God has played a mean trick on us all!"

"What's wrong? Why have you left Aureliana? Is she well?"

"I find you alive when we were told that you had been killed! What punishment!"

"For the sake of all the gods, woman! Why are you here?"

"She thought you were dead! She thought she had lost you in this world and sought to find you in the next! Oh, this is ill news, Lord Horsa, and I am nearly broken by the burden of it. Lady Aureliana took her own life! She thought she would never see you again and could not bear it and so committed the worst of all sins!"

Horsa felt as if every ounce of warmth and happiness had been suddenly sucked from him, leaving him hollow and cold. "She … is dead?"

"We are all punished for our part in this foolish play! Dead! My baby!" and she fell to weeping on her hands and knees in the mud.

Horsa staggered backwards as if struck. He could not believe it. His Aureliana, the one thing he had left to live for was dead because of a lie.

They rode to Hengest's camp in silence. Seren sat behind Horsa for she would allow none of the others to touch her. Horsa felt as if he were being swept along on

195

the winds of autumn with no control over what direction he might take.

Hengest listened to Seren with interest as she related her tale in his tent. His eyes flicked to Horsa, briefly, showing some compassion.

"And you were riding to bring this news to Aurelianus?" he asked her.

She nodded, biting down on a handkerchief to keep another bout of sobbing away.

"You were not headed for the Britons' camp," he went on. "My riders picked you up by the riverbank many miles south of their position."

"Because I got lost. Every track and trail in this forsaken part of the land looks the same."

"What's to be done with her?" Ebusa asked him. "Shall we keep her confined somewhere?"

"Seems a little harsh," said Aesc. "What threat does she pose? We could just let her on her way. She has just lost her ward. A little kindness is surely no foolishness." He looked about at the other men in the tent as if afraid that his words might be construed as treasonous. But they were all watching Hengest who was deep in thought.

"Yes, send her on her way," he murmured. "See that she is fed and then point her in the direction of her countrymen. Escort her across the river yourself, Ebusa."

This unexpected compassion from their leader had taken all in the tent by surprise.

"We attack at dawn," he said, once the woman was removed from the tent.

"What's changed?" Aesc asked. "We're still outnumbered."

"But tonight Aurelianus will receive news that will suck the battle-spirit right out of him. He'll be devastated by the loss of his daughter. He may not even fight at all."

"And without Aurelianus," said Aesc, "the Welsc will be like a headless snake thrashing about on the sand. They have Vortimer and Cadeyrn of course …"

"But those two fools know as much about winning battles as I do about needlework."

Horsa cleared his throat and spoke at last. "You have my sword and my men, Hengest," he said.

They all looked at him as if they had forgotten he was there.

"You are with me at last?" Hengest asked him.

"Yes," said Horsa. "It was Aurelianus that moved his daughter's hand. It was he who caused her death. We might have lived in happiness had he accepted our love. I want him dead. I want to drive my sword into him myself and bathe my arms in his blood."

Only Hengest seemed to understand his anger. The others merely looked confused by this sudden change of attitude. Hengest merely said, "I hope that you get that chance, Horsa."

Vortimer

Vortimer woke to the sound of confusion in the camp. At first he thought that they were under attack by the Saxons but there were no cries of slaughter or the clash of blades, only concerned shouts from one side of the camp to the other. He rose quickly and threw on his tunic, belting it as he left the tent.

"Aurelianus has left us!" said Cadeyrn, jogging over to him.

"Left us?"

"Deserted!"

"This must be a mistake!"

"No mistake. He was seen heading out of the camp in the night at full gallop."

"Alone?"

"Yes. His men remain but they've no idea where their general has gone."

"This is madness! Send out riders after him!"

"I already have."

A commander came galloping over to them, his face white with fear. "My lords! The Saxons have crossed the river south of our position!"

Vortimer gaped. "How many? Is Hengest with them?"

"They are about three-hundred. On foot. No sign of Hengest."

"They attack just as our general deserts us?" said Cadeyrn. "This cannot be a coincidence!"

"No," Vortimer agreed.

"There must have been some communication between Aurelianus and the Saxons. Do you think that he could have switched sides?"

Vortimer shook his head. "Not Aurelianus. Of that we can be sure."

"I shall ride out to meet this advanced force that has crossed the river."

"I would like to accompany you, but it must be a diversion. Hengest may plan to attack from the north. I need to remain here and defend the road to Londinium."

"I'll need most of our cavalry to overcome his force advancing from the south."

Vortimer was struck by indecision. If he sent too many men with Cadeyrn, he left himself vulnerable but if he did not send enough, then his brother might be overwhelmed.

"Diversion or no, they can't have too many men left to throw at us," said Cadeyrn.

"Very well," said Vortimer. "I will send all of our cavalry with you except two cohorts who will remain here. But take my armour. It was blessed by Bishop Germanus."

"You may need it yourself."

"You need it more. It is you who rides out now. Take it."

"Thank you, Brother. Pray for me."

Hengest

The deserted town of Durobrivae echoed with the tramp of Hengest's cavalry. The bridge beyond the town was a multi-arched construction of crumbling stone caked in moss. The river flowed sluggishly between its mighty legs; dark ripples reflecting the scudding clouds.

He wondered what had become of Vosenius and the gang leaders he had never had a chance to deal with properly. This town had been their little empire. Now it was nothing but shadows and ghosts. He supposed they had all fled and melted into the countryside to find new lives for themselves.

A small Welsc barricade stood at the other end of the bridge, hopelessly inadequate to hold off the advancing force. It was more of a lookout post and, sure enough, as Hengest's troops came into sight, a horseman galloped away from it to warn the camp.

"We don't have long before they are roused," Hengest said to Ebusa. "Take your squad across first and muster on the left to protect our flank while we cross."

Ebusa set off, leading his warriors across the bridge, four horsemen wide, their plumes flailing behind them.

Hengest watched, gripping his reins tightly, cursing the narrowness of the bridge that made such a bottleneck of his army. He wondered if the Welsc were yet alerted to the diversion led by Horsa. How many men would Vortimer send to fight his brother? If Aurelianus was incapacitated with grief or, better yet, on his way to his villa to see his daughter's body, the inexperience of the Welsc leadership would be their undoing.

At last the bridge was clear and Hengest led the remainder of his troops across himself. Aesc rode at his side and the dual horse banner fluttered above them, held steady in Ordlaf's hands. Soon, the two stallions would be reunited on the field once more and there wouldn't be a Briton that could stand against them.

Horsa

Centuries before, the bend in the river had been the site of a battle between the legions of Emperor Claudius and the Britons defending their island from conquest. Now, the Romanised Britons faced another invasion and that river knew the tramp of men passing across it on their way to war once more.

Horsa could see the Welsc approaching by the clouds of dust kicked up against the green hills. He struggled to make out the banners and cursed as they drew near. Cadeyrn's serpent was the only one visible. He had half hoped that Aurelianus would be stubborn enough to remain and fight.

"Form a shield wall!" he bellowed, and the clash of scores of shields clattering together roared like the foaming sea.

They formed a circle, many yards in diameter, shields overlapping and spears held outwards. For infantry to hold against cavalry was near suicide but the plan was merely to draw the Welsc close and then cut a retreat to the bridge. There, Horsa planned to engage them in a bottleneck and give Hengest enough time to attack the main camp further north.

The tension was almost unbearable as they waited for the inevitable strike. Hot, foul breath and humid body warmth collected within the shield wall. Prayers were offered to Woden, Thunor and Tiw. Horsa offered none. He was done with the gods and their mockery of him. His sole purpose in life now was to kill the Welsc.

The thundering hooves drew closer and then, with a sudden jolt that made the shields ripple like disturbed water, the blades and hooves of the attackers descended upon them.

The shield wall held for the most part, pushed and jostled by the sheer press of horses. Horsa's raiders thrust out spears, puncturing breasts and flanks and stabbing upwards at their riders. Some Welsc spears and sword tips worked their way between or over the great round shields, drawing blood from the raiders, but the damage was minimal.

The Welsc cavalry broke over the circle of raiders like waves over a rock; washing around them in a deadly tide. They now stood between Horsa's men and the bridge making retreat impossible until they made a second pass.

"Ready!" called out Horsa, his command passed on by his captains down the ranks. "Lift shields and cut them low this time!"

As the Welsc thundered past them again, shields were flung upwards on both sides of the circle, spears lashed out, axes and swords swiped at legs, hamstringing several horses that fell, screaming and rolling, crushing their riders.

"That's it!" Horsa roared. "Retreat to the bridge! Fast!"

Shields were slung onto backs and the raiders took off at a fast jog to the river before the Welsc had even turned around. They came at them fast, galloping hard on their heels. Most of Horsa's men made it across the bridge in time but several at the rear were cut down before they managed to set foot on it.

The Welsc were forced to slow as they met the river, hooves slithering in the mud, the press of horses, crushing and shoving. Some tumbled into the waters; hooves, manes and men cart-wheeling in silvery spray.

Horsa saw Cadeyrn bellowing orders to back up and his host edged back, foot by foot, clear of the rushing river.

He gave orders for another shield wall to form on their side of the bridge, ten men deep and six men wide. They waited for the Welsc to come to them and come they did; a handful at a time.

Hengest

Hengest couldn't have hoped for more confusion in the Welsc ranks. Men clustered around banners with none of the Roman order and formation he remembered from Aurelianus's command. The sheer panic at seeing Hengest's cavalry approaching caused riders, infantry and archers to hurry about, looking for their commanders and captains.

By the time Hengest's men had crested the slope the Welsc had arranged themselves into some sort of defensive line with most of their cavalry mustered on the right flank.

"They're going to try and outflank us," Hengest said to Ebusa. "You take your squads and guard our left. I'll lead the attack on the centre of their line and smash through them."

Ebusa galloped off to marshal his men. Hengest blew his horn and there came a great roar of elation from the ranks as they slammed the shafts of their spears against their shield bosses, the scent of revenge for all the wrongs they had suffered at the hands of the natives working them into a battle-fury.

They set off at a fast trot leading up into a gallop. The terrified faces of the Welsc loomed before them, pale and wide-eyed. Spears were lowered. Shields were raised.

They ripped into the Welsc like a knife slashing into a side of beef. Men tumbled over and over, trampled by hooves, skewered by spears, knocked from one side to the other by the hot, mad press of horses and the bellowing men who rode them.

Hengest's spear splintered against a Briton's shield and he dropped it, his hand automatically reaching for the hilt of *Hildeleoma*. The glint of that magnificent blade instilled yet more confidence in the hearts of those who saw it and its glimmering, rune-inscribed blade soon turned a metallic red as he ripped it through flesh and mail, shearing bone and parting skulls.

Far down the line, Ebusa's squads met the Welsc cavalry, tearing men from their horses and dashing down standards. They had a hard fight of it, cavalry against cavalry, but the Welsc were outnumbered, most of their riders having charged south to meet Horsa's men.

The screams of horses equalled the howls of men in agony as blades gashed bodies, hooves splintered bones and heads were struck from shoulders by axes and swords, some tumbling to the ground, some hanging by tendons while the blood spurted and the stricken men swayed in their saddles.

The Welsc, knowing that they were beaten, began to fall back. Horns bellowed the call for retreat. Their entrenched camp at their rear was their only refuge now and they made for it in a mad, disorganised dash. Hengest galloped up and down the line, instilling courage in his men and cheering their victory.

Vortimer

Vortimer was nearly the first back to camp. From the rear of the army he had witnessed the destruction of his people by the Saxon charge. They had not been ready. Most of his cavalry had ridden south with Cadeyrn. Almighty God, that had been a mistake! He cursed Aurelianus once more for his desertion. Had he been here, he would have organised a more effective defence. For all his parading about in polished armour Vortimer would be the first to admit to anybody that he knew nothing of warfare.

The Britons limped into camp in small, terrified groups. Vortimer set about placing them in defence of the ditches. The Saxons would pursue their attack, there was no doubt of that, and here they were trapped in their camp like cornered hares! He had to get Cadeyrn and his cavalry back. He didn't care if the Saxon infantry won the crossing in the south. Here, Hengest was throwing everything he had at them!

"Captain!" he shouted to a passing officer in a dented helm and half of his face masked with blood. "Send out a rider to my brother. Tell him to get his troops back here as fast as he can! Quickly! Before the Saxons pen us in completely and we are unable to send out for help!"

Aurelianus

The villa was cloaked in a sombre mood as if it were the centre of a grey thundercloud. Sorrow was written on the faces of Aurelianus's servants as he galloped into the courtyard and dismounted. The stable boy did not speak to him as he took the reins. The housekeeper and the cook stood at the entrance to the main building, their cheeks stained with tears.

He looked at them; his own tears refusing to come yet. *Not yet. Not until he had seen …*

She had been laid out on the dining room table. A physician stood nearby, called for in haste, but Aurelianus could see that there had been nothing the man could have done.

Her face had a pale bluish tint and her lips were dark. Her eyes were closed and she looked so peaceful as if she were sleeping. Then he saw the red band of raw flesh around her pale neck; dark and marring.

"She hung herself from the banister," explained the physician. "Your housekeeper found her. It took three servants to cut her down."

Aurelianus looked up at the banister as if he could still see her swinging there, reconstructing the dreadful act in his mind. If only he had been there … He could have stopped her!

It was then that the tears finally came. He felt his knees buckling beneath him and he stumbled, clutching at the table for support. He sank down and grasped his daughter's hand. It felt so cold! He kissed it and wept.

He had driven her to this. His beautiful, perfect daughter, dead because he would not listen to her. Because he refused to meet her halfway. His hatred of the Saxons and his pursuit of war with them had taken the one thing he loved in the world from him. His wife was gone. Now so too was his daughter and he was utterly alone in the world.

Alone but for his hatred of himself and the Saxons and all they stood for.

Horsa

"They're retreating!" shouted Beorn over the din of battle.

Horsa peered over the rim of his blood-spattered shield. The Welsc had fallen back and were cutting a retreat north, following the river. The battle on the bridge had raged all morning and everybody was weary.

Horsa had been replacing the front lines with troops from the rear every few minutes to keep them fresh and to plug any holes in their defence caused by fallen warriors. The river below was almost clogged with bodies and the waters ran red. The surface of the bridge was slippery with blood, intestines and shit.

"Makes no sense," he said. "They had us beat here. They only had to keep pressing."

"Your brother has probably decimated their camp and they need reinforcements," Beorn replied.

"Then we pursue!" If Aurelianus was still with the army than he was most certainly leading the defence against Hengest. And Horsa's bloodlust was still not sated though his sword arm was tired and his tunic was soaked with blood and sweat.

They set off at a measured jog, shields on backs and weapons cleaned and sheathed. The afternoon was hot and the sun beat down on iron helms making them unbearable. Mail weighed them down and the boggy scrubland sucked at their feet. But none fell behind for fear of shaming themselves in the light of their leader who ran on ahead of them like one possessed.

Hengest

They had them surrounded. Their camp with its ditches and barricades was hemmed in on all sides by his cavalry. Arrows soared out of the camp and fell short. Hengest was sure to keep his men out of range.

"We could starve them out," said Aesc.

Hengest shook his head. "I don't want to get drawn into a long siege. They may get reinforcements from any part of Britta soon. I want to crush Vortimer and Cadeyrn and smash their army so that no Welsc warlord will ever dare threaten Cent again."

"Their main gate is weak and hastily built," said Ebusa. "We could build a battering ram like you did when we attacked Gwrangon's villa."

"Not many trees about for timber," said Hengest, looking around at the flat scrub and marsh that was gradually turning to gold under the setting sun. "Send out parties to look for wood anyway. We may be able to assault the main gate tonight. I don't want to give them a moment to rest."

Men were sent out and construction of a ram and shelter was begun. Dusk turned all to a bluish fog over the muddy flats and the smell of roasting meat and fish began to waft from the campfires of Hengest's warband. No smells came from the Welsc camp other than those of shit and fear.

A faint trail of torch lights appeared in the south. Cries of alarm went up from Hengest's men and riders threw down what they were doing and mounted their horses.

"Looks like Cadeyrn's men are returning," said Ebusa, strapping on his helmet. "I'll lead a scouting party and see what's left of them."

Hengest suddenly felt guilty that he had not spared a thought for Horsa recently. If Cadeyrn's men were returning, did that mean that Horsa had failed to defeat him? Was he dead? No, most likely Cadeyrn had received word that his brother was under siege back at his camp and was riding to his rescue. *Well, let him come.*

"Everyone mount up!" he called. "We ride out to meet Cadeyrn and I want to see him smashed! Do not let them get through to Vortimer! Ride!"

Darkness was upon them when they met Cadeyrn's returning riders. The torches were the first things that were flung at them, sailing through the air, spraying embers. They bounced off shields and rolled to the ground, some spreading their flames to the dry reeds and grass and starting fires that the evening wind quickly spread.

Hengest saw Aesc beside him and was proud of his boy, at his father's side here on the battlefield that would determine the fate of their kingdom. After this there would be no more question. Cent was theirs, paid for in blood and witnessed by the gods of Britta and Germania. Here they stood, fighting for a homeland that would not be denied to them no matter how hard the Welsc fought.

And they fought hard. Horsa's attack had, after all, only been a diversion and many of Cadeyrn's warriors had survived to ride back north. Shields slammed against shields and spearheads grazed helms in the thrust and pull, dodge and dash of horse-borne battle.

Hengest's face was wet with blood and scorched by the blaze of the fires that surrounded them. He felt as if he were battling through the realm of the Fire-Ettins, fighting his way to freedom, to blue skies and cool breezes and the glory of triumph.

"Folcwalda!" came Ebusa's cry. "Vortimer's warriors are escaping! We do not have the troops to contain them! They're heading for Londinium!"

Hengest cursed. "We cannot disengage! Cadeyrn's men will be at our heels every step of the way! Fight on! Fight on!"

Ahead, through the press of Cadeyrn's riders, he could see men on foot bearing round shields, cutting away at the rear of the Welsc.

"Horsa!" he shouted! His brother was alive and had followed Cadeyrn all the way here, on foot! "Press through!" he roared at his men. "Press through! Horsa and our countrymen stand on the other side of these whore-sons!"

They renewed their attack with fresh vigour, thrusting faster, harder, penetrating deeper, deeper into the Britons. Blood flowed from a hundred torn torsos that tumbled from their saddles, only to be trampled by the indomitable march of hooves, spurred on by frantic, eager heels.

Over the wavering banners and fire-tinted helms, Hengest believed he could make out his brother leading the attack, his blood-spattered shield half hacked away, his glinting blade swinging, hacking closer and closer, increasingly isolated and surrounded by hostile Welsc riders.

"Get back, Horsa!" Hengest bellowed. "You're too far forward! Get back to your men!"

He watched in horror as Horsa pressed on, dodging spears, hacking at shafts and flanks, dwarfed by the Welsc who towered above him on their steaming steeds. A madness had possessed him, that much was clear even from a distance; a madness that Hengest knew the cause of. His brother, who had been so distant to him over the past year, was mourning for a love he had lost, a world that didn't understand him and a brother who had failed him.

"Horsa!" Hengest found himself bellowing, as he saw the Welsc spear puncture his chest. His brave brother seemed momentarily shocked by it and then, as if in defiance, ignored it and fought on, restrained by the long, bloody shaft that transfixed his body.

A second spear found its way past his shield and he dropped it, gasping. He brought his sword up and hacked through the shaft, and again at the rider who wielded it, slashing through his belly and pitching him from his saddle.

A third spear drove cruelly into his thigh making him buckle and sink to one knee. A fourth and a fifth shaft speared his body, turning him into a grotesque puppet before he toppled over, his face a silent mask of pain.

Hengest covered his streaming eyes. He could not watch any more. He felt the rush of his own men flood past him, pursuing vengeance for the death of their leader's brother. The battle became muted in his mind. He heard the clash of iron and the screams of the dying, but it was a far away sound, like noises in a dream.

Horsa is dead.

In that moment, it was all he knew.

They had won the battle. Vortimer and the remnants of his troops had fled back to Londinium and Cadeyrn's force had been routed and mostly slaughtered. Hengest's men were scouring the moon-lit countryside for stragglers, cutting them down. But all knew that it had been a costly battle and the victory could only be bittersweet.

The dozens of fallen warriors and their horses that littered the battleground reminded them that all victories have a sour aftertaste and, as news of Horsa's death spread, this one in particular became almost intolerable.

Hengest gazed upon the lifeless body of his brother in the confines of his tent, pale skin waxy in the torchlight. There was nothing to be said now between brothers. Horsa had been led by one of his blind rages; a rage that Hengest had encouraged because it had aided his plans.

"I'm so sorry, Horsa …" he mumbled, as he cupped the side of his brother's face.

"Folcwalda," said Ebusa, poking his head through the tent flap. "We have captured Cadeyrn. His horse stumbled as we pursued. There is nothing left of his cavalry now."

Hengest rose without a word and left the tent.

Cadeyrn was a broken man on his knees, his hands bound behind him. Blood streamed down his face from numerous blows. Ebusa's men had not been gentle.

"We could hold him for ransom," said Ebusa. "Or trade him for terms. Cent could be safe from attack for generations."

"Or trade him for another hostage," put in Aesc. "Hronwena perhaps …"

Hengest barely heard these suggestions. Even the mention of Hronwena fell upon numbed ears. He felt only rage as he walked around the Briton; his eyes spitting fire down at the trembling form.

In a sudden movement, he seized Cadeyrn's hair in a tight fist and drew his saex with his other hand. Before anybody could object, he placed the long blade against Cadeyrn's exposed neck and drew it quickly across.

Blood spurted from the ruptured flesh and Cadeyrn coughed and gargled. His lips showed red and his armour became awash with the stuff. Slowly, like a performing dancer at the end of their act, he bowed forward and slumped face down in the dirt.

"Well, so much for ransom and hostages," muttered Ebusa.

"Send his carcass to Londinium," said Hengest. "Let Vortimer know how it feels to lose a brother."

PART IV

(Ear) "Ear byþ egle eorla gehwilcun,
þonn fæstlice flæsc onginneþ,
hræw cólian, hrúsan ceosan
blác to gebeddan; bléda gedréosaþ,
wynna gewítaþ, wera geswícaþ."

(Grave) "The grave is horrible to every knight, when
the corpse quickly begins to cool and is laid in the
bosom of the dark earth. Prosperity declines, happiness
passes away and covenants are broken."

Vortimer

The mood in Londinium was a sullen one. Defeat for the Britons was no new feeling – they had been weathered by decades of inter-tribal conflicts and Pictish invasions – but to be defeated by mercenaries in their own employ was something new. That they could fail to win the war had not even been considered and the citizens of Londinium were divided on whom to place the blame. Many cursed Vertigernus for giving the Saxons so much land in the first place while others cursed Vortimer for failing to crush Hengest and his vermin.

For his part, Vortimer cursed Aurelianus. His absence from the field had been the one thing that had swung the battle in the Saxons' favour. He had dispatched messengers to the general's villa but all had been turned away. Aurelianus was holed up within its walls and had guards loyal only to him protecting the perimeter as if it were a tiny fortress. The word was that his daughter had hanged herself and Vortimer wondered if it had anything to do with Horsa. Not that it mattered. A good soldier did not abandon his duty no matter his personal troubles.

And it seemed that Horsa hadn't been assassinated after all. His sudden appearance on the battlefield had been a surprise to them all, and for Vortimer it had been yet another blow to his confidence in his authority over his agents. Maelona had either failed or betrayed him. Perhaps Antoninus had been in on it. He wasn't sure of anything these days.

News had reached him that Horsa had finally been killed during his mad battle-charge but Vortimer found himself unable to rejoice at this. To learn of an enemy's death when you believed him to be dead already was a small thing to celebrate. It hardly mattered anyway. Hengest was still alive and was no doubt celebrating his true victory.

Scouts reported that the Saxons had returned to their homes, confident that their kingdom was safe from attack for a while. It most certainly was. Vortimer doubted that if every last hill chieftain and Pictish ally sent every man they had, he would not have the manpower to oust the Saxons now.

And Cadeyrn was missing. That boded ill. It was the engagement of his forces with Hengest's army that had allowed Vortimer and his men to escape. He would never forgive himself if anything had happened to him. He had men scouring the countryside and reports were coming back to him that the Saxons had joyfully cut down Cadeyrn's fleeing men.

Dishonourable, murdering heathens!

Footsteps echoed down the hallway. A captain in full armour approached. "Lord Vortimer, I am afraid that I bring distressing news."

"Well out with it, then," said Vortimer with a sigh. "More ill news will hardly sour my mood further."

"The Saxons have sent us one of our dead."

"*One* of our dead when our men litter Cantium's fields in their hundreds? What jest is this?"

"It's your brother."

Vortimer swept from the room and bounded out into the courtyard. A cart with mud-caked wheels awaited him, a motionless figure laid on top of it. Two servants had removed his armour and were in the process of cleaning the pale skin with damp cloths. Vortimer elbowed them aside.

It was Cadeyrn all right. His boyish face was tilted up and his eyelids were open just a fraction as if he were peeping at the stars. The servants had barely begun to clean him up. Clotted blood masked his chin, neck and chest and the ugly gash in his throat showed the tendons and severed windpipe. Vortimer looked away sharply.

"This is no battle wound," said the captain at his side. "They killed him in cold blood."

"They shall pay," said Vortimer. "If it takes me ten years to raise another army, I swear by God they shall pay."

"My lord, look!" said one of the servants who had been cleaning Cadeyrn's armour. He held up the breastplate he had removed. It was Vortimer's own breastplate with the serpent, eagle and fish. *So much for Bishop Germanus's blessing ...*

"There's something written here," said the servant, handing the breastplate to him. "Inside the rim of the neck. It's not Latin, whatever it is. I can't read it."

Vortimer peered at the inscription. "I can't read it either. All I know is that they are runes. *Saxon* runes."

Hronwena

Hronwena's cell had a small barred window that let in a little light. The view was of some kind of yard within the palace walls. She could hear the faint murmur of the streets on the other side of the walls as well as the cawing of gulls high above. The palace itself was morbidly quiet as if it were in mourning.

When she had been sent to Londinium from Vortimer's camp, she had been put up in one of the guest rooms with a guard at her door. Although she was a prisoner, conditions had not been too bad. A comfortable bed, hot meals, clean clothes and handmaids were things she had grown accustomed to since her marriage into the most powerful family in Britta. She was even allowed to roam the palace at will, although never without a guard accompanying her.

But there was little to see or do in the palace anyway. She knew nobody and nobody was interested in making her acquaintance. The only person of any status she recognised was Vortimer's wife. They talked on occasion and the lady of the palace did not show any particular dislike of her which was a pleasant surprise. She too was a warlord's daughter who had been married into this family of vipers. But she had accepted her position which was something Hronwena could never do.

All her freedoms had been snatched away from her the eve of the army's return. Vortimer's wife had received news of it in advance and set about preparing the palace for her husband's arrival. That they had lost the battle – and possibly the war – was clear as soon as the returning commanders set foot in the palace.

The reception halls were filled with wounded screaming out at the touch of the physicians. Soldiers in muddy, bloody armour warmed themselves by the fires and gorged themselves on the palace stores that had been laid out for them as if they hadn't eaten in days. Vortimer had only given his wife the briefest of greetings before disappearing to his chambers. He did not acknowledge Hronwena.

She had cursed to see him alive. Her rune spell had failed. Or she had failed to inscribe it properly. Vortimer should be dead. But she had other things on her mind. She asked everybody for news of her father and brother but none of them wanted to talk with a Saxon woman after so bloody a defeat at the hands of her countrymen.

They had come for her that night. There were no words of explanation. Two guards seized her while a third led the way down to the cells in the bowels of the palace. She had writhed in their grip and reminded them in no polite terms that she was still the wife of Vertigernus and step-mother to their master. It made no difference. The cell was cold and stank, and the slamming of the door behind her was like a slap in the face, bringing her to her senses. She was not lady of the house. She was a Saxon in a British camp. And she was a prisoner.

Not long after she had finished her breakfast of bread and water, keys jangled in the lock and the door to her cell creaked open. Vortimer stood, framed by the light of the torches behind him. Even in the dim light she could see that his eyes were red-rimmed as if from weeping.

"Why am I here in this cell, my lord?" Hronwena asked him. "Have I displeased you? Have I shown myself to be untrustworthy?"

He did not seem to hear her. "The war is over. We lost. But not before your uncle, the mighty Horsa, was cut down and pierced by a dozen spears."

Hronwena blinked. Was this a lie? She made no reply. Inside she burned to know the truth but she would not give this bastard the satisfaction. He was tormenting her with the information. But why? He had never shown such malice to her before.

"Despite his death your father is no doubt celebrating his victory by getting drunk and fucking his whores."

Hronwena ignored the insult to her mother and instead gloried at the revelation that her father was alive. *But what of Aesc? What of all the others?*

"I nearly didn't make it back to Londinium," Vortimer continued. "You would have liked to have seen me cut down while fleeing, eh? Well, my brother took my place in your villainous scheme."

Hronwena didn't understand what he was driving at.

"We found the runes you sour-hearted witch!" he roared. "The Saxon runes nobody in my camp knew but you, you who was only passing through and had opportunity to scratch them into my armour! I gave that armour to my brother who now lies cold and dead by your hand! It was your pagan sorcery that killed him and soon all shall know that!" He was interrupted by a sudden bout of coughing that had him doubled over and tears streaming down his red face. He wheezed and straightened, catching his breath. He did not look well at all.

"You doubtless played some trick on my father to worm your way into his bed – my mother's bed," he continued. "I don't know if you poured some herbal concoction into his wine or scratched your damned runes on to his goblet and I don't much care to learn the wicked ways of the Saxon faith. All I can tell you is that you will die as all witches should. In public and in agony!"

He whirled and turned away from her, slamming the cell door behind him. She could hear him coughing and hacking as his footsteps echoed down the corridor.

He sounded more than sad and defeated. He sounded sick.

Vortimer

Cadeyrn was buried on a dim and dismal day. It did not rain but the sky was a threatening grey as colourless and grim as the tombstones in the cemetery on the outskirts of Londinium.

As Bishop Calvinus read out the rites Vortimer looked around at the crumbling stones and the dank moss and fungi. How many generations upon generations of Britons and Romans lay here in eternal sleep? Here was where dreams went to die. He felt weak and had a raging headache. He wished that the bishop would hurry things along a bit. He needed wine and rest.

"Are you alright?" his wife whispered to him.

He realised that he had his eyes closed and had been swaying.

"I'm fine," he told her.

He wasn't fine. They were burying his brother; a brother he had only recently come to accept after years of resentment. Cadeyrn had proved to be a good commander and even a good friend. Their time as true brothers had been so cruelly short.

Back at the palace, he drank heavily and would see nobody. Eventually, exhausted and drunk, he retired to bed, slipping under the sheets next to his sleeping wife.

He awoke drenched in sweat and wracked with shivers.

"What's wrong?" his wife asked him. She reached out and touched his chest but withdrew her hand as if burned. "You have a raging fever!"

"I am not well …" he mumbled, and the exertion of speaking brought on a fit of coughing that had him doubled up, struggling for air. Liquid hit the back of his throat and he spat, spraying the sheets with dark blood.

"My God, Vortimer!" his wife wailed, rearing up and leaping from the bed. "You have the plague!"

She fled from the room and called for the palace physician, who stumbled along, rubbing the sleep from his eyes. After a few tests, the physician admitted that yes, it was the plague.

He and Vortimer's wife left the room quickly and Vortimer listened to their voices outside the door.

"None must know of this," his wife said. "If word gets out that plague has infected the palace there will be a panic."

"He must be kept confined," the physician said. "I will visit him but no other must see him. We shall burn incense and pray but there is little else that can be done."

"Do you think …?"

"It's possible. Once the fever has set in there is nothing to do but to pray and trust in God."

"Then we must be doubly sure that nobody knows. My husband has many enemies. Should they find out that he is weak or his life is in danger, then they will not hesitate to strike."

Vortimer wept tears of frustration as he listened to their receding footsteps. He lay awake, alone in the darkness for many hours, praying and praying. His words died on his lips as he drifted off into dark and frightening dreams.

Hengest

Horsa was not to be buried on land. The sea had been his true home and it was the sea that would carry him to Waelheall. Hengest demanded that he be given a burial fit for a hero in one of the old tales and so the funeral for Cent's mightiest warrior was prepared in earnest.

The *Bloodkeel* was a fine vessel, perhaps the finest they had, but sacrifice was one of the hallmarks of a Germanic funeral. Hengest consulted with its crew and all agreed on the ship's final voyage.

Horsa was laid in the hold and surrounded with bundles of wood and brush. Gold in the form of trinkets, belt buckles, cups, horns and arm rings were placed in the hold with him; gifts from the men who had fought and bled alongside him in life. For two days people came and the *Bloodkeel* began to weigh low in the waist with its precious cargo.

On a cold, misty morning the *Bloodkeel* was towed out to sea and a fire was kindled in its belly. Hengest and his family watched from the headland. Beorn, who had insisted that he be the one to set flame to his old vessel, rowed ashore as the fire began to lick up the mast and the smoke gathered about it.

Songs were sung as the ship continued to drift, further and further out, carried by the tide until it was a faint glow on the horizon. Perhaps it would wash up in Gaul as bits of charred driftwood, or perhaps it would sail on, blazing merrily until its flames were extinguished in clouds of steam and its cargo would sink down to be forever at one with the sea.

Beorn wept uncontrollably. In one day he was saying goodbye to his best friend and the best ship he would ever know. Horsa was destined for Waelheall where he had earned his place and the *Bloodkeel* would carry him there, like Earandel, sailing upon the starry mists to the songs of the Waelcyrie.

Hronwena

The first indication that something had happened was in the expression of the gaoler's face as he brought Hronwena her evening meal. He was about as friendly as might be expected for one in his job, but as he deposited her tray of bread, broth and sour ale, he cast a foul look of scorn over her.

"Should have hanged you when he had the chance," he spat.

"What?" Hronwena asked him.

"He's dead now, the Lord Vortimer, although I expect you've already seen that with your witch's sight."

"Dead? How?"

"Save it. Nobody in this palace is fooled by you anymore. Your time will come. They're arranging your execution as we speak, but if it were up to me I'd kill you here and now before your sorcery claims any more lives."

"I don't know what you're talking about. I did not kill Cadeyrn and as for Vortimer, how could I when I have been locked up here for days?"

He did not answer and left her with her meal to muse over this new turn of events. *Vortimer, dead?* How had that happened? It couldn't have been a battle or an assassin else the gaoler wouldn't have blamed her. He must have died of some sickness. He hadn't seemed well when he had come to visit her a few days ago. Perhaps the illness had quickly manifested and now all in the palace blamed her who had so recently had contact with him.

Whatever the cause, he was dead and that meant bad news for her. Who was in charge of Londinium now? Who was in charge of Britta?

The days that passed were agonizing for her. Every morning she expected guards to march into her cell to drag her away to her execution, but every morning came and went and still the gaoler deposited her food with only a sneer by way of communication. She was tempted to pry some answers out of him but her pride refused her to. She would not let him know that she was so desperately afraid.

She heard the disturbances just after the bells calling for Vespers finished tolling across the town. It seemed there would be no time for prayers that night. The palace guard marshalled in the courtyard outside her window. At first she thought that her father was coming for her, tearing Londinium apart to free her but the words of the soldiers soon dashed such hopes and she felt foolish for letting her imagination run free. It was a riot. Mobs ran amok in the streets and the guards were being organised to protect the palace.

Before night had fallen, Hronwena could smell acrid smoke on the breeze and hear the clamour of the citizens coming ever closer. She wondered if the town was showing its contempt of a new ruler. Or perhaps there was some sort of coup underway. It became clear that they were at the gates and she could hear the panic in the corridors beyond her cell door as people fled or barricaded entrances. The mob was winning, it seemed.

She called out to her gaoler as he hurried past but he ignored her. Heavy blows sounded on the door at the end of the corridor and, through the bars, she could see the gaoler arming himself with helm and spear.

"Let us in!" cried a voice without.

"Get back!" the gaoler shouted. "I take no orders from drunken plebs!"

"Let us in at the bitch! You can't hide her from us!"

And with an awful sinking feeling, Hronwena realised that the mob's anger was directed at her.

The door was broken down in minutes and the mob forced their way into the cells. The gaoler was knocked down and stamped upon. His cries elicited a pang of sympathy from Hronwena for, although he was her gaoler, he had been the only man left between her and the mob.

His keys were seized and they began peering into the cells, seeking her out. She seized the clay water jug and scrambled under the straw that was her bed and desperately tried to flatten it down on top of her. They began unlocking doors and ransacking the cells. The other prisoners let out cries of freedom.

Finally, they came to her door. They unlocked it and fell in, ripping the straw from her.

"I've got her!" cried one of the mob, as Hronwena swung the clay jug with all her might down on to the man's nose.

Both jug and nose shattered on impact and a mixture of blood, water and snot splashed down onto the stone floor. The man cried out and two others jumped on her. She still held the shattered jug handle in her hand and swiped at their faces viciously but it was useless. She was disarmed in moments and dragged roughly out of her cell.

The mob had filled the courtyard outside and were baying for her blood. She had never heard anything more terrifying. Torches lit angry, hateful faces and curses in a variety of languages were thrust out at her like knives.

Real knives tore at her hair, cutting rough fistfuls free, making her scalp bleed. "Hang the witch!" cried out voices. "Death to the sorceress!" demanded others.

Her dress torn, she was dragged through the streets. Stones and shit were flung at her and her knees and feet scraped painfully along the cobbles as they pulled her along.

Up ahead she caught a glimpse of a beam that had been laid across two crumbling pillars. A rope with a noose hung down like a pendulum. *Oh, gods, they really do mean to hang me!*

Chants were taken up by the mob accompanied by cheers, jeers and laughter. The noose loomed closer and Hronwena could see the faces of her executioners lit like demons by torchlight.

There came a confused screaming as horses stampeded through the crowds, trampling and barging their way through. The crowd parted as several huge warhorses clattered down the street towards the impending execution. Hronwena was dropped to the hard cobbles as her captors tried to defend themselves against their assailants. Hot blood from a severed shoulder splashed on her face and she hid her head in her hands, wishing that she would awake from this nightmare.

She found herself being seized by arms once again and bourn aloft a horse. Stones and refuse continued to be pelted at her with an increased ferocity but a shield was held up to protect her from the worst of it. Soon they had left the mob in the streets behind and gates of the palace were being closed behind them.

Hronwena was taken into a reception hall and seated in a chair. Her rescuers seemed merely content to have saved her life and extended her no further kindness. No water was brought either for drinking or for washing her face.

She waited a while, shivering with fear and cold, holding the torn remnants of her dress to cover her body. Eventually a side door swung open and a figure entered. He was tall and elderly. A grin was stretched across his whiskered face that brought more terror to Hronwena's heart than the thought of the noose or the mob.

"Greetings, dear wife," Vitalinus said. "It has been too long."

Hengest

On the third day of feasting, messengers arrived from Vertigernus. It was known that Hengest's old ally had retaken power in Londinium after his son had mysteriously died. There had been riots in the interim but now those had been quelled and there was talk of a truce. There were also mutterings that one Briton was as bad as another and none were to be trusted, but Hengest agreed to receive the visitors as guests.

They found the hall drunk and melancholy. The feasting had switched between bouts of raucous drinking and song singing and deep slumps of sore brooding. Such were Germanic funerals and the Christian Britons looked about in astonishment as they were ushered before Hengest's table.

"As you can see, we are in the process of bidding farewell to my brother, Horsa," Hengest told them. "He was killed by British spears so if I were you I would speak my piece quickly and choose my words carefully."

The messengers took the hint and ploughed ahead, clearly eager to be done and out of the hall as soon as possible. "My lord Vertigernus extends the bough of peace to you once more, mighty Hengest," said the first messenger. "He regrets the bad blood that has passed between our two peoples but is confident that you know that it was not of his doing. His rebellious sons caused the grief and both are now dead."

"I have no quarrel with Vertigernus," said Hengest. "Indeed, he is family for is my daughter not his wife?"

"She is and it is my lord's most ardent wish that the treaty between Briton and Sais be renewed. He therefore presents you with these gifts."

Servants were called forward bearing a succession of shields, arms and drinking vessels in styles that ranged from East to West, Celtic to Roman to Byzantine.

"Tell your master that I thank him and that there is no bad blood between us. He lost his sons, I lost my brother. Let that be an end to hostilities. We have our mourning in common. I shall send gifts of my own back with you."

The messengers bowed and gratefully scurried out of the hall.

"Gifts?" exclaimed Halfritha in their bedchamber that night. "Your brother is dead and our daughter is in the hands of the enemy and you send them gifts?"

"It was not Vertigernus who began the troubles between our peoples," Hengest said in a tired voice. He was drunk and all he wanted to do was to sleep and to forget.

"The Welsc have been hostile to us ever since we set foot on their island," Halfritha went on. "This treaty was only ever a ploy for Vertigernus to control you and to get Hronwena into his bed."

"Gods, woman! What would you have me do? Continue the war with him when he offers us peace? Would you lose more of us in battle? Aesc perhaps? Or me?"

Halfritha narrowed her eyes. "I'm not one of your strategists, Hengest, but the way I understand it, you have the Welsc on their knees. Their army is smashed, their general is in hiding mourning the loss of his daughter, and their leaders are snivelling cowards who are forced to sue for peace rather than continue the fight they started. For all your ambitions, Husband, you

236

are showing a real reluctance to strike while the iron is hot."

"What need do I have of striking the Welsc now? I have my kingdom. Would you have me rule the whole island?"

"Your kingdom! Your bloody kingdom!" Halfritha exploded. "Is that all you think about? You have lost our daughter!"

She wept now and lay down on the bed, drawing the furs up over her.

Hengest stared into space. He continued staring long after Halfritha's breathing slowed to a low sigh. He left her then and went out to the stables. The gentle nickering of the beasts in their stalls comforted him and the smell of them was a pleasant reminder of happier times. He bedded down on the straw and thought long and hard until the light of dawn was shining in through the wooden bars of the window.

Hronwena

Hronwena had mixed feelings about her return to the west. She had not stopped wondering if Deilwen and Britu had made it back to Din Neidr safely and she desperately wanted to find out what had become of them. But on the other hand, after having come so close to her estranged family, to be carted off back into the British hills was heart-wrenching.

And the manner of her return was what upset her more than anything; a prisoner, a disgrace. *A witch*. The memory of her audience with her husband burned like a sore. He had not allowed her to wash up. She had sat there in that draughty hall, smeared with blood and shit, her dress torn and damp while he had questioned her as if she had instigated the rebellion herself. Her hatred of him had reached new heights.

With his two sons dead and Aurelianus vanished under unclear circumstances, there was nobody to stop Vitalinus from reclaiming control of Britta. Those spineless worms Elafius and Marcellinus had repented their oaths against him and came grovelling back, claiming that the rebellion had been cooked up by Vortimer and Aurelianus and they had been threatened into assisting them. Whether Vitalinus believed their lies was immaterial. He was back in charge and there was nothing they could do about it.

He spoke of the war as if it was a brief hiccup in the ongoing treaty with the Saxons and mentioned envoys sent to Thanet bearing gifts of peace. But any hopes Hronwena had of seeing her family again were cruelly dashed when he made it clear that he had not forgotten her treachery against him and her part in bringing his sons to turn on him. Her punishment was yet to be decided as was her guilt in the death of his two sons; traitors though they were.

She was to be sent back to Din Neidr and kept under close guard to await his return. There would be a trial, he had assured her, and if she had indeed played a part in Vortimer's and Cadeyrn's deaths, then she would die for it, his wife or not. He had saved her from death at the hands of a mob only so he could take his own vengeance on her.

How very like him.

The carpentium rattled into the fortress with none of the fanfare that had accompanied her first arrival over a year ago. The guards who had been loyal to Cadeyrn had been replaced and Hronwena was half expecting to see Marchud reinstated as captain of the guard but was relieved to see that he was nowhere in sight. She was promptly escorted to her chambers where a guard was placed at her door.

It was not long before a maid arrived bearing a meal for her and Hronwena nearly wept with relief to see that it was Deilwen.

"My lady, I am so sorry!" the handmaid said, as soon as the door was closed and they were alone together. "We have been hearing terrible things from Londinium. There is talk of riots and of you being accused of witchcraft and … oh Lord! Your hair!"

Hronwena automatically put a hand to the bare patches on her scalp where her beautiful golden locks had been hacked off. "Never mind that, Deilwen, I am here and alive. Now tell me, what happened after Vortimer's men took me?"

"My lady, I wanted to help and would have had I not had Britu with me. I headed north and we nearly starved on the way home. I am so sorry for leaving you, but what else could I do?"

"Hush, Deilwen, you did right. There was no way you could have helped and I am so very happy to see you here. But tell me, what of Britu?"

"He is safe with my family as he was before."

"And there has been no word from Gaul?"

"None. I doubt Germanus has even seen the boy yet and when he does he won't remember what Britu looked like. We did it, my lady! We saved him!"

"And Enys?"

"Lives here in the fortress but goes to visit her son whenever she is able."

"Thank the gods," Hronwena muttered. "You have done so well, Deilwen."

"It wasn't easy, my lady. It was a long trek back as you know, with bandits and mercenaries infesting the hills and forests. We slept during the day and travelled at night so as to avoid encounters, but with little food to be found along the way I praise God for giving us the strength to come through. And all the while I was thinking of your fate! What happened? They say that you worked some sorcery against Vortimer and Cadeyrn which brought about their deaths!"

"I will go into that later. Right now I need this food and a hot bath."

Aesc

"Why am I not to be at the feast, Father?" Aesc asked.

"Because the Welsc are tricky bastards, as we both know," Hengest replied. "I am taking a great risk in inviting their leaders here and I don't trust them. I have already lost one of my children to them, I don't intend on losing another."

Hengest had called the feast to reinstate the peace between their people and Vertigernus. The war had been unfortunate and had likely opened wounds between the two peoples that would take generations to heal. There were many who were sceptical of inviting the Britons to Thanet but there were also many who were sick of bloodshed and saw the reinstatement of Vertigernus as the leader of the Welsc as a good thing.

Octa fell into the former camp.

"Can't understand it," he said to Aesc. "Your father has always shown the highest of minds in dealing with those Welsc scum but now, so soon after they killed his own brother, he wants to welcome them here as friends!"

"He takes the view that it was Vertigernus's sons who broke the treaty," Aesc explained. "Not Vertigernus himself."

They were in one of the store rooms at the rear of the hall. Halfritha had set them the task of stocktaking. She needed all the help she could get in preparing for the feast.

"You seem a bit glum, young Aetheling," said Octa. "What's up?"

"Father doesn't want me at the feast," said Aesc. "I don't understand why. He wants to prepare me in every way to be his successor as Folcwalda and yet when the most important diplomatic event comes up, he shuts me out."

"Did he say why?"

"Something about it being for my own safety. Doesn't trust the Welsc. He knows I can handle myself! I've proven it again and again. I'm only just a man and I've already fought my first war!"

"I'm sure your father knows best," said Octa.

His mother walked in and planted her hands on her hips at the sight of them. "I didn't send you both in here so you could sit on your backsides shirking," she snapped. "Have you taken stock of the cabbages yet?"

Octa was already on his feet looking busy. Aesc didn't move. "Are you attending Father's feast, Mother?" he asked.

"Try and stop me," she said, as she began counting clay pots of honey. "Although the whole thing is the most disgraceful farce. Just another one of your father's bloody power games. Feasting with the enemy! I ask you! The smoke of the dead has barely dissipated. My only consolation is that it may lead to your sister's return to us."

"Oh? Is Father going to arrange for her return?"

"If he has a single honourable bone left in his body then he will make her return to us a condition of his bargaining. In any case, I will at least be able to see my daughter once more. Though I don't know how I will be able to stand seeing her at the side of that vile old creature."

Aesc gaped at his mother. "Hronwena is coming to the feast?"

She wheeled on him. "I should jolly well think so. She is, after all, the wife of our so-called ally. I made it quite clear to your father that I wanted her here so that

242

I could see with my own eyes if she has been mistreated in any way."

Having finished counting the honey pots she left the store house.

"She's been in an even worse mood than you recently," Octa said. "Begging your pardon."

"My sister will be at the feast," said Aesc. "So why then am I not allowed?"

Vitalinus

"And our weapons must be left at the doors?" Vitalinus clarified.

"No weapons in the presence of my lord and his family," said the Saxon guide. "He hopes that you understand, Lord Vertigernus, that this is not out of distrust of you, but certain others in your retinue have recently been at war with him."

Vitalinus felt Elafius and Marcellinus shifting uncomfortably behind him. He smirked. *So they should.*

"And the Saxons will also follow this rule?" Elafius asked. "There are to be no blades worn by either party?"

"That is correct," the Saxon answered.

"What about those great long knives you all carry with you everywhere?" asked Marcellinus. "Are they to be prohibited also?"

The Saxon smiled at him coldly and rested his hand on the handle of his saex. "These are our eating knives."

Vitalinus forced a smile. He felt the apprehension of his colleagues. They were venturing deep within the heart of Saxon Cantium. All the remaining members of the council had been invited to this feast that was supposed to heal the wounds caused by the war, including Aurelianus. Hengest had not yet been informed that the general had been struck from the council for his betrayal in the final battle and besides, the man would not even respond to messengers sent by British lords, let alone Saxon ones.

Naturally Hengest's invitation had been met with a near insurmountable level of opposition by the council. Lords Elafius and Marcellinus were quite rightly mortified at the idea of wandering deep into Saxon territory with no army to protect them. It was most probably a trap, Elafius had exclaimed. Why was a feast needed to cement friendship anyway? Marcellinus had asked.

Had either of the two lords any say in the matter they would have remained tucked up in their palaces but, as it stood, Vitalinus had them by their shrunken ball-sacks for their betrayal of him, and if he said that they would respond favourably to Hengest's request, then they had better start picking out outfits to wear.

And so, accompanied by a handful of guards, the remnants of the ruling body of Britannia rode into Cantium. A party of Saxons sent by Hengest met them in Rutupiae to ferry them across to Thanet. Elafius and Marcellinus looked at the shambling, festering town around them with the expressions of those who might be stricken with the plague any moment. There had been few reports of the pestilence in the south-east and Vitalinus knew that their revulsion was more due to the Germanic tongues wagging all around them and long-haired barbarians swaggering past.

Bishop Calvinus offered up prayers to God and sprinkled holy oil on the waves that rolled past the keel as they traversed the small body of water. It was as if they were embarking on a journey into the underworld. Vitalinus rolled his eyes at the cowardice of his fellow countrymen. He himself was eager to see how these Saxons lived and was intent on making a mental note of every characteristic of their camps and military defences. Should war ever break out with these savages again he wanted to be prepared.

Hengest did not meet them on the docks. A small retinue of his warriors escorted them up to his Great

Hall. Vitalinus had never seen anything like it. There had been various examples of Germanic architecture on their journey through Cantium in the form of smallholdings and the halls of minor chieftains, but this enormous construction of gables and thatch was a monument to a leader who wanted to stamp his mark on the land.

The guard that Vitalinus had brought were ushered away to their temporary lodgings. As requested, Vitalinus and the other council members unbuckled their swords and gave them into the keeping of the gatekeeper before being admitted into the hall.

Hengest greeted them as a king would greet his subjects and this attempt at power-play was not lost on Vitalinus. The hall was decked out with tables spread with food. Pigs roasted on spits over the great hearths and the Saxon lord's retinue stood on ceremony as the guests were led past the crackling flames to the dais.

"Welcome to my kingdom, lords of Albion," said Hengest in flawless British despite his heavy accent.

"I like what you've done with the place," said Vitalinus.

Hengest smiled. At his side sat his wife whose name Vitalinus could not remember at present. She was beautiful, that much he remembered. It had been a long time since he had seen her at the palace in Londinium and he was struck by how much she resembled her daughter. He wondered, briefly, if she was as savage in bed as Hronwena, and cursed the fact that he was unlikely to ever find out.

"Please be seated here, at my table," Hengest said.

Spaces were afforded the guests at regular intervals along the table with a Saxon between each. As far as Vitalinus could make out, it was for the sake of symbolism. There were to be no sides or factions here. They sat down.

"Where is my daughter?" Hengest asked. "Why have you not brought her?"

"She is unwell, I am afraid," said Vitalinus. "She so desperately wanted to come and see you both, but her illness prevents her from travelling."

"How ill is she? It is not the plague?"

"Goodness, no! A minor malady. We must arrange a meeting in the near future when she is recovered." Vitalinus smiled, as his lies were taken in. He could never have brought Hronwena here in her current state. If these Saxons took one look at her shorn locks and bruised face, he would never make it off Thanet alive. The only one who did not seem to believe him was Hengest's wife who fixed a cold glare on him that did not waver.

The feasting commenced and there was much horn lifting and rising from seats to proclaim everlasting peace and friendship between Saxon and Briton. Vitalinus eyed Hengest's wife. She had a face as sour as a crab apple. He knew that look. He had seen it on the face of her daughter at every banquet. It was the face of somebody who would rather be having their toenails pulled out, one by one, than sit through a formal dinner. She did not raise her cup whenever a toast was made and Vitalinus was left with no misunderstanding as to where Hronwena got her lack of discipline from if this was how Hengest allowed his females to act.

Hengest and his wife conversed in their own tongue and the words grew extremely heated. Vitalinus stifled a smirk. This fearsome leader of the Saxons was receiving such a thorough brow-beating from his wife that it was quite amusing to see. Hengest then spoke in a commanding voice. He seemed to be sending her away. She rose and left the table, her fine curves switching in irritation as she moved. She was indeed her daughter's mother.

"You must excuse my wife," said Hengest. "Her disappointment at not seeing our daughter overcomes her."

To lift the mood one of their bards was commanded to strike up a song. He strummed his odd harp quite pleasantly but the meaning of his words was utterly lost on the Britons who did not understand a word of Saxon. They continued to eat and the food was surprisingly good. Contrary to Vitalinus's expectations Saxon diet did not consist wholly of pork. There was game and fish and vegetables. Cheeses and fruits were abundant too and the bread, coarser than the stuff the British nobility were used to, was still good.

But most abundant was drink. Celts were not unknown for their capacity for alcohol, but these Saxons seemed intent on putting even the most debauched British chieftain to shame. Mead was the drink of choice for the Saxons but several barrels of imported wine had been opened, apparently for the benefit of their guests. Vitalinus enjoyed a drink with his meals as much as the next man and the serving girls who replenished their cups were nothing to complain about, but he became increasingly conscious that drink was being foisted on him and his countrymen with an almost aggressive generosity.

The feast was not even halfway over before they were all roaring drunk. Bishop Calvinus kept drifting off into a stupor and narrowly avoided planting his head face down on his platter on more than one occasion. Paciacus, the Master of Coin, roared with

248

laughter at the badly phrased jests of his Saxon dining companion and even Elafius and Marcellinus seemed to be enjoying themselves a little, their cheeks rosy and their lips stained purple from the wine.

Vitalinus tried to engage Hengest in banter. "These serving girls, Lord Hengest! By God! I would purchase a dozen from you to liven up my own mealtimes back at the palace!"

"They are not for sale," the Saxon chief replied. "Free-born women. Daughters, sisters and nieces of my thegns."

"Saxon women are fine creatures," Vitalinus went on, eyeing the cleavage of one who was leaning forward to pour Paciacus some more drink. "As tranquil on the outside as they are ferocious on the inside."

Hengest's face turned suddenly sour. He rose from his seat and barked out an order. All the serving girls put down whatever they were holding and filed out.

"You're spoiling the fun, Lord Hengest!" complained Vitalinus. He was suddenly aware that he might have offended his host. He was, after all, married to his daughter. But these Saxons pass their women around like whores, surely? What did he expect?

Hengest drew his saex, holding it high in the air so that the firelight glinted off its keen blade. It occurred to Vitalinus that he had not seen a single one of these wicked-looking blades being used for eating as the Saxons had claimed. And yet they are all wearing them as if they were religious talismans.

The words that spilled from Hengest's mouth were alien and ferocious to Vitalinus's ears. The rest of the Saxons in the hall had risen too and drawn their own blades. None of them seemed drunk anymore.

Aware that they might be misunderstanding some heathen custom, the Britons could only gape at their hosts, not knowing what to do. Vitalinus looked around the hall. The doors were closed and men had been posted to guard them.

When Hengest had finished speaking, the Saxons at the high table fell upon their British neighbours. Vitalinus's cry was caught in his throat as he saw a blade being drawn across Marcellinus's jugular, spraying the golden platter before him with crimson droplets.

Elafius struggled against his own attacker who held him in his seat with a meaty arm, reaching around and slitting the Lord of Britannia Secunda's throat as if it were old rope. Bishop Calvinus's face was already down in his dinner, this time put there for good by a Saxon blade, his blood pumping across the dark oak. *A man of the cloth, by all the demons in Hell!*

Vitalinus slithered down beneath the table and scurried along on his hands and knees towards the door from which the guards had left to join the fray. He reached it without obstruction and heaved at its carven handle. It did not move, bolted from without.

"Vertigernus!" roared Hengest from the other end of the hall. "There is no escape!"

Vitalinus looked around in horror. They were all dead; all his countrymen. Why had he been spared? What slow horrors awaited him at the hands of these savages and their long blades? He was aware of his bladder giving out and a spreading warmth at the front of his breeches. One of the Saxons guffawed and made a grab for him but Vitalinus was too quick, powered by terror. He scuffled under the nearest table; seeking shelter like a snake from a sharpened stick.

The table was flung aside with a tremendous clatter of goblets, horns, food and platters. Hengest, his blade still drawn, seized him by the scruff of his neck and hauled him over to the blaze of the hearths.

"Y …you … you betrayed your oath!" Vitalinus stammered, feeling the heat of the flames on his back. "We came in peace, you madman!"

"There will be no peace!" said Hengest. "Do you think I would trust a Briton after what your people have done to me? My brother is dead! Hundreds of my countrymen are dead!"

"That was not my fault!" Vitalinus cried. "My sons! My sons betrayed me! They betrayed our treaty!"

"How do I know that you will not betray me too? By bringing you to your knees, that's how! Look around you. All your leaders are dead. You are the only Briton of any note left and had my daughter been here, you would be dead alongside them. Now we both know that I can crush you any time I like. You will return my daughter to me immediately for I'll not have a child of mine in your viper's nest."

"M … my … my wife?"

"My *daughter*! And if she is harmed in any way, I will see that a similar fate is exacted upon you."

Vitalinus thought quickly, recalling the rapes, the threats and the beatings he had inflicted upon this lunatic's daughter since their marriage. If he returned her to him he would have a Saxon army on Londinium within days. He had to keep her! "I'll give you anything! Land! Provisions! But leave me my wife! She's all I have in the world!"

"Land I have, Briton."

"Cantium? Cantium is a timber yard compared to what I could give you! I'll extend your lands in every direction! I'll ensure that a yearly tribute of food and provisions is sent to you!"

"We do need grain," said one of Hengest's men.

"You'll get it," Vitalinus replied. "And more!"

Hengest appeared to consider this. He barked an order in his own tongue and somebody went hurrying off, returning promptly with a map.

The map was unfurled before Vitalinus. A debate then followed with much pointing and shouting, resulting in lands north of the River Tamesis including the old Roman capital of Camulodunum being ceded to the Saxons as well as lands along the south coast which provided fine hunting in the forest of Anderida. These were sizable territories and surrounded Londinium on three sides. Hengest's kingdom would be vast.

And yet they still wanted a yearly tribute of grain, leather and wool that would cripple the coffers of the Britons. Poor Paciacus, who lay face down with blood running off the table into a slowly congealing puddle on the floor, would never know the administrative hell his death had saved him from.

"Now that you have ruined Albion and made your kingdom the richest on the island," whimpered Vitalinus, "what surety do I have that you will not annihilate us?"

Hengest eyed him dangerously and he wondered if he had spoken too boldly. "What surety do you need?"

"Leave me my wife. I love her and her presence in my palace would be a gesture of peace between us. You know that I would not dare harm her after what has passed here tonight."

Hengest considered this. "Done."

With oaths and promises extracted from him, Vitalinus was escorted out of the hall and down to the harbour. The guards who had accompanied him were not present and Vitalinus was forced to assume that they had met a similar fate as his fellow council members. He was placed alone on the boat that would take him back to the mainland where he intended to gallop without stopping for the safety of Londinium.

Aesc

Aesc found out why his father had forbidden him from attending the feast on the morning that directly followed it. He had smelled the smoke before he had seen it. The foul, acrid stench was familiar to him for he had been present at many funerals in his short life. There was plenty of grumbling throughout the settlement and Aesc got the feeling that he was the last to know something.

From the western side of the hall he could see the flames of several pyres. Only a few men attended them, his father among them. There was no ceremony accompanying the burning of the dead and most of the villagers seemed content to watch from afar with sour expressions. As Aesc approached the pyres he recognised the cut of the cloth and the mail of those who burned and knew then that these had been their guests the previous night.

"Either you didn't trust my sword arm or my stomach, Father," he said.

His father turned to him. His face was grim. "Son, I trust you more than anybody. This was a nasty business in which I took no pride and it was because I wanted you to have no part of it that you were not at the feast."

They watched the bodies burn in silence for a while.

"Are they all here then? All of the Council of Britta?"

"No. I let Vertigernus live."

"The most dangerous of them all? Why?"

"He is the most dangerous because all the other Britons fear him. He will keep the rest of them in check. No other can."

"What of Hronwena?"

"Your sister is to remain his wife. Their marriage was always a union between our peoples and so it shall remain. I have merely reduced his power drastically and earned us even more security and prosperity."

"So it was all about land?"

"No. I wanted him to bring Hronwena to me. Then I would have killed him with the rest. As it stands, I cannot kill him for that would leave your sister alone in the hands of his followers."

Aesc's mother approached them. Her eyes were red-rimmed and blazed with a fury Aesc had never seen in them before. He guessed that she had heard of Hengest's deal with Vertigernus. She stopped within two feet of him and struck him hard across the face with all her might. Jaws dropped. Hengest wiped the back of his hand across his mouth and smeared away blood. She whirled and strode away, the wind whipping at her long dress.

"Father … I," Aesc began but didn't know how to finish. He felt bad for his father to be shamed like that in front of him. In front of everyone.

"Don't you worry, boy," he replied. "Women are even more temperamental than horses."

He had tried to make a joke of it but Aesc could see the pain in his eyes. He saw that he had been deeply stung and shamed.

Hronwena

Hronwena's attendance at her husband's welcoming party was entirely involuntary. Had it been up to her, she would have remained in her chambers and left all the grovelling to the sycophants Vitalinus had filled his fortress with. But, as wife of the restored ruler of Albion, she was expected to be there to greet him in the courtyard and her guards made sure that she was dressed, presentable and standing to attention along with everybody else.

Well, she would not cower, of that they could be damn sure of. Now that he had returned her trial would no doubt be held within days. Her fate, whatever it was, was drawing near. She thought of her mother and tried to draw strength from the memory of her, distant though it felt. She would not shame her by being weak. She would look him in the eye and meet whatever he doled out to her.

Her mother, at least, was somebody she could remember with fondness. Aesc too. But as for her father, may the worms devour him!

News had spread across Britta of the slaughter on Thanet. On all corners of the island Britons cursed her people for their treachery and her father in particular. But none felt a hatred of him equal to hers.

He abandoned me.

The feast had been a chance for him to send for her, to repent for his decision to marry her to a monstrous, incestuous rapist. But he had thrown that chance away for yet another land grab. Her father had died in her heart the moment she had heard that. It was clear to her that dirt and farms and livestock meant more to him than family. She knew that she would

256

never return to Cantium again. Never see Aesc or her mother again. Her hatred of her father would not allow her to go within a hundred miles of Thanet, even if she had been free to do so.

Well, she would die soon anyway. Maybe then, when her father received news of her execution for witchcraft, he might regret his actions. For all the consolation it brought her, she hoped that he would suffer for it the rest of his life.

She felt her flesh crawl as the carpentium trundled into view. Her stomach churned, not at the fate that awaited her, but at the occupant who stepped down into the courtyard. This man and her father were the two men she hated more than anyone.

For all the shame he must have felt at his humiliating defeat on Thanet, Vitalinus held his head high and walked with a slow, deliberate step, daring anybody to disrespect him. He approached Hronwena and she saw a glint of hatred in his eye for her. Nevertheless, he took her hand and raised it as he had done the day he had first brought her to Din Neidr. There was clapping, as there had been that day, and all were reminded that in this fortress at least, Briton and Saxon were united.

Later that night Hronwena prepared for bed. Deilwen brushed her hair in front of the large, bronze mirror. There was the sound of angry voices in the corridor outside. Deilwen went to see what the trouble was.

A kitchen servant was engaged in heated argument with the guard at the door.

"This fool wants her ladyship to go down to the kitchens," said the guard.

"There is a dispute over a delivery of salted beef," said the servant. "The head cook says he didn't order it and the trader won't leave until he's been paid."

"Well, the Lady Hronwena is confined to her chamber, you dolt!" said Deilwen. "Lord Vitalinus would flay us all if we broke his rules."

"What shall I tell the head cook?" the servant asked.

Deilwen let out an exasperated sigh. "I'll come and deal with it myself but give me time to finish up here."

The servant nodded and left. Deilwen resumed brushing Hronwena's hair.

"You can get off now, Deilwen," Hronwena said. "I'm quite capable of brushing my own hair. You'd best see to this dispute in the kitchens."

"I'm sorry about this, my lady."

"Pay it no mind. Rules are rules."

"I don't know what that trader thinks he is playing at, making deliveries at this time of night. Sleep well, my lady."

"And you Deilwen."

With the door bolted behind her and locked from the outside, Hronwena climbed into bed and lay her head down on the cold pillow. It always took her a long time to sleep knowing that there was a guard outside her door to prevent her from escaping.

Her eyelids had just begun to feel heavy when she heard more voices in the corridor outside. She was just about to get up and tell them that prisoner or no, she was entitled to a decent night's sleep like anybody else, when a key grated in the lock and the door swung open. Three armed men entered and for a horrible moment she was reminded of the mob storming her cell in Londinium.

"You are to come with us, my lady," said one of them.

"Where? Why?"

The man did not answer and the other two went to seize her by the arms. They did not give her time to put on anything more modest and she found herself being marched down the hallway in her nightshift. It was not long before she realised where they were taking her and only then did she realise. Deilwen had been called away for it was Deilwen alone who would try to defend her now. She began to struggle.

"No! Please! I beg you!"

The door to Vitalinus's chamber loomed ahead. They entered without knocking and dragged her to the feet of her husband. He stood over her with a smile. His arms were crossed and in his right hand he held a short horsewhip.

"Check her," he said.

Hronwena winced in humiliation as one of the guards ran his hands up under her shift and around her bare thighs to make sure she did not have a concealed weapon. Of course she did not. The dagger Deilwen had given her had been confiscated when she had been taken to Vortimer's camp.

"Bind her," Vitalinus said, handing one of the guards a leather thong.

Her hands were fastened tightly behind her back and she was forced down over the edge of the bed.

"Not her legs. I want them open. Good. Now, leave us."

Bent over in this humiliating position, Hronwena heard the guards file out of the room and the door swing shut followed by the key turning in its lock.

"Now then, wife of mine," Vitalinus drawled, turning from the door and stowing the key behind his tunic. "Finally I am free to tame you."

His fist gripped her hair and pressed her face down into the bed sheets. She struggled but found herself utterly at his mercy.

"I have been looking forward to this," he hissed. "For all the disrespect, for all the injuries you and your family has shown me, finally you are mine to do with as I please. My treaty with your father prevents your execution, but perhaps I can find a fitting accident that will not arouse suspicion. But first, I intend to enjoy your suffering as payment for the suffering you have caused me."

As he lifted her shift and exposed her bare skin to the coldness of the room and his icy touch, Hronwena came to realise that it was never going to stop. It would never be over. Not until he was dead.

Aesc

Germanic custom forbade hostility to guests. It was a strong taboo, so the victory over the Britons and the furthering of Cent's borders was not met with uproarious cheer. Vertigernus had been defeated once and for all. The rulers of Britta who had opposed Hengest were ashes on the wind and the standard of the dual horse had been planted so firmly on the island that nothing would ever threaten it again. *But at what cost?*

Aesc could sense the bad feeling in the settlement. Only a handful of his father's men had known about or been involved in the plot. There were many who said, although not in his father's hearing, that a grave crime had been committed, a crime that had not gone unnoticed by the gods. Slaughtering guests sounded like a good way to lose one's seat in Waelheall.

When Aesc's mother had struck his father, it had been as if she had acted on behalf of all his followers. The blow symbolised their outrage at his actions and, while she merely thought of her daughter, they thought of the honour lost.

Her anger at him had not been sated by the slap and she had taken to sleeping in an adjacent chamber at night. This had not gone unnoticed and served to further fuel the gloomy atmosphere on Thanet. If the Folcwalda and his wife could no longer share a bed, what did that say for the rest of the kingdom?

His father tried to ignore it all by throwing himself into his work. There was much to do. Fortifications needed strengthening, ships outfitted, settlements supplied and warriors trained. Aesc rode to Dubris with his father and Beorn to oversee the construction of

261

some new ships when his father was struck another blow.

It was Aesc who noticed the three small boats that were being loaded down on the wharves. The men loading them were ceorls: traders, butchers, tanners and potters. They had their families with them and seemed to be loading every item of their livelihoods into their vessels.

"What is that lot doing?" his father said. "They look as if they're making ready to leave!" He strode along the wharf to them and demanded to know what was going on.

One of the men – a potter – explained without meeting his eye. "We're heading back to Jute-land. There's no place for us here."

"No place?" Hengest exclaimed. "I have just assured us a generation of peace, you fools!"

Only then did the man's eyes meet his. "But was it a peace bought honourably?"

Aesc saw his father's face redden and he grew worried that he might strike the ceorl. "What do you mean by that remark?"

"I meant no offense, Folcwalda, but enemies or no, it bodes ill to slaughter them when they are our guests. We are not the only ones who are afraid that the gods have been displeased. Crops have not been good this season."

"And you think that has something to do with me?"

"The holy men say that the connection between land and ruler is strong, lord. If a ruler fails his land, his land fails him. That is how it has always been."

"What is there back in Jute-land for you? Poorer crops, tribal wars and licking the arses of Danish kings?

I have forged a kingdom here for you all and you repay me by abandoning it?"

The ceorl did not have an answer and they continued loading in silence. Aesc could see that his father knew it was useless to argue. He turned from the wharves and strode to the nearest tavern. Aesc followed.

There were few people in the tavern at this time of day and his father's guards stood watch at the entrance so their lord would not be disturbed. Hengest went over to the hearths. Aesc drew up a bench and joined him. "I'm losing my grip on my people, Son," he said.

"A few ceorls don't speak for the whole kingdom," Aesc said, dutifully trying to raise his father's spirits.

"I have the horrible feeling that they do. How have I made such a mess of things? My wife won't share my chamber. My daughter is lost to me. Do I still have you, at least, Aesc?"

"Always, Father."

He smiled and patted him on the shoulder. "That gives me great comfort, boy. At least when my business on Middangeard is done I will know that my kingdom will be in safe hands. I have raised you and trained you to be a king, Aesc, you do realise that, don't you? That is why I have never worn a crown myself. I wanted you to be the first King of Cent. The first of the dynasty that your father and uncle forged out of blood and fire. Do you feel ready?"

Aesc paled. "No Father … not yet!"

"Of course not!" his father replied with a smile. "A true king never feels ready for his responsibilities. That is how I know that you are fit to rule. So tell me now, young Folcwalda, king to be, what should I do?"

Aesc was lost for words. "About what?"

"About this damned situation I've got myself into. If I don't find a solution I risk losing more and more of my followers daily. Pretty soon I won't have a fyrd left to defend Thanet and then any Welsc warlord can take it from me. I'm asking you for help, Aesc."

Aesc thought for a moment. His father had never asked his advice on anything. All his life he had looked up to him and strived to please him. This sudden plea for help was both embarrassing and worrying. "What happened at the feast is done and cannot be changed. But ... mother still might be won back to your bedchamber."

His father narrowed his eyebrows at him. "It's your sister, isn't it? Do you miss her?"

Aesc nodded. "It was not for me to disagree with your decision to marry her to Vertigernus. And perhaps it was necessary for the treaty."

"But look at that treaty now. It has cost me nearly everything."

Aesc suddenly felt angry at his father, sitting there moping when he had always been a pillar of strength for everybody around him. "Then take it back!" he found himself saying, perhaps a little harshly. "Don't let everything you have fought for go drifting off on the morning tide. Fight to keep it!"

His father looked a little surprised but also a tad proud. "How? Where do I start when my own wife and half my followers have lost their faith in me?"

"Get Hronwena back."

He shrugged. "That would please your mother, I'm sure, but my followers don't care about my family or my marital troubles."

"That is where you are wrong. Hronwena is a symbol of the honour we have lost. And a leader's followers put much stock in the health of his marriage. Reclaim her and we reclaim what the Welsc have taken from us. Give our men something to fight for. All this sitting around has turned your men fat and irritable."

"You want another war?"

"Vertigernus is a shadow of what he once was. He is a wounded old boar that awaits only the killing thrust."

His father straightened as if filled with new vigour. "I never had you down for beating the war-drum, Aesc, I must admit. You have grown so much in the past year and I am so very proud of you. Londinium is poorly defended. I have no doubt that we can take it if we wish to. But think on this: is it just? I have already shamed myself in the eyes of my people by slaughtering guests. Would not an attack on our allies bring more shame upon me?"

"As I said, that damage is done," said Aesc. "And war is war. The only way to regain some honour is to create such a bloody havoc on this island that the gods themselves would be impressed. That's the sort of thing Uncle Horsa would have said."

That almost drew a smile on his father's worried face. "Aye, it certainly is," he said with fondness. "You are perhaps more his nephew than you are my son."

"Take Londinium, Father. Kill Vertigernus and bring Hronwena home. Besides, our men would be so dazzled by the chance to loot Londinium and spill Welsc blood that they would quickly forget that a taboo had been broken."

"Do you think my men will follow me still?"

"The sooner we ride the better. Ordlaf and Ebusa would follow you into the realm of mist and shadow. Octa too is as loyal as a wolfhound."

"And Beorn? Your uncle Horsa's men look to him as their leader now, not me."

"I do not know. But you must make them follow you."

They returned to the wharves where Beorn was still going over plans with the master shipbuilder. They explained their plan to the scarred sea-raider. He looked Hengest directly in the eye.

"I did not agree with the massacre of our guests, Folcwalda," he said. "I thought it shameful and an offense to the gods. But honest war is no shameful thing. And I welcome the chance to spill a river of blood in Horsa's memory."

"Then you and your men are with us?" Hengest asked.

"Your brother trusted you in the end. And I trusted him like no other. If he saw you as the rightful Folcwalda of our people then so do I. You have our blades, our ships and our hearts."

Hengest

Hengest wanted to come upon the Welsc by surprise and give them no chance to send out to any of their allies in the west or the north for assistance. He instructed Beorn to take their fleet up the Tamesis, ready to reinforce his warband which would follow the Roman road. They carried no wagons of supplies nor drew any camp followers. This was to be a quick strike and once victory was secured, Londinium would yield more than enough food, loot and women for all of them.

They left the deserted town of Durobrivae and crossed the river into Welsc territory. Hengest was surprised by how many Germanic settlements existed outside of Cent's borders. Men and women flooded from their homesteads to see the passing warband and when they were told what their destination was, many took up arms and joined them. Soon his ranks had swollen significantly, not with warriors, but with farmers, tradesmen, shepherds and villagers. *Let them join*, he thought. This battle was for all of them: every Germanic settler who had crossed the sea seeking land and favourable crops and who now struggled to survive in a hostile land. *Let them partake in our final victory.*

The road to Londinium was in poor condition. Grass poked up from loose cobbles; grown bold during the lull in trade due to the recent unrest. Where the road crossed a tributary of the River Tamesis a Roman trading settlement had been built around the ford. The Romans had called it *Noviomagus Cantiacorum* but the local Germanic speakers simply referred to it as Crecganford: 'the ford on the creek'. Timber watchtowers guarded the wooden bridge and the settlement lay abandoned. Framed between the two towers was a hill, distant in the mist, where a third watchtower stood. Around the foot of that watchtower many tents had been set up.

This was where the Welsc planned to make their stand.

Hengest knew that news of their advance would reach Londinium before long and he was pleased they had managed to get this far unopposed. The ford was a natural defensive point and as they approached, the Welsc mustered themselves and formed a line on the western bank. Beyond the silent watchtowers he could see the standards of their enemies: the fish of Londinium, the serpent of Din Neidr, along with the family sigils of several petty local nobles. It was a small force and nowhere could he see the standards of Ambrosius Aurelianus. He was almost sad. He would have liked to cut down that snooty bastard here at the end of all things.

Hengest drew his warband up and sent riders to call Beorn's raiders to make landfall and join them. They vastly outnumbered the Welsc and it should be a short battle despite the bottleneck of the ford. Barricades were being constructed between the watchtowers but it would do no good. The tide was on its way out and soon the river would be shallow enough for Hengest's warband to cross the mud wherever they liked and flank the enemy on both sides.

Hengest organised his warriors – giving Aesc control of the right flank. It was time for the lad to be given more responsibility and, by being closest to the River Tamesis, his flank would soon be bolstered by Beorn and his raiders when they arrived.

The lust for battle hung over them, and although Hengest was not much for gallant speeches the like of which they heard in the songs, he felt that the time called for a quick address that would remind his followers of why they were here.

"Follow me close," he said to Ordlaf.

Together they rode out in front of the warband. All eyes were on the fluttering banner with the dual horse-heads.

"Men of Cent!" Hengest cried, making his voice carry as far as it could. "Jutes, Saxons, Angles, Danes, Frisians and all the rest of you who are under my standard! You who came across the sea hoping to find a home and those of you who had homes here ere I came! You all followed me and did me proud. But in return you have suffered betrayal. Betrayal by our Welsc allies and betrayal by my own weaknesses! Now I ask you to ride into battle once more, but not for myself! I ask you all to ride for your families and your homes and all that you hold dear!

"We have fought and carved out a kingdom here in Britta, a kingdom that those across the river have tried to take from us! This is our land now! Ride and fight with me so that your children's children can live in peace in a land that they will know without question belongs to them! Ride now for home! For family! And for our united people!"

There was an uproarious cheer that startled Hengest. He did not know if his speech had indeed united them in a common cause of if the tension before battle had been seeking an outlet and had finally found one. Either way these men screamed and shook their spears with such vigour and gusto that it brought a tear to his eye.

269

He turned and faced the Welsc host. He drew *Hildeleoma* and let the light shine along its blade. He did not even give the signal to attack. His men had taken it upon themselves and rushed past him, making his mount step nervously from side to side until he spurred it on, not wanting to be left behind.

Welsc rule was over. Britta would never be the same again.

His two flanks splashed through the river, the mud sucking at them and the slow current tugging at their thighs. The centre ranks pushed and jostled each other as they squeezed onto the bridge, six men wide, shields held up, spears bristling. Arrows sailed out from the west bank, and as they drew closer, javelins were hurled, thudding into shields, punching through leather and mail or vanishing into the churning river.

The men on the bridge broke upon the barricade and began tearing and hacking at it while the Welsc hurled their missiles from behind it. Hengest and his cavalry followed the left flank, which was already scrambling up the west bank, tearing down the flimsy palisade that joined the watchtower. They met British spears which thrust and stabbed, trying to keep them in the shallows which already ran red from the drifting corpses.

Hengest urged his mount around the mass of warriors who were locked in battle with the defenders and, the mud sucking at its fetlocks, forced it up the embankment. They had successfully flanked the enemy which was too engaged with the infantry to notice. Hengest rallied his men into a loose formation and charged, spears lowered. They cut through the side of the Welsc ranks like a knife through butter and Hengest heard cheers from the bridge and the river. The Welsc turned and fled from his charge, leaving the bridge defences unmanned.

Up ahead, Hengest could see Aesc and his riders charging the Welsc on their right flank, bolstered by many footmen which he could only assume were Beorn's raiders from the ships. The Welsc were outflanked on both sides. The men on the bridge finally forced themselves through the barricade and formed a shield wall between the two watchtowers. The wall advanced, pushing the enemy away from the river.

It was over. The Welsc turned and fled back to their camp atop the hill. Hengest's warband went wild. They took the hill from two directions, Hengest leading the left flank and Aesc the right. In the middle marched the horde of footmen, those with shields and spears at the forefront.

It was a massacre. Exhausted and on foot, the Welsc scrambled up the hill but were ridden down by the Saxon cavalry. When they reached the encampment, Hengest ordered the tents burned as well as the watchtower. By the time the infantry crested the hill, the camp was a roaring inferno and the fleeing remnants of the Welsc resistance could be seen in the distance, trickling back up the road to Londinium.

"It's like the old days, eh, Beorn?" Hengest said, as they took a moment to fill their bellies from the stores that had been rescued from the burning camp. They stood by the road, the hill with its blazing watchtower behind them and the way to Londinium open before them.

Beorn nodded. "Almost."

Hengest knew what he was thinking. *Horsa should be here.*

"Your brother lived for this life," said Beorn after a while.

"We'll avenge him, Beorn. A hundred times over."

"Your son did well leading the right flank."

Hengest looked over at Aesc who was laughing and sharing a skin of mead with some of the thegns. "The time has come for him to lead our people. I won't be around forever and he must command the fyrds without my help."

"He's a good lad. A good head on his shoulders. They'll follow him well."

"Will you follow him when I am gone?"

Beorn looked around at the trees and fields and sniffed. "Britta is my home now. My family live here. I grow my crops here. And, if I have to fight until the end of my days, no Briton shall take my hides from me. If your son is to lead us after you are gone, and if the gods allow me to live long enough to see it, then I'll follow no other but him."

Hengest smiled and knew then why his brother had loved and trusted this man as family.

Aesc

The attack on Londinium was to be a three-pronged one. Beorn was rowing his fleet up the Tamesis where he would lay waste to the town's docks while Hengest led the larger portion of the warband north of the town to engage whatever forces the Welsc had left at the fort. During this diversion, Aesc's warband would come upon the town's southern gate and force their way in. This triple attack would overwhelm the Welsc and win the town within hours, or so Hengest hoped.

Aesc sent out scouts and they returned with word that no Welsc companies could be seen. Many farms and homesteads lay between them and Londinium and Aesc forbade the pillaging of them. This was not out of some sense of kindness, rather he wanted no delays en route to their destination. They marched on; a trailing column of tramping hooves, fluttering banners and helms plumed with horsehair and topped with gleaming boar shapes. The Welsc who saw them pass fled in terror, taking their families and possessions with them, certain that their world was over.

The suburbs on the marshy islands south of the town were deserted. These inhabitants, at least, had got wind of the attack and had fled. As they approached the bridge with its watchtowers Aesc could see the burning docks. Beorn's ships were riding the tide in the middle of the river; the *Fafnir* and the *Raven* shooting fire arrows at the warehouses, while several smaller vessels had been beached on the mud and the men were now storming the wharves.

The diversion had drawn the defenders from the watchtowers to the town wall directly above the wharves. The helmed heads of the Welsc as they hurled missiles down on the attackers were nearly obscured by the swirling smoke.

Aesc parted his men so that the battering ram could be brought forth and set against the bridge gate. With no defenders left on the watchtowers, it was down in moments and Aesc struggled to keep up with his men as they crossed the bridge.

Their advance was noticed by somebody on the walls and clusters of bowmen could be seen hurrying along to defend the southern gate. Arrows began to soar down on them. Somebody had the bright idea of sending fire arrows and two had found their marks in the hide covering of the ram before the first stroke had fallen against the gates.

Each pounding stroke was accompanied by a cheer from Aesc's men. He squinted through the ash and smoke and could see Beorn's men hurrying along the mud to join their assault, the blazing wharves at their backs.

"We'll have that down in no time," Beorn said, jogging over to Aesc, his bald pate beaded with sweat and the head of his large axe red and sticky. "Any orders for when we get into the town?"

"Why bother?" Aesc replied. "This lot will run riot and no orders will keep them in check. This is a looting expedition for the most part. Let them loot. I myself shall proceed to the palace and find my sister. I shall need a good body of fighters with me."

"You can count on me. Shall I pick some men from my raiders?"

"Do that. Only hurry. Those gates will come down at any moment."

True enough the massive iron-bound gates splintered and tumbled inwards much to the elation of the attackers. The arrows from the towers had ceased now and Aesc guessed that the defenders had either fled or were regrouping somewhere behind the walls to meet them once they were inside.

They swept into the capital of the Welsc with gleeful abandon. The southern part of the town was mostly houses and shops and these were the first to meet the wrath of the ransackers. Doors were booted in and women dragged screaming out into the street while the contents of the homes were looted.

Aesc felt as if all control had been wrenched from him in mere moments. Most of the men he saw doing the looting were unrecognisable to him. So many hangers on had joined them on the march that he felt like a stranger amongst the looters.

Fires had already broken out in some dwellings due either to carelessness or arson. Up ahead loomed the forum and the ruined basilica, and to the looters, that meant booty. They surged ahead, hacking down any Welsc they saw. Aesc darted to the left side of the street; his sword drawn.

"Beorn! Where are you?"

"Here!" came the reply, and Aesc saw the bald head bobbing through the throngs towards him. He had twenty-odd men with him.

"Follow me," said Aesc. "The palace is only a few streets over."

They met little resistance. A few barricades were in the process of being hastily built but the Welsc who were building them fled at the sight of Aesc and Beorn's men advancing. The invaders tore down the barricades and hurried onwards.

The palace gardens were surrounded by a high wall set with iron gates. A few guards had marshalled in the courtyard and were hurling cobblestones over the walls at them.

"Fetch a timber or something," Aesc instructed his men.

A beam from a nearby dwelling was quickly commandeered and, shields held high, ten men began denting the gates inwards. It did not take long and soon they were in and on the defenders. The courtyard became slippery with blood that reflected the fires of the burning town. More Welsc appeared from the gardens and Beorn set off to meet them.

"We'll handle these if you want to get in and find your sister," he shouted.

Aesc just had time to see the sea-captain wheel his axe around and embed it in the skull of one Briton before the lot of them vanished into the shadows of the cypress trees.

"Come on," Aesc called to those of the men who had remained with him.

They used the same ram to batter down the doors to the palace and sent servants and maids screaming from them in a panic. Aesc vaguely remembered the layout of the ground floor and made his way to the rooms they had stayed in when they had been guests of Vertigernus. They were empty. How could he hope to find Hronwena in this maze of mosaics, marble busts and richly decorated chambers?

She would most likely be held on the upper floor and he darted for a wooden staircase, only just aware that none of his men were with him. He was suddenly alone. More chambers with bright hangings and objects of wealth greeted him. It was deathly quiet up here and he wondered how many Britons were hiding behind curtains or in cubby holes. The sound of the slaughter below echoed like ghostly memories as he passed from room to room, bedchamber to dining hall, looking for whatever room Vertigernus kept his sister in.

A sudden thought struck him. If Vertigernus himself was cowering somewhere up here then he would be the one to finally butcher the old goat. How fitting for Cent's first king to kill the last ruler of the Welsc!

He heard a faint screaming from some chamber near to him and ran, following the noise. He came upon several of his men who, apparently having made their way up a separate staircase, were assaulting a servant girl on a wide, silk-covered bed.

"Stop that!" he said.

"You can't deny us the spoils of conquest," said the man who was leaning over the girl and trying to force his way in between her thighs.

"Do you recognise me?" Aesc demanded. "It's Cuthlaf, isn't it?"

He was not surprised that he could remember this young thug's name for whenever there was a chance for swaggering, bullying or brutalizing women, Cuthlaf was bound to be involved. He was about the same age as Aesc, with darker hair and a permanent sneer of distaste on his ugly face.

"Fuck off," Cuthlaf said, and continued trying to force himself on the girl.

"I am your commander and I order you to stop!" Aesc roared. He had never faced direct insubordination before and it made him angry. He wasn't going to let this low-born oaf undermine his authority on the most important mission in his military career so far.

Cuthlaf got up off the girl and faced him. "Or what?"

Aesc's grip tensed on his sword and he made sure Cuthlaf saw it. "I need to find my sister. This girl might know where she is being kept."

"Fine," Cuthlaf said. "Be my guest. Only I get to have her when you're done."

Aesc glared at him as he helped the girl to her feet. She was weeping and through her tears he could see that she was very beautiful.

"Don't be afraid," he said to her in British. "I won't let anyone harm you."

She glared at him under her bedraggled hair which was black and hanging loose, torn free from the pins that had held it up. Her eyes were filled with a hatred of him that almost overrode her fear.

"What's your name?"

"Aeronwen," she replied.

"Do you live here in the palace?"

She nodded. "I am a chambermaid."

"Do you know the Lord Vertigernus and his wife?"

At the mention of his name she seemed to flinch. Then she nodded.

"Where are they?"

"Gone. My lord left over a week ago and her ladyship long before then. Before the treachery of you Saeson at your feast."

Aesc's head whirled. "Gone? Where?"

"West. To his lands in Britannia Prima."

Aesc could not believe it. It had all been for nothing. They were laying this town to siege for nothing! Vertigernus had lied to his father. Hronwena was already long gone when he had said that she was in Londinium. Now he had fled west too and with him their chance to end this thing.

Vitalinus

Vitalinus awoke drenched in sweat. He had been dreaming that Londinium was burning. He had seen his prized town – symbol of power in Britannia – blazing with a hundred fires and he had heard the screams of the people as they fled. He had smelled the stink of white-hot terracotta, burnt plaster and roasting flesh. Thank God it had only been a dream!

He yanked the covers off to dry the sweat that made his nightshirt cling to his chest. He was still so hot! The darkness of his bedchamber was thick. He was alone in his bed. Hadn't his wife been here with him earlier? Or had that been yesterday? He couldn't remember. She had become much more docile recently and he had stopped leaving her tied up after he had finished with her.

He sniffed the air. He couldn't tell if what he smelt was real or simply some lingering vestige of his dream, but he thought he could smell burning. Faintly below him, he heard somebody screaming. He sat up in bed. Somebody else screamed from a different part of the fortress and there came the shouts of men. The smell of burning was steadily growing stronger.

Fools! Some careless idiot had caused a fire! If he ever found out who, then he would make them sorry they had ever been born. He got up to put on his robe and as soon as his feet touched the floor, he withdrew them in shock. The wooden boards were painfully hot! The fire must be directly below his own chamber!

Forgoing his robe he hopped and danced over to the door and yanked on the handle. It didn't budge. Something had been jammed against it from the other side. He was trapped!

In a panic he began to tug and wrench at the door and call at the top of his lungs for assistance. Surely there must be some guard in the corridor who would hear him? But no, they would all be too busy fighting the fire on the floor below.

The heat was unbearable now and Vitalinus hacked and wheezed for smoke was seeping up through the floorboards and filling the room. He ran to the window but knew it was useless to even consider it. His chamber was too high up and he'd be killed if he jumped.

Down in the courtyard he saw soldiers running to the well and back with pails of water. He screamed at them and waved his arms but they could not hear him over the din of confusion and crackling flames.

Sweat ran down his face and the soles of his feet began to blister as he ran around the room in a state of madness. There was no way out! He doubled over in a fit of choking and stumbled headlong to the floor, unable to catch his breath. He felt the searing agony as the flesh on his hands and knees touched the hot wood but there was nothing he could do about it. His strength gave out and he collapsed face down on the floor.

He was not conscious to feel his nightgown and hair catch fire as the flames began to lick between the floorboards to consume the room, and him in it.

Hengest

The plains before the walls of Londinium were littered with the corpses of men and horses. The stench of blood and shit was nauseating and the carrion birds were already descending. Hengest looked around at his cavalry as they rode around in squads, dispatching those who cried out in their agony for death. Their losses had been slight. The Welsc had hurled every soldier they had left at them and had been entirely wiped out.

"They're refusing to open the gates to us," Ebusa said. "Don't they know when they're beaten?"

"They're just being stubborn," Hengest replied. "We would be no different. Aesc and Beorn must be tearing through the southern quarters of the town by now."

"We have some prisoners. Shall I order them to be executed within sight of the walls?"

"Good idea. It might persuade them to open up, if only to send whatever is left of their troops against us in anger."

"We have one of their crosses too. Great heavy iron thing they were carrying before them. Symbol of their crucified god. Fat lot of good it did them."

"Hack it to pieces next to the prisoners. I want them screaming with outrage."

The orders were carried out but neither the death-screams of the prisoners or the dismantling of their holy cross seemed to move anybody behind the walls.

"Pig-headed bastards!" Hengest cursed. "What does it take to tell them that they have lost?"

"They've stopped shooting arrows at us too," said Ordlaf.

"Maybe they've run out." He said it in jest but if it were true then an assault on the gate would be a very low-risk strategy. "Start building a ram. If they won't open up, then we'll have to force our way in."

It soon became apparent why nobody was answering from behind the wall, verbally or otherwise. No arrows assailed them as they began ramming the gate and once it was down there was nobody on the other side to challenge them.

"They've gone!" exclaimed Ebusa, looking around at the deserted guardhouses and empty stables.

Hengest dispatched men to climb the gate towers to make sure nobody was lurking about. "Either we've frightened them off or there is nobody left to guard the northern gate."

"My lord!" cried one of his men from the top of one of the towers. "Come up here!"

Hengest hurried up the steps to join him. The view of the town from the tower was a panorama of fire, smoke and destruction. The entire southern residential quarter was ablaze. Black smoke billowed out from the church in the forum and the screams and cries of a dying world were carried to them on a foul-smelling wind.

"Aesc certainly didn't hold back on the looting and sacking," Hengest said, not without a touch of pride. "I didn't think he had it in him."

Ebusa called up to him that refugees were flooding towards them. He peered over the battlements and saw rag-tag groups of Welsc carrying sacks of food, possessions and supporting the wounded and the elderly between them. Children cried as they were dragged along by their mothers and older siblings. Their misery was the song of the defeated and the ruined.

"Let them pass," Hengest said. "They have lost everything. Further abuse gains us nothing. But keep your eyes peeled for any signs of Vertigernus or my daughter!"

When the last of the refugees trailed past his line of men, Hengest descended the tower and rejoined Ebusa. His men were sheltering their horses in the stables of the deserted fort and seeking out food and water for them. "Form up!" Hengest ordered. "We take the streets in groups."

"Surely we are not going into that blazing hell?" Ebusa asked him in astonishment.

"My son and daughter are in there somewhere," he replied. "And this isn't over until I have Vertigernus's head on a pole! Prepare to advance!"

Aesc

Aesc gripped Aeronwen's arm as they headed down corridors, turning this way and that. He didn't know why he was bringing her. There must have been dozens of women in the palace left to their own defences. But he had stopped Cuthlaf from raping her and for some reason he felt responsible for her further safety.

Cuthlaf and the others tagged along behind; ordered by Aesc to escort them out of the palace. He didn't want to leave them to assault any more women on this floor and he needed a bodyguard in any case.

As they reached the staircase it suddenly became apparent that they would have to find another exit. Below was an inferno that roared and crackled. Flames licked up the wood and the heat was unbearable.

"The mad bastards!" cursed Aesc. "They've set the damned palace on fire!" Where were Beorn and his men? Surely they knew that he was still inside? He turned to Aeronwen. "Where is the nearest set of stairs?"

"Down the corridor over there," she indicated. "But …"

They took it at a run; spurred on by panic at being trapped inside a burning building. The corridor led to a large set of doors. To Aesc's relief they were not bolted and they swung them open to reveal a large chamber that may have served as some sort of dining room once.

"No!" Aeronwen cried. "Not through there! You're all mad! Let me go!"

Aesc held her tightly and Cuthlaf asked; "What's she babbling about?"

The light in the room was dim and they could make out the shapes of many occupied beds set out in rows. The prostrate forms made no sound as they entered and it was only the occasional movement of some limb that told them that this was not a mortuary.

"Some sort of infirmary?" Cuthlaf noted, pulling the covers off a whimpering man. "But they don't appear to have very serious wounds."

It was true. Aesc had spent enough time among the wounded after a battle to have been haunted by the screaming of limbless wretches and men who had to hold their guts in with their hands. There was none of that here, only sad, still silence.

Cuthlaf inspected one of the patients closer suddenly drew back. He let out a scream at the sight of the raw rash and blistering pustules and staggered backwards. "The pestilence! It's a plague ward! Get out of here!"

They stumbled out, fighting to get through the door while holding their breaths, each of them terrified that they had been infected already. They slammed the doors shut behind them and wheezed for clean air.

"We can't go through that way!" said Cuthlaf. "We'll all be smitten!"

"It's either that or through the fire," said Aesc.

"Well you can take your chances with those seeping wretches in there, but I'd rather leap through flames!"

"Wait a minute, there must be another staircase. You lot were up here before I was and I'm sure you didn't pass through the plague ward without noticing it."

"True, we came up another stairway," said one of the others. "But that's way over on the other side of the palace."

"Well come on, then!" Aesc shouted.

The heat from the stairs had seeped into the corridors and filled them with black smoke. It was a hot, mad run accompanied by hacking coughs as their lungs felt like they were blistering. Their hopes were dashed as they rounded the corner and found the other staircase ablaze as well.

"The fire must have swept the entire ground floor!" said Aesc.

"What now?" demanded Cuthlaf in a panicked voice. "We'll be roasted alive!"

Aesc poked his head out of a window. "There's a roof below us. Must be part of the kitchens. We can climb onto it and jump down."

"Looks too far," grumbled Cuthlaf.

"Then stay here and burn!"

Aesc climbed out first, his feet slipping on the loose tiles before helping Aeronwen out. He held on to her tightly and sank to his knees to spread his weight. They edged towards the lowest side of the roof and Aesc cursed as several tiles skittered past him, set loose by Cuthlaf and the others scrambling out of the window behind them.

He gripped the edge of the roof and swung his body over before letting go. The fall was a short one but long enough to knock the wind from him and give him jarring pain in his ankles.

"Alright, Aeronwen!" he called. "Slide off and I'll catch you!"

The girl still did not look like she trusted him but she had run out of options. Aesc blushed at the feel of her slender muscles under the fabric of her dress as he caught her. She was not heavy and he would have gladly carried her but she squirmed about at his grasp so he set her down. At first he thought she was going to make a run for it but the grounds of the palace were filled with roaming bands of his men, drunk and noisy, so she remained with him.

Cuthlaf and the others slid down, one by one, and landed with varying degrees of gracefulness. "Well, thank the gods we got out of that one!" Cuthlaf said, his relieved grin eclipsing the cowardice he had shown only moments previously.

Some of Aesc's men wandered past rolling a barrel of wine between them. One of them carried a screaming Welsc girl a little older than Aeronwen over his shoulder. "Looks like we're missing out on the party," Cuthlaf said. He eyed Aeronwen. "Let's get some of that wine and have a party of our own, eh? How about that, my Weslc pretty?"

Aesc shook his head. "This building behind us is going to come down at any moment and engulf the gardens in smoke and hot ash. I'm going to order all my men to pull out. Besides, I need you to accompany me north to meet up with my father."

"Are you serious?" Cuthlaf demanded. "We haven't had a drop of drink or a sniff of cunny yet while the rest of our boys have been tearing up the town! I'm tired and fed up with taking orders from Hengest's runt! You got what you wanted from this bitch and now she's mine so hand her over!"

"Forget it," Aesc said through bared teeth. "She's coming with me."

Cuthlaf laughed. "Are you in love, runt?"

"I am an Aetheling of Cent and your future king!"

"King is it? So your father has been grooming you for a crown eh? Well, there are many in his warband who might have a thing or two to say about that. Most of us are sick of his bloody lordly ways and think that once he's dead there should be a change in leadership. Who knows? Maybe he's dead already!"

Aesc drew his sword. "I'm not taking any more shit from you, Cuthlaf."

"Oh?" Cuthlaf replied, drawing his own sword.

Aesc was quick, as Octa had taught him. He swung at Cuthlaf and nearly finished the fight there and then but Cuthlaf was no amateur and he batted Aesc's blade aside, nearly losing his nose in the process.

Aesc swung again, overhead this time and Cuthlaf brought his sword up to meet the blow. Their comrades stood around with their jaws open; not knowing whom to support.

Aesc had given up his initial offensive and ducked and dodged Cuthlaf's blows. He heard Octa's words in his mind, 'If an opponent seems too strong or too skilled, try and wear him out.' And Cuthlaf was tiring. That was visible by his grunts and the spittle flying from his mouth as he lunged and swiped, growing ever frustrated at Aesc's evasiveness.

Aesc let his blade drop and sidestepped as Cuthlaf's whistled down next to him. It was a trick Octa had shown him. When Cuthlaf's sword embedded itself in the dirt, Aesc swung his blade up with both hands and drew it fast and deep across his abdomen.

Cuthlaf gasped and leaned forward on his sword pommel. The blow had shorn through mail and leather and opened a gash in his belly from which his intestines bulged. He coughed in agony and the entirety of his guts fell out to land on the ground with a horrible wet sound.

He stood there for a while, breathing heavily, the tendrils that dangled from his wound glistening and steaming. Then, unable to stand any longer, he fell forward to lay face down over his own stinking guts.

Hengest

When he got word that Aesc and several of his men had made it through the chaos to the northern section of the town and that they had a girl with them, Hengest's heart soared. But when he set eyes upon the girl's black hair, he could not hide his disappointment.

Aesc's face was marred by soot and scorched pink in places. He and his men were exhausted and, although he was pleased to see his son, Hengest could not refrain from demanding a report.

"Vertigernus left the city days ago," Aesc told him, accepting a cup of wine from somebody. He drank thirstily. "Hronwena too. They're gone."

"He took her west?" Hengest asked. "To *Britannia Prima*?"

Aesc nodded and called for another cup of water.

It was a crushing anti-climax to their victory over the town. It had all been for nothing. As Hengest looked about at his men piling up goods looted from the fine town houses and smashing open casks of wine and ale with their axes, he knew that they would never see it that way. As far as they were concerned they had got what they had come for. Once the victory celebrations had started there would be no stopping them until the light of dawn awoke them from their drunken slumbers. He had failed. He had failed Halfritha, he had failed Hronwena and he had failed himself.

As Londinium burned behind them they camped and feasted in the shadow of the northern gate. With the madness of destruction and looting still continuing on one side and the stinking corpses of the battle grown cold on the other, to Hengest it felt like he was at the world's ending.

He had no appetite although Aesc ate ravenously, chewing on meat stolen from some cellar and roasted over their campfire. He occasionally passed scraps to the Welsc girl he had rescued who sat by his side. She begrudgingly took the tidbits and sipped at the wine he also to passed her, her empty belly clearly getting the better of her pride.

"What do you plan to do with her?" he asked Aesc.

Aesc shrugged. "I can't let her go wandering off. She has nothing in the world and you know how our men would treat her if they got hold of her. I'm her protector."

"And when we return to Thanet? What then?"

Aesc was silent. He clearly hadn't thought this through.

"Are you planning on keeping her?"

"Yes. But not as a theow."

"As what then?"

"Well … I don't see any reason why we couldn't …"

"Couldn't what?"

"Be … *friends*."

"Why don't you ask her?"

Aesc turned to the girl and spoke to her in British. "Aeronwen. You have lost everything and I can't leave you here in Londinium. It's not safe. Will you come back to Thanet with me?"

She glared at him. "As your slave?"

"No. As my …" he struggled for the British word and used one that meant something between companion and whore. Hengest winced.

Her eyes spat fire at him. "Take me if you want, Sais, but know that I will never willingly lie with you!"

"That's not what I meant!" said Aesc in a panic. "I want us to be friends."

"Friends? You have burned and sacked my town to the ground. You have killed my masters and as we speak your men are raping and stealing from my countrymen. Why on God's earth would you think that I want to be friends with you?" She got up and went and sat down next to a few barrels that had been put aside. She clearly didn't dare go too far despite her fiery words.

"I rescued her from being raped by Cuthlaf," said Aesc. "I never meant her any harm. Why does she hate me so much?"

Hengest sighed. His son had matured so much in such a short period of time. War could do that to a boy. But he was still a boy after all and had much to learn about women. "It's a mistake to try and make friends with these Welsc," he told him. "Take it from me. I think our peoples will be at war until the gods fall."

With morning, Hengest woke early and began giving orders for the warband to move out. Half of the men were still drunk and were sleeping it off. The other half had ferocious hangovers and were in no mood for having orders barked at them.

The warband assembled themselves sluggishly outside the northern gate; their noses wrinkled at the stink of the corpses. Ravens cawed angrily at being disturbed.

Ebusa and some other thegns had been dispatched to find any salvageable carts and horses to draw them. They were piled up with the looted goods and given an escort to take them back to Cent.

"Why don't we accompany the loot ourselves?" Ebusa asked. "We are more than enough escort."

"Because we're not returning to Cent yet," Hengest told him.

"We're not?"

"Vertigernus has my daughter locked up in his fortress in the west. And that is where we shall march."

His thegns gaped at him. "It's too far!" protested Ordlaf. "We are not equipped to march across the whole island."

Hengest was not interested in such talk. "If Vertigernus took my daughter to his Christian Hell with him it would not be far enough to dissuade me."

"My lord," said Ebusa, "our men are tired. We have just won a victory the like of which they have never dreamed of."

"Then now that their morale is so high it is the perfect time to look to other goals," Hengest argued.

His thegns were not convinced and neither were the rest of his warband when he put it to them. There were audible cries of protest from the ranks and Hengest scanned their faces, trying to pick out the dissenters but he could not find them. He told Ordlaf to gallop ahead so that they could all see his banner and, with curses and threats, he and his thegns managed to get the band moving if only at a slow shuffle.

The day was a long one. Most of the men had raging hangovers and did not appreciate the hours of marching. By nightfall they camped by the side of the Roman road and when Hengest awoke the next morning, he found that a large percentage of them had deserted.

"They've got homes and families to get back to," Ebusa said to him. "And loot to divide up."

"So, they only followed me for the chance of looting," said Hengest. "Ungrateful wretches!"

A scout came in at a gallop, his horse lathered with sweat. "My lord! An army approaches from the north-west! They're coming down the road towards us!"

"An army?" asked Hengest incredulously. "What army is left in Britta but my own?"

Ebusa and Aesc rode out with him. In the distance, they could see a marching column of armoured soldiers stomping up dust as they went. Hengest squinted and made out large oval shields painted with what looked suspiciously like the Chi-Rho symbol. Banners fluttered above the column; banners that he had seen before.

"Aurelianus," he said, as if invoking the name of some demon.

"Then he is alive," mumbled Ebusa.

"He must have marshalled every hill tribe and rural militia on the island," Hengest added.

When they got back to the camp they found it in the process of disbanding.

"Who gave the order to strike camp?" Hengest demanded.

"There's an army coming!" said one of his thegns. "We're not strong enough to fight another battle."

"And so you retreat without striking a single blow?" he said.

"We are far from home," said another thegn. "We didn't set out to conquer the whole of Britta."

"And we didn't come here to rescue your daughter!" cried one of the men from the ranks. There were murmurs of agreement at this.

"We've got our own families!"

"We're going home!"

Hengest could only watch in anguish as tents were pulled down, carts were loaded and, piece by piece, his army began the journey back east. The dual horse banner fluttered where it had been thrust into the mud, left by Ordlaf who had also disappeared. Even Ebusa had turned and led his cohorts in retreat.

"I think this is the end of the road, Father," said Aesc.

"But what of your sister?" Hengest demanded.

Aesc shrugged. "I want her back too, but as you said, she was a piece to be played in this game with the Welsc. And she has been played."

"I've lost her," said Hengest, a sob welling up deep in his chest. "Gods help me, I've lost her!"

"You have achieved more than any of us ever dreamed of," Aesc continued.

"And in doing so I've lost my daughter to a wicked tyrant and my wife will never look on me with love in her heart again. I've lost all that is important! Horsa was right. He knew the price was too high. And I lost him too!"

He felt like weeping but could not bring himself to do that in front of his son. He still had enough pride left for that.

"You have your kingdom," Aesc said. "There was always going to be a high price for that. And our descendants will thank you for it."

Hengest looked at him and, for the first time, he saw his boy as a man. He saw him as a *king*.

"Come on, Father," said Aesc. "Let's go home."

Hronwena

They watched the smoke from afar. Din Neidr would burn for many days and nights. The fire had won out and the people had abandoned the fortress, trickling out into the countryside to make new lives for themselves. Vitalinus – *Lord Vertigernus* – was dead. His tyranny was over at last.

"What now, my lady?" Deilwen asked Hronwena.

"You stop calling me 'my lady', that's what," Hronwena replied. "I am no Lady now. We are on equal terms, Deilwen, and I wouldn't have it any other way."

Behind them Britu began to sing a song in his mother's arms. They had three horses between them, snatched from the fortress stables during the confusion. They had enough food to last them several days and some gold trinkets and coin to barter. Hronwena had spent days preparing before she kindled the fire below her husband's chamber.

"Will you return to your family in Cantium?" Deilwen asked her.

Hronwena shook her head. "I have no family now but you three."

"And we have none but you," said Enys. "But we are glad to have you."

"You still have Pasgen," Hronwena told her. "He was out on patrol when the fire broke out. I made sure of that. We could take you to him. He'll be lord of these lands now. Aurelianus will probably support his claim. He'll be a good ruler."

Enys shook her head. "I love my twin brother dearly and perhaps, in time, I will go to him. But for now it is best if I disappear for a while. I need to spend time with my son. My family has wounded me too deeply already. I just want to live my life and not be afraid anymore."

"Then let us live it together," Hronwena replied. "The four of us. We'll find a place somewhere where the troubles of the world will never find us again."

They turned and descended the rise but before the smouldering ruins of Din Neidr passed from view, Hronwena gave it a final glance. It occurred to her that as her brother and father were witnessing the birth of a new kingdom in the east, she was watching the death of an old one in the west.

She turned her back on it and they faced the rising of the sun that stretched their shadows long and thin.

EPILOGUE

The Monastery of Escanceaster (Exeter), the Kingdom of Wessex, 892

Eanberht set down his paintbrush and pulled his monk's habit up tighter around his neck to keep out the chill. It was after vespers and with an hour to go before compline, the day was drawing to an end. Outside it was snowing and the air inside the monastery was bitterly cold.

By the flickering oil lamps, the breadth of Britta lay before him, painstakingly painted on parchment over many days and nights. It had been commissioned to show the new layout of an old land with an uncertain future.

A generation ago, such a map would have shown the four kingdoms of their people; Wessex, East Anglia, Mercia and Northumbria. Now, most of it was ruled by Danish law.

The lands in the south west showed the fragile kingdom of Wessex ruled by Aelfred, the only king left. The people he ruled had now been forged together by a sense of camaraderie in the face of the Danes. Gone were the days when Saxons, Jutes and Angles had fought each other as they had fought the Welsc in days gone by. Now a word had started to emerge that bonded them all by a sense of unity: 'Angelcynn'. *Kindred.*

The door to Eanbehrt's cell swung open and Bishop Asser strode in. "Is that map finished yet, Eanbehrt?"

"Nearly done, your Grace," Eanbehrt replied. "I just need a little more yellow ochre for the edging."

Bishop Asser tut-tutted. "I had hoped to present the map to the king when I visit him next Thunorsdaeg."

"It will be finished by then, your Grace."

"You have forgotten that I am travelling to Aethelinga Island in the morning to oversee the monks at the new abbey there. I will not be returning before my audience with the king. You ever were a forgetful boy, Eanbehrt. I knew this when your father delivered you to me in Dyfed all those years ago."

Eanbehrt said nothing to this. His abandonment by his father and subsequent education in the Welsc monastery under Asser was the reason he was here in Wessex now.

Asser leaned over his shoulder and peered at the map. "Hmm. It may all be for nothing if the Danes attack in the spring. Guthrum may be dead but his successors are keen to prove themselves. And Aelfred grows ever weaker."

"Is the king sick again?"

"He is sick every winter, more or less. His will is as strong as ever but he feels God calling to him. His remaining years with us are few, I fear."

Whatever his physical shortcomings, none could doubt King Aelfred's determination. In the years of peace since his victory at the battle of Ethandun he had begun a task some said was more ambitious than the defeat of the Danes: the education of the Angelcynn.

Learning had been devastated across the land by the attacks of Guthrum and his warriors. In response, Aelfred had gathered monks and bishops from the Carolingian Empire, the Welsc kingdoms, Erin and other places where Christian learning had continued more or less uninterrupted and set them to translating documents from Latin to Anglisc. The compiling of a massive chronicle of their people was underway detailing everything from the birth of Christ to Aelfred's own time.

Such an undertaking was a testament to their king's belief in their future as a people. For all his reforms, coin striking, ship building and town fortifying, there were many who felt that it might all be swept away should war consume them once more. South of the Danelaw, the threat of imminent destruction had been a bedfellow to the Angelcynn for over a generation.

But the hatred of the Danes was more than just a hatred of their thieving, brutal ways. For the Angelcynn, looking at the Danes was like looking at themselves through the mists of four hundred years. After all, Danes had formed a large part of Hengest's war host and the Jutes, Angles and Saxons that made up the rest of his following had been little different in those pagan times.

Eanberht often found himself thinking of the legendary founder of their people who had landed his three ceols on the shores of Cent and had wrestled a kingdom from the Welsc. Clerics like Bishop Asser would never see him as anything more than a pagan sea-wolf, no better than Guthrum, but Eanberht, like many of his countrymen, recognised Hengest and his brother, Horsa, as the true founders of their people.

The beginnings of Cent had been well recorded but the eventual fate of Hengest, son of Wictgils, had been forever lost to time. Whether he had died of some illness or fell on the battlefield was not known. His son, Aesc, had succeeded him and, under the guidance of his father's faithful steward, Octa, had founded the royal house of the Aescingas who had ruled Cent until its absorption into Mercia and eventually, Wessex.

Though a good king, Aesc was never possessed of the fiery determination of his father and, apart from a brief alliance with King Aelle of the South Saxons which was sundered by the disastrous Battle of Mount Badon, he spent the majority of his rule defending the borders of his own kingdom. It had been left to other kings like Aelle of Sussex, Penda of Mercia and Aelfred of Wessex to forge the lands of the Angelcynn into what they now were and attain the illustrious title of *Bretwalda*: 'wide-ruler'.

Bishop Asser had left him now and Eanbehrt could hear him in the next cell, packing his things for tomorrow's journey. He returned his gaze to the map of Britta. The kingdom of Aelfred faced aggression on both sides. In the west they suffered constant raids by the Welsc and in the north east, annihilation by the Danes. Hengest's legacy was a whisper away from doom.

But Aelfred had a dream. Some said that it was nothing but a dream; a dream of vain hope and false promise. It was a dream of a united people; a kingdom of kingdoms that would last the ages. Perhaps it would not happen in Eanberht's lifetime, certainly not in Aelfred's, but it was a dream nonetheless. And Eanberht believed in his king's dream.

Eanberht took up his quill and began to write a word across the map. Bishop Asser would no doubt berate him for his presumption and likely cast the map to the flames, but he could not help himself. The word stretched across what was left of Hengest's legacy that had been founded on blood, justly or unjustly, and which was determined to survive in the face of foreign oppression.

This word was the name of his dream and of Aelfred's dream and of the dream of many of their people, peasant or noble. It was a single word; a word for the land of the Angelcynn that would one day be known across the world. That word was;

ÆNGLALAND

AUTHOR'S NOTE

The tale of the destruction and eventual death of Vortigern (Vitalinus/Vertigernus in this novel) is dominated by the figure of Bishop Germanus of Auxerre. *The Life of Saint Germanus*, written in about 480 A.D. by Constantius of Lyons, states that Bishop Germanus and his companion, Bishop Lupus of Troyes, originally voyaged to Britain in about 429 A.D. to combat the Pelagian Heresy. There, through debate and preaching, they won many back to the Augustinian teachings.

As with the lives of many saints, miracles were also performed including the healing of a blind girl by the holding of Germanus's reliquary to her eyes. Germanus even leads a British army against a confederation of Picts and Saxons and, by chanting the "Alleluia", manages to rout the enemy without even having to strike a blow.

A later chapter reveals that Germanus returned to Britain (possibly around 447 A.D.) as Pelagianism was once again on the rise. A healing miracle is performed once again, this time for the crippled son of Elafius; a leading man in the country.

The Life of Saint Germanus makes no mention of Vortigern but Nennius's part-legend-part-chronicle *The History of the Britons* further elaborates on Germanus's second visit to Britain beginning with his confrontation of a tyrannical king called Benlli (there is an old hill fort called 'Foel Fenlli' in Denbighshire, Wales). After

Benlli's city is obliterated by "fire from heaven" Germanus raises a peasant called Catel Drunlue (Cadell Derynllug in the Welsh genealogies) to the position of king.

Germanus then goes to the court of Vortigern who has, much to everyone's outrage, married his daughter and sired a son on her called Faustus. Germanus gives the boy razor, scissors and comb and tells him to present them to his true father. The boy gives these items to Vortigern who "arose in great anger, and fled from the presence of St. Germanus, execrated and condemned by the whole synod."

Nennius follows this with a version of the fairly well-known fairytale 'Vortigern and the two dragons'. Meanwhile, Vortigern's son, Vortimer, rises to the position left vacant by his father and wages war on Hengest and Horsa, driving them back to the isle of Thanet. Three more battles take place, the first upon the River Darent, the second at 'Epsford' (possibly Aylesford) where both Horsa and Vortimer's brother Catigern are slain. The last battle was "near the stone on the shore of the Gallic sea, where the Saxons being defeated, fled to their ships." The Anglo Saxon Chronicle puts these battles in a slightly different order and names them; Aegelsthrep (where Hengest's brother Horsa is slain), Crecganford (identified as Crayford where the Britons forsake the land of Kent and flee to London), Wippedsfleet (where Hengest and his son Esc slay twelve British leaders) and a final unnamed battle where "the Welsh fled from the English like Fire."

Vortimer then mysteriously dies and, in an aping of the Welsh tale of Bran the Blessed, commands that his body be buried upon the spot where the Saxons first landed so that they may never land there again. His commands are ignored of course, resulting in the eventual Saxon conquest of most of Britain.

Nennius makes it clear that Vortigern returns to power on the death of his son. Hengest invites Vortigern and his followers to a feast where, in the original Night of the Long Knives, his men butcher them all except Vortigern whom Hengest hopes to ransom for his daughter's return. More land is turned over to the Saxons including "the three provinces of East, South, and Middle Sex."

On the run again from the fury of Germanus, Vortigern flees to "the kingdom of the Dimetae where, on the river Towy, he builds a castle, which he names Cair Guothergirn" (literally 'Castle Vortigern'). Fire once again falls from heaven and destroys this castle, killing Vortigern, Hengest's daughter and all its other inhabitants.

Nennius claims that Faustus was brought up and educated by Germanus in Gaul and went on to become Saint Fautsus of Riez. The Pillar of Eliseg – a ninth century monument erected in Denbighshire, Wales – names the sons of Vortigern as Pascent and Britu and makes no mention of Vortimer and Faustus. It claims that Britu was blessed by Germanus and, for the sake of a good story, I equated him with Faustus; a British boy given a new Latin name. Germanus himself died at Ravenna in about 448.

The rune poems that accompany each segment of this novel are from a 10th century manuscript from the Cotton library which, unfortunately, was destroyed in a fire in 1731. Luckily, the scholar George Hicks published a facsimile in 1705 and the particular translation I used is from the *Runic and heroic poems of the old Teutonic peoples* (1915, pp. 12-23) by Bruce Dickens.

I hope you have enjoyed the *Hengest and Horsa Trilogy*. If you did, you could do me a huge favour by leaving a review on Amazon. This would be greatly appreciated. Read on for a sneak peek at *Sign of the White Foal*, the first book in the *Arthur of the Cymry Trilogy* which is a sequel to the *Hengest and Horsa Trilogy*.

Sign of the white foal

CHRIS THORNDYCROFT

"Then Arthur along with the kings of Britain fought against them in those days, but Arthur himself was the leader of battles."
-     The History of the Britons, Nennius

PART I

"My poetry,
from the cauldron
it was uttered.
From the breath of nine maidens
it was kindled."
-    The Spoils of Annwn, Book of Taliesin

Venedotia (Gwynedd), 480 A.D.

Cadwallon

Night cloaked the coast, turning sand to silver and the hills to slumbering shadows. The moon was shrouded by shifting clouds and beyond the lapping waves the sea was an impenetrable, black void. Cadwallon mab Enniaun sniffed the air. The tide was going out; there was no mistaking that stink. But there was something else there too. Perhaps it was his imagination but there was something on the wind that was not *right*.

"An ill night, lord," said the young warrior beside him, as if reading his thoughts.

"Aye," Cadwallon replied.

The small camp had overlooked the Afon Conui, nestled on the wooded slope that ran down to the marsh at the water's edge. The fire had been stamped out and not long ago either. Smoke still curled up from the ashes and the stones that surrounded it were warm. The corpses of the three sentries were warm too, but only barely.

"Poor Gusc," said the young warrior looking down at his slain comrades. "He owed me money."

"There wasn't much of a fight," said the second warrior, an older man whose name Cadwallon seemed to remember was Tathal. "Looks like they were come upon by surprise; Gusc here only had his sword halfway out of his scabbard before some bastard's knife cut his throat for him."

"Should we expect an attack?" asked the young warrior, a touch of fear creeping into his voice.

"I don't know." Cadwallon looked at the long reeds of the marsh below them. That dense foliage could easily conceal a band of warriors. So could the trees of the wooded slope upon which they stood for that matter. *Enemies could be everywhere.*

"Lord, return to the fortress," said Tathal. "We can deal with this. It's not safe for you to be here without an armed escort."

Cadwallon ignored him. Though he was right, of course. His presence wasn't strictly necessary and it was probably a little reckless for him to be there, but in truth he had welcomed a break from the side of his father's deathbed. News of three dead sentries and no sign of their attackers had drawn him from his father's chamber with eager haste.

It was the smell that got to him the most; the smell of death. Not the fast death of slaughter on the battlefield (and at thirty-five summers, Cadwallon had smelt enough of that), but the slow death of old age and sickness. The burning incense did little to mask the stink of sweat and shit, only contributing its own heavy fug to the mix. He had longed for the cool night air and salty tang of the sea. Now he wasn't so sure.

At their back, straddling twin hills connected by timber palisades, was Cair Dugannu, his father's fortress; the mighty royal seat of Venedotia. On fine days those twin hills afforded a wide view of seaweed-strewn mudflats, wavering marsh reeds and the deep blue of the ocean, its glassy surface broken only by the curve of the fishing weirs. Further along the coast, the earthworks of the old Roman fort could be seen shielding the port of Penlassoc; a snug little haven where vessels were beached on the mud to trade wine for fish and the fine pearls of the blue mussels that clustered at the mouth of the Afon Conui.

Such were the fine images of youth forever imprinted on Cadwallon's memory. But tonight it felt as if the darkness was pressing in on all sides, cutting him off from memories of sunshine and cawing gulls, obscuring his sight and threatening to overwhelm him.

He tried to shrug off his foolishness. He was no bard to wax poetic about doom and fate. The kingdom was on the verge of change; that was all. It was natural to feel some apprehension.

And yet … Here lie three dead sentries.

"What's your name, lad?" Cadwallon asked the young soldier.

"Gobrui, lord," he replied. "Son of Echel."

"How long have you been in my father's guard?"

"Six months, lord. My da was killed in that border dispute with Powys when I was nine. He always wanted me to be a warrior like him so I joined as soon as I was sixteen but …" his voice trailed off. Cadwallon smiled. He knew that the lad had been about to voice his shame that he had not yet made it beyond a night sentry but had thought better of complaining to his lord.

"I'm sure you will become a warrior to match your father's good name and make his shade very proud one day," he reassured him. "But take it from me, be careful wishing for war and glory. War is seldom glorious. Take these poor men here. They were come upon by surprise and left this world before they knew what was happening."

"Are we truly at war, then?" the lad asked.

"Difficult to say until we know who did this," said Tathal.

"Could've been robbers," offered Gobrui.

"Robbing sentries?" Tathal replied. "Our lads had precious little to steal apart from blades and leather and those were not taken." He looked at Cadwallon. "You don't reckon it was … *them* do you?" He jerked his head in a north-westerly direction.

"They haven't attacked in a decade," said Cadwallon. "Why would they now?"

Yes, why now? He thought. *Why tonight, of all nights?*

He gazed beyond the headland at the narrow straits that separated the mainland from the isle of Ynys Mon. That slim stretch of tidal water was all that stood between them and their age-old enemy. It had been ten years since they had returned. Gaels, *Scotti* in the Latin tongue; wolves from across the sea seeking land and plunder. Ynys Mon was theirs, ceded to them after years of bitter conflict. The Britons held one side of the straits while the Gaels held the other. He shivered and lied to himself that it was just the chilled night breeze from the river. To stare at death every day and trust their lives to the whim of the tides! Manawydan protect them!

"Remain with the bodies," he ordered, his voice suddenly more assertive. "I will send down a patrol to bring them back to the fortress."

"Will you send out troops to scour the woods and marshes?" Tathal asked.

"No. I want all our men within the palisades tonight. I won't risk ambush by sending out small patrols."

"My lord, there could be a warband lurking nearby. Shouldn't we at least …"

"No!" he didn't know why his voice had snapped like that. Was it fear? As Gobrui had said, tonight was an ill night …

He left them then and headed up the slope towards the fortress.

Cair Dugannu had been fortified by his father after his grandfather's original holdfast on Ynys Mon had fallen to the Gaels. The return of the hounds of Erin had been a sore blow to the dynasty that had driven them into the sea a generation previously. After Rome had abandoned Albion, Venedotia, like the rest of the province, fell vulnerable to those who had never borne the yoke of the iron legions. Gaels plundered and settled in the west just as the Saeson did in the east and the Picts in the north. Facing barbarians on all sides, the Council of Britannia, an assembly which was hastily formed to administer their newfound independence, struggled to keep the old province together. Out of desperation, the Council's leader, Lord Vertigernus, had decided to fight fire with fire.

In the north dwelt a client tribe who had served as a buffer zone between Rome's northernmost border and the howling, blue-painted Picts that lived in the hills beyond it. Cunedag was their leader and a more ferocious warlord Albion had rarely seen. His standard was the red dragon, the origins of which lay in the carven standing stones of the Picts, for that people's blood flowed strongly in his line.

Cunedag was descended from Padarn Redcloak; a Pictish chieftain who had accepted a military rank from Rome and swapped barbarism for toga and trade. As Lord Vertigernus aped his Roman predecessors, so had Cunedag followed in his ancestor's footsteps. He and his sons took up the offer of butchery for pay and marched south to Venedotia.

Nine sons of Cunedag there were; Tybiaun, Etern, Ruman, Afloeg, Caradog, Osmael, Enniaun, Docmael and Dunaud. Together they brought fire and sword to the Gaels and forced them back in battle after bloody

319

battle until only the island of Ynys Mon held out against them. That battle was the bloodiest. Tybiaun and Osmael fell but the Gaels were finally sent back across the sea whence they came.

The dragon standard was planted deep into the soil of Ynys Mon and the sons of Cunedag came to be known as the 'Dragons of the Isle' with Cunedag as their chief; the *Pendraig*. Before he died, he divided his kingdom between his surviving sons. To Etern went Eternion, to Ruman Rumaniog, to Afloeg Afloegion, Caradog Caradogion and Dunaud Dunauding. Meriaun – the son of Cunedag's fallen firstborn who had excelled himself by slaying the Gaelic chieftain Beli mac Benlli – was also given a portion; Meriauned.

The only son who did not receive a kingdom was Cunedag's seventh and favourite son Enniaun, known as 'Yrth', the impetuous. Cunedag had groomed Enniaun to rule as Pendraig after his passing. But when old Cunedag finally died and Enniaun succeeded him as High-king of Venedotia, the other rulers began to grumble at being subservient to their younger brother.

Envious eyes looked upon the dragon standard but the return of the Gaels had kept the Venedotian kings too busy to do anything about it. The wars were long. Ynys Mon was lost and the Dragons of the Isle grew old. One by one they died and were succeeded by their sons but family rivalries still burned deep. When King Afloeg died without an heir, Enniaun Yrth absorbed his kingdom on the Laigin Peninsula into his own lands, an act which caused further grumbling.

Although a fragile peace between Briton and Gael had reigned for many years now, the wars had turned Enniaun Yrth into a battle-hardened old warrior every bit as ferocious as Cunedag had been. None of the other kings dared act on their resentment while he still lived. Instead, they bided their time, knowing that one day a new king must be crowned Pendraig.

Cadwallon strode in through the west gate and made his way up the north hill where the Great Hall stood. He gave orders to a sergeant to dispatch a patrol to retrieve the slain sentries. A servant was relighting the torches that were sputtering low. All were still awake and about their duties. Few would sleep that night, least of all him.

The night was dark. The enemies innumerable. And in a chamber on the upper floor of the royal quarters, the Pendraig was dying.

The attack came before dawn. Enniaun had died in the small hours. Cadwallon was in the Great Hall, a horn of mead in his hand. He wasn't grieving. The old warhorse had been over sixty and had been a difficult man to like at the best of times. No, his thoughts dwelt on the immediate future.

To all intents and purposes, he was now the Pendraig, High-king of Venedotia. There would be a coronation ceremony of course and all the other kings – his cousins and remaining uncle – would come to pay him homage. Some had already visited his father's deathbed when it became known that his time was near. Some had been conspicuously absent and their names had been noted.

His wife, Meddyf, entered the hall and joined him at the table.

"How are the boys?" he asked her.

"Sleeping, at last," she replied. "They were tired but they did their duty and paid their last respects to your father."

"How are they?"

She shrugged. "Maelcon acted like he didn't care which may be the truth for all I know. Guidno was upset but I think he was just scared. They weren't close to your father, after all."

"No," Cadwallon agreed. "Few were."

She poured him some more mead from the jug and took the horn from him, drawing a long sip herself before setting it down. "Will you be coming to bed soon?"

"No. I can't sleep."

"Thinking about the future?"

"I've been thinking about the future for many years now for all the good it did."

"Surely after so long you feel ready to be a king?"

He looked at her. "Do you feel ready to be a queen?"

She was silent for a while and then placed a hand on his arm. "We have known this day was coming for a long time," she said. "All is as it should be and that must be enough for us. Let us rest our heads in the lap of fate and be content."

He didn't answer her. As always, she sensed his mood and was trying to quell his concerns, good wife that she was. He couldn't hope for a better one and he needed her now. He wanted to tell her about the dead sentries. He wanted to tell her his deepest fears, not just about that night but about all the nights and days to come. But what sort of a husband would that make him, to burden her with his own troubles? *What sort of a king?*

The door to the Great Hall crashed open and Tathal staggered in. "My lord!" he wheezed, evidently having run up the north hill. "We are under attack!"

Cadwallon felt the warmth the mead had brought him suddenly drain from his face and a chill came over his heart. He slammed the horn down and stood up. "Bar the gates!" he said. "Man the palisades! Wake every warrior! Why do I not hear the warning bell?"

"The guards on the western palisade have been slain, lord. Nobody can get to the bell. They came upon us under cover of darkness and scaled the palisade with ropes and grappling hooks."

"Who, in the name of the gods?"

"The Gaels."

Cadwallon felt his stomach sink. What a fool he had been! They must have crossed the straits at the Lafan Sands at low tide earlier that day and waited in the marshes and woods. They had even slain his sentries and still he had not sent out patrols!

"They have us pinned on the north hill," Tathal went on. "The southern hill and the lower fortress fell but not before I sent a messenger out the east gate. With any luck he will make it through to Din Arth and get word to your brother."

Cadwallon turned to Meddyf. "Go and stay with the boys," he told her. "Bar the door."

"Where are you going?" she asked.

"I am the lord of this fortress now," he replied. "My place is on the palisades."

Tathal followed him out of the hall and they crossed the enclosure to the palisade that ringed the north hill. The gate was barred and every remaining warrior had marshalled on the rampart that faced south, overlooking the small valley between Dugannu's two hills. In that dip lay a cluster of roundhouses, pig runs and workshops. As Cadwallon climbed up to the rampart, he could see the Gaels ransacking and burning the homes of his people. On the other side of the dip the southern hill with its barracks and granary was already under Gaelic control.

"I've failed them …" he muttered. "May the gods forgive me, I've failed them!"

They could hear the screams of the fortress's inhabitants as glowing sparks whirled up into the night sky. *The sun has not yet risen on my reign and already I am defeated! How had they known? How had they known?*

The Gaels marshalled on the footpath that led up the side of the north hill. Cadwallon's men had a few bows between them and several arrows were sent down into the mob who quickly raised their shields and advanced on the gate.

The defence did not last long. A battering ram was brought forth and heaved against the gate by ten men, shields covering their heads. Cadwallon, Tathal and the remaining men on the palisades descended to ground level and formed a defensive line in front of the gradually splintering gate.

"You should go and be with your family, lord," said Tathal.

"No," Cadwallon replied. "I brought this upon us. My fate will be no different to yours. I should at least be able to die in battle."

The gate came down and the Gaels spilled in, falling upon the spears of the Britons with blood-curdling war cries. The line held for a moment but eventually, inevitably, the Britons were overwhelmed. The line broke and the fighting descended into the chaos of one-on-one combat.

Cadwallon roared as the pent-up shame and fear finally found an outlet and he reddened his sword in Gaelic blood. Tathal, loyal warrior that he was, kept himself ahead of his new king, hacking and slashing like a man twenty years younger.

The Gaels seemed to part as several of their warriors shouldered their way through to the front ranks. As soon as they saw them the Britons fell back in sheer terror. Cadwallon had never seen anything like these men. They were like nightmares from a mist-shrouded age. They were naked but for masks that concealed their features and those black, soulless eye sockets told him that these were masks fashioned from human skulls. They fought like demons, screeching and howling, all traces of humanity blasted from their minds by the battle fury.

"Gods, what are they?" Tathal uttered.

Focused solely on slaughter, the skull-faced warriors seemed impervious to pain, ignoring the wounds inflicted on their naked, woad-stained flesh as the Britons desperately tried to fight them off.

Cadwallon could see that it was hopeless. These monsters were driving a wedge between them while the rest of the Gaels flanked them on either side. They were as fish in a barrel. Tathal fell, his shoulder blade splintered by the axe of a skull-faced howler. The rest of Cadwallon's warriors rallied to him with cries of "To the Pendraig! To the Pendraig!"

He could have wept at their loyalty for there could be none among them who did not know that they would all be slaughtered within minutes. But the Gaels seemed to hold back, fresh spearmen pushing through the ranks to hold the Britons at a distance and, at the same time, drive back their own wild warriors.

"Which of you is Cadwallon mab Enniaun?" demanded a voice in British with a thick Gaelic accent.

All were silent but for the groans of the dying and the heaving breaths of the living. Cadwallon straightened and stepped forward. "I am he," he answered.

A large Gael wearing a tartan cloak and the torc of a chieftain shouldered his way forward. "I am Diugurnach mac Domhnall," he said. "Surrender this fortress and your remaining men will live."

"And what of my family?" Cadwallon asked.

"All will live if you throw down your weapons now. If you do not, all will die."

Cadwallon felt the eyes of his remaining men upon him. It had been selfish to think that he could die in battle. He had the lives of his people to think of. He tossed his bloodied sword to the mud. A heartbeat passed before all British blades and spears fell to the ground in unison.

The Gaels herded them into the Great Hall while the skull-faced warriors capered and foamed at the mouth amidst the blood and the entrails outside. All of the women, children and servants were roused from their quarters and marched into the hall. The chamber echoed with frightened weeping. Cadwallon looked for Meddyf and saw her clutching the hands of Maelcon and Guidno. She was visibly shaken yet her face remained brave and defiant.

The one called Diugurnach mounted the dais at the head of the hall and spoke to them. "I have taken this fortress and you are all my prisoners. Cadwallon mab Enniaun, step forward."

Cadwallon took a pace towards the dais, conscious of Meddyf, his sons, *everybody*, watching him. He must

326

not fail them now. He was still their king. His courage must hold strong.

"Do you yield to me, princeling?"

"I yield this fortress to you to save what is left of my people," Cadwallon replied. "But I am no princeling. I am the Pendraig, the High-king of Venedotia. My uncle and my cousins all owe me allegiance. By tomorrow five-thousand British spears will be upon you and you will rue the day you set foot on Venedotian soil."

Diugurnach ignored the last and addressed the hall; "You all heard him! This fortress is mine! I offer food and plunder to any warrior who wishes to join me and pledge their allegiance. Step forward now!"

He knows he is vulnerable here, thought Cadwallon. *Otherwise he wouldn't recruit warriors from the enemy.*

Several of Cadwallon's warriors stepped forward to the disapproving hiss and grumble of the assembly. Cadwallon saw young Gobrui among them but found that he could not begrudge the lad. They were all so frightened. One by one they knelt and kissed Diugurnach's sword before taking their places among the Gaels.

All warriors who did not pledge allegiance were taken outside where the skull-faced still howled. As Cadwallon and his family were escorted to their quarters, they heard the screams as they were butchered behind the Great Hall. *That they should remain loyal while I surrender*, he thought miserably. *That they should die and I should live!*

They were taken to the royal apartments at the rear of the fortress and left with their sorrows. The celebrations of the conquerors could be heard drifting through the thatch of the Great Hall and up through the open windows.

"Are they going to kill us, Da?" Guidno asked, his face as white as a sheet.

"Of course not," Maelcon snapped at his little brother. "Else why would they keep us alive now? We're far too important to kill."

Maelcon was ten and already showed much of the surliness of young manhood.

"Maelcon is right, Guidno," Cadwallon said. "We are royalty. They won't touch us. They won't dare." *Gods, I hope I'm right.*

"There are no guards outside our chamber," said Meddyf, peeping into the corridor beyond.

"Diugurnach can't spare the men," Cadwallon said. "They are needed on the palisades. He has enough warriors to seize Cair Dugannu but not enough to hold it."

"Or to keep its inhabitants from escaping …" Meddyf suggested.

"Escape?" he regarded her with surprise. "There is no need to be foolhardy. All we need do is sit tight and await the marshalling of the teulu. Once Tathal's messenger reaches Din Arth, my brother will have all Venedotia coming to our rescue. These Gaelic wolves don't know what they've done in attacking us."

The Teulu of the Red Dragon was the standing army of Venedotia. Formed by Cunedag in the old days, every king contributed warriors to its ranks. It was headquartered at Cair Cunor in the south and could reach the coast within two days.

"Someone is coming," Meddyf said.

The door opened and Gobrui entered. He was armed.

"Not drinking your king's mead in the Great Hall with your new friends, traitor?" Meddyf spat. "Or have your new masters already got you running errands?"

The boy blushed but he appeared to have something of import to say. "I know you have little reason to trust me, my lord, but I have prepared a way out, if you are willing."

"A way out?" said Cadwallon "Too risky. I'll not endanger my family on some reckless escape plan when all of Venedotia will be coming to our aid tomorrow."

"All of Venedotia?"

"Tathal was able to get a messenger out before the east gate fell. By midday tomorrow Owain and Cunor will be mustering the teulu."

"Begging your pardon, my lord, but the messenger did not get through. They led his horse back in with his carcass slung over its saddle not an hour ago."

"Damn!" Cadwallon cursed. "Damn these bastards!"

"There's more, my lord. Diugurnach did not act alone. He has support from somebody in Venedotia. My Gaelic isn't too good but they seem to be awaiting the arrival of somebody of great importance tomorrow. You are being kept alive for an audience with them. What your fate will be afterwards, I do not know."

"Diugurnach may have orders to keep you alive only long enough to be used as a pawn," said Meddyf. "Once you have served your purpose we may all be killed. Look what happened to those soldiers who remained loyal to you even after Diugurnach promised to spare everybody. I say we make a run for it. If we can reach Owain at Din Arth we will be safe, at least until the teulu can be mustered." She glanced at Gobrui. "How is it to be done?"

"It will have to be on foot," the youth replied. "Diugurnach has few warriors but we can't reach the stables without being seen. I have taken care of the guard at the east gate. The way is open but only for so long. If we are to leave then it must be now."

"Very well," said Cadwallon. "If you get us out of this, lad, you will be the hero of Venedotia. Come! Lead the way!"

They stepped out onto the gallery. Dawn was still a few hours away and the lamps burned low. Drunken singing could still be heard down in the Great Hall but all elsewhere was silent. Gobrui led them right along the gallery towards the west wall.

"Hold," said Cadwallon in a low whisper. "Wait here for me." He turned and Meddyf seized his arm.

"What are you doing?" she hissed.

"Just give me a moment," he replied, shaking himself free of her grip.

He hurried down the gallery and descended a couple of steps to the standard bearer's quarters. It was pitch black inside so he took one of the lamps from the gallery to light his way. Bronze and silver glinted in the darkness. He wove his way between the racks of spear shafts to the iron-bound chest at the back of the chamber. He opened it and took out what he wanted, bundling it under his arm before re-joining his family.

"What's that?" Meddyf demanded, her eyes on the bundle of red cloth under his arm.

"My father's dragon banner," he replied.

"You went back for that?" Her eyes blazed in the darkness.

"This is the very standard Cunedag brought with him from the lands of the Votadini over forty years ago," he said. "It is the symbol of our dynasty and I'll be damned if I'll leave it in the hands of the bastard Gaels."

"We're trying to escape with our lives and you tarry to collect a battle standard?"

"I am the Pendraig now. I am its custodian. Where I go, it goes. Else all is for naught."

"If you dare to suggest that a piece of brightly coloured cloth is equal to the lives of our sons I'll leave you right here in in this fortress!"

Cadwallon looked at the two frightened faces of his boys. Maelcon looked upon his father with his mother's scathing eyes while Guidno seemed on the verge of weeping. *They don't understand,* he thought. *How could they? But they will someday. Maelcon especially if he is to succeed me …*

They headed to ground level and skirted the Great Hall. Gobrui pulled them into the shadows of the palisades as a drunken Gael stumbled out of the building and vomited under the eaves. They waited while he staggered to his feet and urinated before shambling back indoors, tying his breeches as he went.

They hurried over to the gate which had so recently been breached. Its shattered timbers lay all around. The corpses had been carried off but the ground was damp with the blood of the fallen.

"They leave no guard at the north gate?" Cadwallon asked.

"They see little need to," Gobrui replied. "They fear only attack from without and have all their guards on the palisades looking outwards."

As they descended the footpath they could see the ruins of the settlement between the two hills. Roundhouses still burned but the flames were low, licking at charred timbers which poked up from the ruins like blackened skeletons.

The east gate was closed and Cadwallon helped Gobrui heave it open just enough to allow them to slip out.

"How did you persuade the guard to leave his post?" Cadwallon asked him, looking up at the gatehouse.

Gobrui didn't answer but as soon as they left the fortress they saw the guard's corpse impaled on the defensive spikes at the foot of the wall, his body pierced in at least three places.

Cadwallon was impressed but the need for haste was too great to bestow compliments. They had escaped the fortress but it was a long trek to Din Arth and when the Gaels realised their prisoners had escaped, they would be after them in hot pursuit.

They heaved the gate shut for the sake of appearances to buy themselves a little more time. Cadwallon scooped Guidno up into his arms and Meddyf led Maelcon by the hand. At the foot of the hill the treeline was a black haze that signified concealment and shelter. They hurried towards it; fleeting shadows in the pale light of dawn.

Printed in Great Britain
by Amazon

24498843R00199